T0130079

GOD CHILD

ALSO BY MICHAEL BAPTISTE

Cracked Dreams

GOD CHILD

MICHAEL BAPTISTE

SBI

STREBOR BOOKS
NEW YORK LONDON TORONTO SYDNEY

Strebor Books
P.O. Box 6505
Largo, MD 20792
http://www.streborbooks.com

Cover design: Michael Baptiste

ISBN-13 978-1-59309-044-9
ISBN-10 1-59309-044-7
LCCN 2004118318

First Strebor Books trade paperback edition November 2005

10 9 8 7 6 5 4 3 2 1

Manufactured in the United States of America

For information regarding special discounts for bulk purchases, please contact Simon & Schuster Special Sales at 1-800-456-6798 or business@simonandschuster.com

DEDICATION

Your strength gives me power. Your perseverance gives me determination. Your principles influence my values. Your sheer unwillingness to submit to all of life's trials and tribulations is evidence that a strong woman *can* raise a strong man. If I had your heart, I would probably have already succeeded in and surpassed all of my hopes and dreams! Here I am, a 25-year-old published author, out there relentlessly chasing more dreams than a little bit—at the same time holding down my responsibilities on the home front—and you're *still* stronger than me! You're my mother *and* my father. Mommie, I love you. I dedicate this—my second major step toward reaching my dreams—to you.

Marie Lourdes Baptiste
December 1, 1949 — August 19, 2005

R.I.P.
We will all continue to treasure your memory, never forgetting how much you meant to everyone in this family! You were strong for all of us, and now it's time for us to be strong...for YOU!

I LOVE YOU

ACKNOWLEDGMENTS

First and foremost, I'd like to acknowledge my family starting with my grandfather, Franck "Papam" Mirvil, who is no longer with us. He and my grandmother, Saintulia "Yaya" Mirvil, who passed almost two decades ago now, did the best jobs parents could do raising their children and their children's children...and their children's children's children!!! If, and when, I have kids I'd be striving to do it up big like them. They raised nine strong, bright, successful men and women: Geurda, Frantz, Marie-Lourdes (my momma-duke), Micheline, Mireille, Josee, Francois "Frenchie," Nicole (my godmomma-duke), & Mimose. They, in turn, raised a host of wonderful children (apparently too many to name without forgetting a couple here and there)...ha ha! In any case, I'll just send a big WHAT UP to all my cuzzos...one love! One love to my big brother, Supreme; and my older sister Rachel, too! Of course, I can't forget the younger generation: Andrew, Craig, Saintulia "Tuli" (my goddaughter), Ebony, An-yah, Stanley "Doodie" Jr., Star, Sky, Sole, Jasmine, & Jada. Last, but most certainly not least, I'd like to stand up and salute Marie Ivana "Tun Doudone" Mirvil (the only remaining Mirvil of all of her brothers and sisters). She, like her brother Papam, raised some fine children...love you! To the fam' that may have gone unmentioned, charge it to my head and not my heart...love all ya'll!

Secondly, to my hood fellas: Chris "C." (hold ya head, hommie, you'll be here soon), Mikey, Psychem, Louie a.k.a. Peri Ping a.k.a. Cuban Lou, Des a.k.a. Starchild, Bill a.k.a. Illz, El Don, Poncho, Tone, Rob a.k.a. Robbery, & Jeanique (the first lady of the Time Bombs).

224th Street STAND UP: Eddie a.k.a. Green Eyes, R.I.P. Donda, Treshaun, Takwan, One Face, Two Face, Big Pete, Trish and the rest of the Johnsons, Greg, Gary "G." and the rest of the Tyners, Original, Sandra and the Strong fam, Leon, Irving, Crazy Lou, Glen, Jason "J.", Freda and the rest of the Hargroves and Joneses, Essae, Dre, Camille and the rest of the fam, Ronald D. (in the place to be!), Pito, Willie, Bradley (no, that's a slaughter!), Takesha and the whole fam.

To all the hoods in the Bronx that rep this and hold it down always: Castle Hill, Powell, Gun Hill Rd., Burke Ave., 219th, 222nd, Bronxwood, Vyse "Vyse City" Ave., East Tremont, White Plains Road, 228th, Bronxwwod, Barnes Ave., Boston Road., Allerton Ave., Wallace Ave., Onlinville Ave., Bronx Blvd., Co-Op City, South Boogie...of course all up and down the 4th and across the Ave.... keep repin' that Boogie! The Bronx, Brooklyn, Manhattan & Queens...oNe!

Much love to all the street vendors: Sidi and the rest up and down 125th Street in Harlem, 149th & Grand Concourse, Fordham Road, 28th & Broadway, and all the rest...keep holdin' the kid down! The Urban Literature genre would be lost without you. I know everybody ain't warm up to putting all their credit info over the Net to cop a book off of Amazon. I'll holla when I'm passing through!

Much love to Charmaine and the rest of the Strebor staff and authors: D.V. Bernard, Tina Brooks McKinney, Laurinda D. Brown, Shonda Cheekes, William Fredrick Cooper, JDaniels, J. Marie Darden, Cheryl Faye, Shelley Halima, Lee Hayes, Allison Hobbs, Keith Lee Johnson, Rique Johnson, Darrien Lee, Jonathan Luckett, Nane Quartay, V. Anthony Rivers, Harold L. Turley II, Michelle Valentine, A.J. White, Franklin White, Shonell Bacon, Mark Crockett, Michelle De Leon, Laurel Handfield, Dr. James D. Roberts, Sylvester Stephens, Jimmy Hurd, Nikki Jenkins, Janice Pinnock, ReShonda Tate Billingsley, David Rivera, Jr., Naleighna Kai, J.L. Woodson, Suzetta Perkins and Kimani Kinyua. Keep up the good work, everybody! Let's keep the fam tight!

Much love and respect to Zane. I thank you inside every time I look at those pictures from the '04 Baltimore Book Festival, when I opened that first box, and held for the first time, my first published book—*Cracked Dreams*. The feeling was indescribable. I ain't ever seen my face lit as bright as in those pictures. My guess is I'll be even more thrilled this time around, as I am so much more involved in the creative process as a whole. I wish you continued success in all of your endeavors...peace!

To my future in-laws, Ms. Diane (mom), Mrs. Kinard (granny), Deborah (auntie), Lillian (auntie), Big Yolanda (aunt), Kenyetta (cuz), Candice (cuz), Aliah (cuz), and of course Raean a.k.a. Mrs. Rule (cuz), Mr. Taylor (future father in-law), keep your head up and I can't wait to see you on this side!

Last, but not least (by far), I'd like to acknowledge my fiancée, and soon-to-be wife, Yolanda. You are the reason all of this is possible. Without your influence and motivation this would not be a reality that I would've foreseen. You told me that my work was good enough to be published, and made me believe it when we first began getting interest from publishers. Now that we're taking that step toward the next level in our relationship, I couldn't be happier. No matter what some people may think, I know in my heart that what we have is FOREVER! I won't settle for anything less; just promise me you won't either! All the little bullshit that we're going through only makes us stronger. I just thought that EVERYBODY should know that! Love you, *Mommy!*

...oNe...

CHAPTER 1

"L*ord, I'm begging you…PLEASE!!!"* she cried. "That's my baby boy, my only child! He's only twenty-five years old! He's too young to go…he's just way too young. I can't bury him, I *won't*! I'll die without him…God, please just bring my boy back! Take me instead…take *ME!* But, please, just bring my baby back!" She grabbed onto her son, and almost pulled him from his casket as she tried repeatedly to wake him. She hadn't come to the realization yet that he was in a place that he couldn't come back from. She could try with all of her might to pull him from death's clutches, but it wouldn't be doing any good.

At the ripe age of twenty-five, he was dead and gone, caught up in some bullshit that wasn't even worth it. What so many die for in the street for nothing. So many lives taken as a result of petty, small-time, low-level bullshit…it's a shame. Now, he was a statistic, nothing left to carry on his legacy but a small four-year-old daughter and a baby's momma. He had nothing else to show for his existence…and then to catch a slug over smalltime packages worth thousands on the street? Was this worth dying for? Was it even worth fighting for? Hell no! But, that's what it was. The fucked-up reality of it was that it wouldn't stop here. This one meaningless killing would lead to much more bloody murder; there was no getting around that. But, for what? Nothing, reputation, bell-ringing… bullshit! The only thing he should've been ready to die for was his little girl, and that's it, nothing else. Now, besides Mommy, she only had her godfather to look after and protect her from the street. He'd make sure she didn't end up like her father, even if it killed him!

***

"What the fuck? I know I'm forgettin' somethin'!"

It appeared that there was nothing left to do now. All the preparation it took to be ready for the day had been done and them some. Shit, a few things were even done a second and third time to make absolutely certain. He was ready to go now…right? Still, there he stood before the mirror hanging on the wall in his bedroom. Staring. Thinking. Contemplating what he may have forgotten. Something had to have been carelessly overlooked.

The black silk tie he was wearing was tied in a perfect Four-in-Hand knot tightly around his neck. At least after nearly twenty tries, it wasn't gon' get any more perfect; that was for damn sure. The suit he wore was the same deep, dismal color, and it was spotless and creased sharply. A few dozen passes of a lint-brush made sure of that. His slide-in shoes couldn't be any crispier, as he had shined them relentlessly until he could check out his fresh haircut in the reflection.

So, that was it…right? He took one more look at himself in the mirror. He was brown-skinned and about five feet eleven inches tall. His perfectly shaped facial hair was a rarity. His usual look—messy mustache, nappy beard, and uncombed hair—wasn't exactly appropriate for the day. He was definitely looking his best.

"Shit," he said aloud to himself, finally recalling what he'd forgotten. He reached into the nightstand sitting beside his bed and pulled his black, rubber-handle Glock 9 from the drawer. A quick check to see if it was fully loaded resulted to his satisfaction. He tucked the pistol into the back of his pants, took a quick look at his wristwatch, and he was off.

This was Sylvester. Anyone that knew of him, or heard the stories that circulated in the street about him, was well aware of his rep up in North Philly. To them, he was known as Boom, a heartless, cold-blooded murderer without a care in the world. In the "City of Brotherly Love," this mean bastard's name rang more bells than Owens, McNabb and Iverson altogether!

According to the word on the street, Boom was known by that name for one reason and one reason only; if you had any beef with him, and ran into him on the street, the last sound that your brain would process would be *BOOM!* That was that. You were now reduced to memories. Your boys could reminisce about you crowded around in ciphers, while emptying liquor bottles onto the ground in your honor. They could talk about how much they loved you, and babble on about what they'd do if they ever found out who had done you in. Hmm…yeah they could *talk* all they wanted. But that was all bullshit. They knew as well as you did who heated you down. They probably even knew where the nigga rested his head at. Better yet, they probably even knew where they could find the dude at any given moment. The problem wasn't lack of information like the impression they gave. The absence would be when it came to thoroughness, gulliness, or just straight-up balls. They didn't have the heart or the smarts. Considering that making a move against Boom was almost synonymous with suicide, they were forced to choose living out their own worthless lives as opposed to taking it to the streets.

Boom, on the other hand, held court in the street on a regular basis. It was only because his reputation was so tuff, that he was forced to slow his roll this last year or two. He was finally about to lean back into his heavy street cred' and employ some fresh thoroughbreds to make his extortion collections in his name. That would've been the plan, had a nigga not begged for his presence to be known in these streets once more. If only he could relax for a hot minute...but damn, this nigga was askin' for it!

You see, what had Boom so anxious about leaving his place this afternoon was the fact that he wasn't quite sure if he was ready to face his right-hand man, Ivan, in his current state. Ivan was Boom's homey since he first moved to Philadelphia from the South Bronx. He was the closest thing to back home he had. Though Ivan was from Jamaica Queens, him and Boom instantly clicked and became the best of friends until...well, let's just say that Boom is gon' have to continue damn near on his own from now on. Apparently, some coward-ass, jealous, so-called thug nigga put a slug in his boy's back, so now Boom was cocked and loaded ready to heat up the streets until the boy was dead and gone. Now that he had his spurs back on, the fool that did Ivan dirty like that would soon hear his last sound, but for now, he had his own shit to handle.

***

After fifteen minutes of sitting in his car double-parked a block away from Baily's Funeral Home, where the proceedings for Ivan had begun a few hours ago, Boom was just about ready to enter the building. The hurting feeling he felt deep in his gut wasn't going anywhere anytime soon. He just had to bear the pain. He exited the car and walked down the block toward the funeral home. Every step he took made him more and more anxious. As he stepped inside, his slim frame just seemed to be swimming in his own sweat beneath that suit. His upper lip started to twitch. He took one deep breath at the end of the corridor, and swung the door open. He was immediately welcomed by Ivan's mother, who could no longer take the sight of her only son lying in that coffin looking bloated and pale. She was wearing a black blazer and a long black skirt. She had a black hat on with a veil that covered her distraught facial expression. She lifted it enough to give Boom a kiss on the cheek. They embraced. She didn't want to let go and neither did Boom. He knew that as soon as he let go, he'd have to come face-to-face with his comrade. It was killing him softly.

"You and my boy's about the same age, right?" asked Ivan's mother, her eyes looking all swollen and dry.

"Yeah, just about," answered Boom. "I'll be twenty-five soon, so he only had me beat by a few months."

"Well, I know you know my son could be a mean bastard when he wanted to be, but he was still a sweet, wonderful person. He chose this life for himself; I don't doubt that one minute, but he was my lil' boy. And he was like a jewel in the middle of all that coal and dirt out there."

"I know that's right," agreed Boom.

"What I'm trying to say is...I don't want you to end up in one of these boxes like Ivan, Sylvester. I want you to do the right thing. You probably know who did my son like this, don't you?"

Boom didn't answer. He didn't have to. The sight of his lips tightening up spoke loud and clear.

"I realize that that sonofabitch ain't worth it, but I've already forgiven him. I don't blame him. But his future has already been written. He'll find his punishment sooner than later. I believe that deep inside of my heart. That's why I can forgive that man, you understand?"

Boom knew where she was going. He knew that she didn't want him to respond to her though, especially if he'd already made up his mind, because he wasn't going to be dishonest. He wouldn't have even sugarcoated it. He'd have told her straight up, *'You goddamn right that muthafucka's future is already written. Shit, couldn't have even been much to write neither...'*

His thoughts were only interrupted by Ivan's mother's voice saying, "Okay, Sylvester, go say good-bye to your friend."

Boom paused, then replied, "You know if you need anything, and I really do mean anything, you won't think twice..."

"I know, baby. Thank you."

Boom turned around slowly and entered the room. He was approached by many people showing their love and respect. Everyone knew how close Ivan and Boom were.

Down the aisle, he was greeted by Shonda, Ivan's wifey and baby's mother. Beside her was Sabra, Boom's four-year-old godchild. Now that Ivan was gone, Boom's duties would be kicking in pretty quickly. He would make absolutely certain that neither one of them ever wanted for anything.

A brief embrace gave Boom what was needed to get up the nerve to walk over to Ivan as he lay, comfortably asleep in his eternal bed.

He knelt before him and said a quick prayer. Then he looked up at his boy with eyes welling up with tears and said, "What up, homey? I'm i-ight," as if Ivan had asked him how he was doing. Given his state, it's a wonder he hadn't flipped out yet. A little imaginary conversation wasn't that bad; shit he could be doing a whole lot worse.

"Listen to me, brother," he continued. "I'm gon' hold it down for you, i-ight... Shonda and Sabra? Oh, that ain't even a problem; don't even worry yourself with their well-being. I want you to rest. Like I said, *I'm* holdin' this shit down like steel, my nigga."

He kissed his forehead, and took a seat beside Shonda as the service was about to begin. When she took his hand into hers, he felt a chill go up his spine. He put his other hand atop hers and they both held on tight.

When the preacher approached the podium, what little discussion that was taking place was lowered to whispers. Following a brief speech about life and death, when you're here and when you're gone, and what's waiting for us all on the other side, he introduced a group of guys that called themselves Insight. They were a local R&B trio that came along with the funeral package. They were there to sing songs; sometimes people made requests. They started out with "It's So Hard."

***

All of a sudden, Boom could no longer focus only on the gentlemen singing. His mind was traveling somewhere else...to another time...years and years into his past. He was remembering things with specific detail that he hadn't thought about in over fifteen years. Now, coincidently, he was seeing these things in front of his face, clear as day, like if they were happening right now, right this minute.

The first thing he realized was the color of the walls changing. From a flat burgundy, they changed to different shades of brown, as if attempts to touch up only the damaged areas in the wall had failed. Where the paint wasn't fresh and glossy, it was faded and chipped.

When his mind took him around the room, he saw images similar to the ones that were currently surrounding him, being that the people were all dreary and bleak. Though it was similar, it was altogether a different room. The well-dressed, respectable men and women were replaced with raggedy custees, deprived and unhealthy-looking individuals. Opposite them were the hustler types. Flashy... loud...gaudy gold rope chains and four-finger rings decorated their persons. Kangols and du-rags covered their heads, and dark black shades shielded their eyes.

The large roomy area was replaced by a small, humid space. The huge stainless-steel coffin that stood before him was replaced by a tiny, cherrywood casket, which looked more like an old chest than a final resting place. The image of the man inside the casket was familiar to Boom. It was his father, Sylvester Sr.

Boom's mind had traveled back seventeen years to 1988, when he was only eight years old. Harmless, shy, modest...these were words that described an eight-year-old Boom, when he was just Sylvester, or "Lil' Silly" as he was sometimes called. He'd grown to become a very different man. Now, he couldn't even begin to imagine what such innocence felt like.

His father had just been murdered, and he didn't have a clue why. The man never even hurt a fly. He had spent some time in prison, but it was for a mediocre car theft, nothing violent. He and Boom were two completely different animals. In fact, had he not been killed while Boom was so young, there's a good chance he would have grown to be a better man; a hard-working, honest-living man. He still had a warm part of his heart left, but it was surrounded by thick, hard ice.

As Boom dove deeper and deeper into his memory, he could remember one of his father's friends speaking on his behalf. He spoke about them laughing and crying together. He spoke about where they first met, up north in the penitentiary. He said that his father always gave twice as much as he was given. He said he never once required anything in return. It was purely out of love. He said that they hadn't seen each other for some years now, and it wasn't because he didn't want to. He knew that with his friend starting a family, that he wouldn't be anything but a bad influence, and he was absolutely right. His frame was already showing signs that he was diminishing slowly.

In the middle of his story, he cracked. He couldn't even speak anymore; the pain he was feeling inside had gotten so unbearable. He simply shut his eyes tightly to hold back the tears and began singing..."It's So Hard." Others sung along to help him through the verses, in an attempt to keep him from completely breaking down.

That's when the doors opened, and in walked a long-legged woman wearing a dingy, gray fox fur coat, fishnet stockings and a denim mini-skirt. She was dressed extremely inappropriate for the occasion, especially for her age. Following close behind her was a short, well-built guy, maybe in his early thirties. He was wearing a pair of acid-washed jeans, a wife-beater and a black leather P-coat. An acid-washed baseball cap turned backward covered a thick, nappy Afro, and he had a scar across his face that started from his right eye and ended somewhere by his left jaw. His ice-grill could give you the chills. He stared down every face that turned in his direction with his lips tightly curled upward. Seconds behind him was a dark-skinned tall, wide-body nigga. He had long dreads that could almost touch the ground as he stood straight up. He wore dark shades and a cleanly shaven face. A long trench coat hung from his huge frame, as he kept his position in front of the entrance with both arms crossed.

Row by row, as this woman and her man walked past, people stopped singing along. They were all so astonished at the sight of the couple that they could no longer concentrate on anything else.

When they finally reached the front row, no one else was singing but Boom's father's comrade. He still kept his eyes shut and deep into his performance for his fallen soldier. It wasn't until Boom's mother lifted her head from her lap, where she had been curled up rocking back and forth with a waterfall of tears running freely down her face, when the guy realized what was about to go down. She squinted her eyes to see a clear picture through the tears, and she was in sheer disbelief at the vision standing in front of her. Through bloodshot-red eyes, she saw the only two people in the world who were able to bring a beast out of her that she had never known. Up until now, she'd relegated to a catatonic state, but now, the blood that pumped through her veins was replaced by a blazing fire. Her eyes grew larger and larger as her face expressed more and more disgust. She lifted up out of her seat and yelled, "Bitch, you got some fucking nerve!!!"

***

"Boom, baby, you okay?" Shonda asked, waking Boom from his daydream. "Boom, can you hear me? It's okay, baby, just let it out."

"Huh?" asked Boom, forgetting where he was for a second. "Wha?"

Shonda looked into Boom's eyes with concern. She knew how much Ivan meant to him, and vice versa. She was worried, though. He hadn't much shown any sort of feeling since he found out about Ivan. She hadn't yet seen him cry or anything. He just kinda wondered around aimlessly, with a blank facial expression.

Shonda and Ivan had been an item now for a long time. She was with him right up until the end. She would ride or die for him. When she found out what had happened, her first reaction was to find out who did it, and to deal with them accordingly. The only thing that held her back from hitting the street was the assurance Boom gave her. He made certain she didn't worry herself with it at all. He'd handle it personally.

She and Boom had gotten closer over the years, since Ivan asked him if he'd be his daughter's godfather. Being so close to Ivan made it easy for her to get to know Boom better because they were so much alike.

Shonda was a beautiful combination of Black and Puerto Rican. She had a light-skin complexion, brown curly hair, and light-brown eyes. She had strong cheekbones, full lips, and a toned figure.

***

Boom finally came back to his senses, and was aware of his surroundings again. But now he was anxious to complete the story. He needed desperately to find out what happened next.

Shonda ironically stated, "You look as if you just saw a ghost."

Boom simply turned to her with a curious look on his face. "You read my mind. I'm gon' get some air."

Boom got up and walked out to the sidewalk. He leaned up against the wall and lit a cigarette. As he blew out the smoke, he put his head back and tried to think. He tried to recall the rest of the story. The last thing he saw was that a confrontation was developing between his mother and a woman that had just walked in. He tried his best to remember, but it wasn't coming to him yet. He shut his eyes and tried harder. He talked himself through it.

"Alright, the broad walks in and Moms jumps up and holla: *'Bitch, you got some fucking nerve!'* Okay, what then? Damn, nigga, think! Think! What the fuck happened after that?"

"What the fuck happened after what?" someone asked in a deep voice to Boom, as he stood there babbling to himself. "You okay, lil' nigga?"

Boom opened his eyes to see Uncle Black. Now Black wasn't really his uncle; that's just what he called him. Since he had taken care of Boom since his father's unfortunate passing, Boom looked at him as an uncle. Besides, Black and Vester—that's what Black called him—they were that close. They might as well have been brothers. Black assured his longtime comrade since little Sylvester Jr. was first born that if anything were to happen that he'd hold it down. He honored that promise.

Now, although Vester and Black were close, they weren't the same, as were Boom and Ivan. It was the opposite with them. They met each other way back in their high school days, but they weren't running partners like that. Black took to Vester kind of like a charity case. He felt sorry for him. He didn't have any friends. He didn't have anyone to watch his back. When they met, Vester was getting picked on by some kids who were bigger than him. Black stepped in and put an end to it. Ever since then, they were inseparable. Vester followed Black everywhere he went...everywhere! Years down the line he even followed him once for a joyride in a stolen car. That's when Black knew that Vester would hold him down, just as he did when they met for the first time. Because when he was caught by the police, Vester never even thought about ratting Black out to get off. He took the rap all by himself.

***

Black was just that...BLACK. With exception to his fair complexion, everything else that represented him was dim. He wore dark clothes, dark shades, and he had a dark persona to match. Besides Vester, Boom was one of the few people that knew of his sensitivity. Everyone else knew a vicious criminal, specializing in burglary, strong-arm robbery, assault, battery, and even murder. Yeah, he'd capped a couple of cats in his time, but it's nothing he's proud of. Being from the street and in his profession made him that way. He wouldn't be able to survive otherwise.

He stood at about six feet two inches tall, and built. The naked eye wouldn't pick it up but Black was seriously in shape. He's what you'd call a sleeper; he wasn't oversized, Venice Beach-brolick, but below his seemingly round frame he was all muscle. He had a bald head and a cleanly shaven face. He kept a cigar in his mouth and a pistol on his side at all times, in a shoulder holster hidden underneath a blazer or an overcoat. He was the physical representation of thorough!

***

"You okay, lil' nigga?" he asked, clipping the tip off of a fresh Graycliff cigar. "You don't look good, man."

"Yeah, I'm i-ight, Unc'," replied Boom. "I'm just trippin' on all of this shit, man. The boy ain't deserve this shit, you know?" Boom paused to take a pull from his cigarette. He blew out the smoke with a sigh. "Besides that," he continued. "The weirdest thing just happened in there, freaked me out. I'm sittin' there, tryin' to make sure Shonda and Sabra is doing okay, and I get like some kinda flashback from way back when I was a kid, and shit. It was crazy, Uncle Black; I swear it felt like I was right there for real. I remember I was wearing a black suit with a white shirt and penny loafers. I even remember the haircut I had...a busted Caesar-fade. I remember it all that clear."

Black drew long pulls from his cigar as he lit it. "What you yappin' 'bout, son," he said. "You ain't making no damn sense."

"It was my father," stated Boom. "I saw him, Unc'. It was at his funeral. I remember being there."

Black took a slow pull from his cigar and blew the smoke out quickly. He was looking all jittery now.

"Listen, son," he said. "All of that is in the past now. I done told you about thinking about all of those things. You just gon' make things worse on yourself. You need not be thinking about all the bad shit that happened to ya twenty years ago, especially not when you got all of this fucked-up shit happening to ya right now! Stop cluttering your head with all that mess, boy!"

"Damn," said Boom as the vision of his boy laid out came back to him. He was sniffling now, trying to hold back tears. "I can't believe my boy Ivan is gone...damn!"

"I didn't mean to upset you, son," said Black, realizing that his words were disturbing Boom. "I'm just worried about ya, that's all. Now, I been there for you from day one, and I'll be there for you 'til I'm layin' up in one of the boxes... me! You hear that, son??" He paused for a response, then continued, "Until the end, boy."

Black pulled Boom close for a hug. He grabbed onto him and held on tight. Boom held on even tighter. He was still holding back, but now at least the pain in his stomach was fading and he felt a little better.

They were interrupted when Shonda came out of the funeral home along with Sabra. "Is everything okay?" she asked as she rubbed Boom on his back. "It's gon' be alright, okay, baby?"

When Boom finally ended his and Black's embrace, he held his head down and looked at the floor, still fighting the tears. He lifted his enough for his eyes to meet with Shonda's. The second they exchanged a gaze felt like an eternity. She could always make Boom feel better; she just had that way about her. She squeezed his left cheek, and pulled him close to kiss the other side. They shared a healthy hug as well.

Black never realized it before, but it was becoming really obvious how close Boom and Shonda had gotten over the years. He could relate. He and Grace,

Boom's mother, were close also. The way he saw it, it was difficult not to love a person like Grace. She had a really positive personality. Besides the fact that she was drop-dead gorgeous, she just always seemed to have a glow surrounding her, like nothing could ever go wrong. Brown skin, shoulder-length hair and a bright smile...that was Grace.

"So, how've you been, Shonda?" Black asked. "You understand that boy is in a better place now, right? Trust me; there are way worse places for Ivan to be in...as fucked up as this world is. He's with God, now, sugar. Can't shit beat that there!"

"I know," answered Shonda. "But I would still rather him be here...with me...with his daughter. Call it selfish if you want, but I don't know what I'm gon' do without that man." Shonda was fighting back tears now, but she wasn't doing too good a job. You could tell by the color of her eyes that she'd already done her fair share of crying. Her eyes were all dry and red now. It wouldn't be long before her tears dried up altogether.

Boom put an arm around her and gently rubbed her back. Black also made an attempt at consoling her.

"Oh, now that's what Sylvester is here for; you still got him," he said as he knelt down to speak to Sabra. "Isn't that right, sweetie? You can count on your godfather, can't you?"

Sabra turned away from Black with a frightened look on her face. She hid behind her mother.

That's when Germ came out to check on Boom. He was a dude that Ivan and Boom kept around, simply because he was just as crazy as them. By their standards, his breed was hard to find. When it came down to it, Germ was the type of dude that would buss his gun the quickest, get knocked, and do the bid without talking. This muthafucka was for real. Germ had dark skin and a slim build. He was older than Boom by some years, but you couldn't tell by his face. He had a light mustache and a non-existent beard. He stood at about six feet flat.

"Damn," he said. "Everybody's out here and shit, huh? What's up, Mr. Black?"

"Same old, youngster," replied Black as he stood back up to exchange a handshake with Germ. "How you holdin' up?"

"Well, you know," he replied. "Just barely. I'll be good though, soon as we see this boy..."

"Come on, man," interrupted Boom. "Kill that shit!"

"I'm ready to go," Shonda said. "I'm not gon' be able to take much more of this before I have a nervous breakdown. I ain't slept in three days, plus tomorrow's gon' be another long day."

"Yeah," Boom said. "You right. You need your rest. Come on, lemme take you home."

Before he left, he gave Germ a pound and a hug. He also gave him a word of advice.

"Call me later about that thing, you heard?" he said. "And stop bumpin' ya gums and shit, man. It ain't always the right time for that shit!"

"Alright, I hear you, brother...holla at ya boy!"

Boom also gave Black another hug before he left and told him, "Until tomorrow, I really wanna finish that talk we were having, cool? I already know what you're gon' say...but it's for me...you know?"

"Okay, boy," Black said reluctantly. "I'll sit with you."

"One last thing," said Boom before walking off. "Let me hold on to that cutter," he said, referring to Black's sterling silver cigar-clipper. "I'll give it right back; just think I'm gon' need it later, that's all."

Black hesitated, but reached into his pocket for his cutter anyway. He reluctantly gave it to Boom, not knowing if he'd ever see it again. Shit, he wasn't even sure if he'd take it even if he did see it again. No telling what the hell Boom wanted it for.

Boom and Shonda walked back to his ride, each of them holding one of Sabra's hands. They jumped into his low-key, charcoal-gray, Lincoln LS sedan, and they were off. They didn't speak much during the ride.

After a twenty-minute drive, Boom pulled up to Shonda's plush loft apartment over on Walnut Street. Boom had been trying to concentrate on his recollection from earlier but as hard as he forced himself, his memory still escaped him. He was really having a bad time with all of the shit going on at the same time. Initially, he hadn't planned on going upstairs with Shonda, but she insisted. She didn't think it was a good time to be alone—for him or her.

Upon entering, Shonda put Sabra to bed upstairs. Next she went into the small kitchen, adjacent to the living room, to fix her and Boom a drink. Boom took a seat on the couch in the living room.

Just looking around the apartment made Boom wonder how his boy Ivan used to lay his head there. It was obviously Shonda's influence that made this place what it was. The décor spoke so vividly of her character. The high ceilings and white walls, the few pictures hanging here and there…the furniture placed perfectly to create a cozy setting…that was definitely Shonda. The floor was oak, and the countertops were granite. On the side of the kitchen were stairs that led up to the bedrooms. It was simple, quaint, and intimate. That wasn't the Ivan that Boom knew. If you knew him, you would cosign.

Boom and Shonda talked for the remainder of the night, mostly about old times. They each recollected memories to top the other's story. They could've gone on all night discussing the kid. This is when Boom got the call he'd been waiting for.

"Yo, what it is?" he shot into his cell. "We in there?"

"Yeah, you know," responded Germ. "Like swimwear. I got the whole shit mapped. Let's do it."

"I-ight then, let's tear into this muthafucka!"

Boom got up to leave, but Shonda quickly stopped him.

"Wait," she pleaded. "I can't stay here all alone; I'll go out of my mind."

"Well, I can't stay any longer, Shonda," answered Boom. "I got some shit to do, you already know the deal." Boom thought for a second of a quick fix. He needed to be leaving soon if he was gon' make this engagement in time. He just spat out the first thing that came to his mind. "Alright, fuck it," he blurted. "You can crash at my crib. I won't be out long, but at least you don't have all kinds of shit reminding you about Ivan over there. I know you just about ready to pull ya hair out and shit. I'll hold you down for tonight, but after tomorrow, we gon' have to work on this. If you gotta get a new place, then so be it."

Boom helped Shonda pack a few things and carried Sabra down to the parking lot where the car was parked. Twenty-five minutes later, they were pulling up to Bustleton Avenue where Boom stayed. He walked Shonda inside while he held Sabra tight in his arms. She was about to wake when he put her down in his bed. He kissed her forehead. "Go back to sleep, little girl," he said playfully.

"Are you gon' be my daddy now?" she asked, still half asleep.

Boom was astonished that she'd ask him something like that out of the blue. "Hmm," he said. "What makes you say that, baby?"

"Mommy said daddy's gone now. He not coming back no more. So I don't have a daddy now. Will you be my daddy?"

He paused. He didn't know how to answer. What could he say, no?

"You know, no one will EVER be a better father to you than your real dad. Me and him are like brothers, you know? So no, I ain't gon' be your daddy. But I'm gon' try my best, okay?"

Sabra gave the nod of approval and Boom was off the hook...*for now!*

"Alright, go back to sleep, now. Nighty-night, baby."

When he felt his cell phone vibrating again, he knew just who it was. "I'm comin', nigga!" he spat at Germ as he left the room. "Hold the fuck on, man! I'll be there in two minutes."

CHAPTER 2

"Come on lovely," said Travis to the young lady he was trying to coerce into his crib. "Just for a second, boo. You actin' like you don't know me now; what up with that?"

"That's 'cause I *don't* know you, *nigga!*" the fiery woman said. "For all I know, you could be some maniac psycho. You act like we go way back...I just met you tonight!"

"I don't even know why you actin' like that, girl," he replied. "Now you wasn't sayin' that shit when you was grindin' on my dick in the club. What's all this new shit you poppin'? I just wanna get to know you, damn! What a nigga gotta do to get to know a lady nowadays?"

"The club is one thing, but..."

"But what?" he asked, cutting her off. "Do I look like I could even hurt a fly?" asked Travis, showing his most innocent face. The halo was shining extremely bright above his head now. "Come on now," he continued. "If you still feel that way in another thirty minutes or so, I'll drive you all the way home without a word...promise."

Travis was pulling out all the stops now. He stood there, attempting his sexiest smile, waiting for the girl to agree with him. All he needed was for her to show just a little weakness, and he had her! All that bullshit about taking her home was all a game, especially if she dissed him. Shit, it'd be hard enough to get him to give her a ride even after she gave him the nut he wanted, let alone if she shitted on him.

"Well," she said, showing signs of vulnerability. "We can just go up for a minute, right? I'll have one drink and that's it, okay? I don't want anything to happen. I mean I am feelin' you, but..."

"'Nuff said," interjected Travis. "Let's do it, then."

Travis led his unsuspecting victim into his apartment building. She couldn't have known that she had just made the worse decision of her life. Just like her, Travis was pleased with himself up until this point. He was looking forward to a long, sweaty night. He didn't know the half.

Upon entering his apartment, Travis suddenly felt a weird vibe. He carried a suspicious look on his face. He started sniffing, as he could get a whiff of something burning. He didn't know what it was, but there was a hint of smoke in the air. He let his nose lead him until he was standing at the living room door. On the other side of that door was whatever he smelled. He proceeded with caution. The young lady had no idea what was going on. She just followed Travis' lead.

He cracked the door until he could get a glimpse of a man sitting on his couch in the dark. As Travis went for his piece, the man lifted his hand to take another nonchalant drag from the cigarette he was smoking. By now, Travis' heart rate had quadrupled. He pushed the door open and busted into the living room with his weapon cocked and pointed.

"Muthafucka, you wanna tell me what the fuck you doin' in my house???" Travis yelled. "You hear me, nigga?" He spat at the man, as he sat without even turning his head to address Travis directly.

Click-clack...that's all he had to hear to let him know he wasn't alone in the room with this strange man. Germ stepped from behind the door and lifted his pistol to the back of Travis' head, while holding a tight grip on his lady friend's neck. He got just close enough for Travis to feel the cold, steel, nine-milly pressed up against the back of his head.

"You stupid muthafucka," he said condescendingly. "That was the easiest shit ever. How that feel, duke?" Germ swung his gat around and landed a blow to the back of Travis' head. Travis, a little dazed, fell to his knees, dropping his burner on the floor as he held his throbbing head.

"Ya'll muthafuckas done seen ya *last* days," Travis said, trying to give a valiant effort to save his ass. "Do ya'll know who ya'll fuckin' with? I'm Travis-motherfuckin'-Strong! Ya *best* motherfuckin' bet is take what you came for and get the fuck outta my house before I get a good look at you. If not, you muthafuckas better be ready to kill me tonight!"

That's when Boom thought he'd bring some light to the situation via the lamp that sat atop the end table beside him.

When Travis looked up, he saw the devil himself sitting in his living room. He couldn't be the bad-ass he wanted to be anymore. At the sight of Boom, he knew that he wasn't gon' have nearly as much fun with the remainder of the night as he'd originally planned. He let out a sound like he couldn't even breathe, like he was choking on his own tongue. Then, when he finally got his wind back, he gasped like he was taking his last breath.

"Travis Strong, huh?" Boom asked, reciting Travis' whole government name. "More like Travis Feeble, ha ha." He laughed at his own joke. "Maybe Travis Frail…Fragile…or just Pathetic! You bitch-made faggot, come over here so I can see you."

Travis Strong…he was the nigga that did Ivan. He was the punk that didn't have the heart to look him in the eyes when he sent him. He didn't have the balls to put the burner up to his temple and see the sweat run off of his brow before he pulled the trigger. He didn't have that urge to make sure a nigga knew why he was about to die, and by whom. He wasn't a killer. He was a gambler. He shot Ivan in the back, while he was on his way to see his probation officer at that. He didn't know he was dead…he only hoped. Of course, Ivan didn't have his whistle on him to return fire. Now, that would've been cool, a sweet hit even, had he just been doing a routine job. It would've been different if he were only executing a murder-for-hire contract, like the many jobs that Boom had taken in his time. But no, this was personal for Travis. He had something to prove. He should've carried out his objective with the streets in mind, especially if he was trying to regain what little rep he had. He knew who Ivan was…*everybody did!* He knew what it meant to cross a dude of his stature, but his better judgment escaped him. He knew that he could very well be starting a war, but he was dumb enough to think he could ride it out. So sad…so sad. He'd be finding out soon enough what he was really made of.

"Nigga, you ain't hear me?" asked Boom when Travis didn't respond quick enough. "Didn't I tell you to come over here so that I could see you?" He lifted his Glock from the coffee table and rested it on his lap pointed in Travis' direction. "You better be quick with it, nigga."

The girl started crying at this point. She couldn't take it any longer. Her fear got the best of her. She quickly began begging for her life. She asked to be spared.

"Ay, shut that bitch the fuck up, man," demanded Boom of Travis. "You hearin' me, nigga; shut your bitch the fuck up!!!"

"Bitch, quit crying, and shut the fuck up!" yelled Travis as his voice cracked. He would soon be joining her as she wept, and he couldn't even conceal it.

The girl went on to explain that she had just met him tonight, and swore *"on her life"* to keep quiet if they let her go. Boom simply giggled at her request.

"Damn," said Boom with a chuckle, as he thought out loud. "I know you gotta be feelin' fucked up about yourself now…fuckin' with this lame-ass nigga." He let out another small giggle. "And don't ever use your life to swear on, sweetie… that's just bad karma. Besides, I already own that. Germ, make sure that bitch don't say nothin' else."

Germ's eyes lit up at Boom's request. He knew just what to do. With a devilish grin on his face, he began to lead the girl out of the living room. Her body was trembling with nervous energy now, without a clue as what the rest of the evening would bring her. She started to hyperventilate and let out a brief scream before Germ covered her mouth with his hand. With the other hand holding his nine-milly, he put it up over his mouth. "Shhh," he warned. "You don't wanna do that," he said, now shaking his head back and forth. He scooped Travis' piece up off the floor, and left Boom to deal with his victim.

With Boom by himself with Travis, he made an attempt to get to know the boy a bit better. He had a few questions he needed answers to. Nothing too serious; he was just curious, that's all.

"You smoke?" he asked.

Travis shook no, with his head down and his eyes welling up.

"You sure?" Boom asked, offering him a fresh cigarette. "I've heard that a lot of people ask for these when they get put in your situation. I guess it's so they relax better, ya know? This shit can be real stressful on a nigga." He paused. "Here, take one!" he demanded.

Travis extended his right hand enough to reach the cigarette Boom held out, without getting too close to him. He was shivering from his fingertips, to his knees, all that way down to his feet now. He couldn't keep still, even if *that* was what he was concentrating on. Nope, his real concern was to keep himself from shitting in his pants.

When Travis finally got hold of the cigarette, Boom took out a fresh one for himself and lit it up. He sat back in the couch, blowing smoke into the air, and made himself comfortable in Travis' simply decorated bachelor pad. He looked around. "Nice little spot you got here, Strong. Not too bad at all." He looked back at Travis. "Nigga, you can at least say thank you!" he insisted.

Travis stuttered the words, "Th-th...tha-thank y-y-yo...th-thank you." He managed to let it out as his jaw began twitching more and more.

"Don't mention it, homey," he replied. "Oh, my bad," said Boom in an apologetic tone. "You need a light? Here!" He tossed his lighter up in the air toward Travis, and when he reached his hand out to catch it, Boom leaped from the couch at him. He knelt down beside and grabbed the back of his head. With the other still holding the freshly lit cigarette, he pulled him closer and closer. When he was close enough, he sunk the lit cigarette into Travis' right eye. He pulled him closer even...close enough to hear the sound of his eyeball sizzling around the burning ashes. Close enough to hear the popping sound the juices made as his eye turned to liquid and came to a boil...*that close!*

He let Travis go to try and keep what was left of his eye inside of his head, as he rolled around on the floor crying out and gasping.

"Shut the fuck up!!!" Boom ordered.

Travis' cries came down a few notches, but he was still unable to bear the pain without letting out small high-pitch murmurs. His eye was leaking through his fingers now.

"That the eye you used to aim at my brother??" Boom yelled. "Huh, muthafucka, you hear me talkin' to you? Is that the one??"

Travis didn't answer.

"Okay," he said matter-of-factly. "Then maybe it was the other one...come over here, nigga!"

"Yes! Yes!" Travis answered. "It was this one. It was! It was the right one! You got it, man!"

"Oh," he simply replied. "Why ain't you just say so then, nigga? Damn, I was about to just pop that left one out of ya dome; good thing you spoke up, huh?"

Boom didn't lose a bit of the sarcasm in his voice. He wasn't at all displaced by the sight of a man, rolling around on the floor, trying to keep his eye from spilling out of his head.

"Hmm," he said, as he thought aloud to himself once more. "So, I guess you right-handed, then? Seeing as how that was the hand you held out to catch that lighter. Am I right?"

Travis didn't want to answer. He was too afraid of what a reply meant. He was well beyond the point of keeping from shitting on himself now. He already let it slip, and now Boom could even smell it.

"Yo, did you just shit yourself?" he asked, disgusted with the sight. "You can't be fuckin' serious, man." Boom took a closer sniff. "Awe, damn! Nigga, you shitted on yourself??"

Travis still couldn't answer. He was breathing uncontrollably now, as the fear of dying a horrible, slow, painful death consumed his heart. He saw no possibility of his life being spared. He could only hope to die quickly. For now, he just tried his best to get as far away from Boom as he could. He wasn't doing that well a job at it either. He was all the way by the living room door when Boom stopped him.

"Come here, you shitty-assed muthafucka!" said Boom, dragging Travis across the floor, scratching and clawing at the hardwood. He walked around to Travis' other side and stepped on his right hand. To stop him from trying to move, he kicked him in the face with his other foot. "Keep still, you filthy fuck! Lucky bastard, I'm gon' have to make this fast now, goddammit! Your nasty ass'll fuck around and make me throw up!"

Boom reached down to where he had Travis' hand down flat with his foot. With his hand, he pulled at Travis' index finger. He pulled it back until he heard it. *snap!!!* "Is that the finger you used, nigga? Huh? Answer me, nigga! Is that the finger you used to pull the trigger??"

"Yes!" Travis yelled, giving Boom what he needed to proceed. "YES!!!"

"Yeah, you bitch. I bet you felt real happy with yourself when you squeezed off that slug, huh? Didn't you, muthafucka??" he yelled. "Didn't you??"

"YEAH! YeAH!" Travis cried. "I DID!!!"

Boom reached into his back pocket and pulled out the cigar-clipper he borrowed from Black. He planted his knee into Travis' hand now to keep him still. With one hand he slid that index finger into the hole. With the other hand, he squeezed… once…twice…three times before he heard another snap as Travis' finger-bone shattered.

"Yeah, muthafucka," Boom said, now pleased with the job he'd done so far. "How it feel, pussy?"

He lifted up from his knees and sunk a kick deep into Travis' ribs, turning him over. He lifted his foot again for more swift stomps into the boy's chest before stopping. He rapped the finger in a black bandana he had in his pocket and instructed Travis to roll over on his stomach so that he could finish him.

Travis welcomed his death now. He wanted nothing more than to stop the pain. He rolled over quickly.

Boom brandished a shiny, chrome blade, flipped it open, and knelt down to lift Travis' head to slit his throat from ear to ear. Before he was able to complete this task, he got another idea. He slammed Travis' head back to the floor.

"Stay there, muthafucka!" he ordered.

He walked back around to Travis' backside. Before Travis knew what was going on, Boom had already got his pants down to his knees. He almost gagged at the sight of his feces running down his leg. He held his breath and lowered his boxer shorts. With the sharp dagger in hand, he swung downward in a swift motion. When he sunk the blade into his target, he twisted it left…then right… then left again.

He couldn't even take anymore before he'd probably vomit all over the place. Funny, it was nothing to see the cat rolling around on the floor trying to put his eye back in its socket, as it dripped down his arm, but now he was uncomfortable. He got up, leaving Travis on the ground crying out in a pitch so high, that it probably woke all the dogs in the neighborhood. He went to go wash his hands in the nearest sink, which happened to be in the kitchen right on the side of the living room. When he was done, he went to get Germ.

He caught Germ in Travis' bed, about to rape the girl he came home with. "Ay, man," he said, disturbing his partner's concentration. "Leave that bitch alone, man, and come here."

Germ quickly got up, after sucking his teeth, and buttoned his pants back up. "Damn, nigga," he said. "Why so fast? I thought you'd be in there takin' it to that nigga for at least another hour; what's up? I'm about to get me some pussy!"

"Fuck that," Boom said calmly. "Now go in there and take that knife outta ya boy's ass. When you get it out of his ass, dig that shit into his chest, and cut his motherfuckin' heart out. Hurry up, too, so we can get up outta here. I gotta get up early in the morning."

After a disappointing sigh, Germ went to carry out the orders he was given. He didn't even ask what the hell a knife was doin' in Travis' ass to begin with... he'd gotten to the point where he just wasn't surprised anymore. He'd been jaded to such gruesome sights long ago.

When he was gone, Boom walked over to where the girl had curled up on the bed shivering. She couldn't even bring herself to look at him in his face. She had a look that let Boom assume that she'd seen and heard enough to keep her mouth shut about what she'd seen and heard. Just to make sure, he picked her skirt up off the ground and searched through it for some extra insurance.

"It's okay, sugar," he assured her, as he sat beside her on the bed. "Don't worry, I ain't gon' hurt you." He flashed her driver's license in front of her face and made sure she saw him put it in his pocket. "But trust," he continued. "You open your mouth about this to ANYBODY, and I'll find you...and it won't be pretty. You hear me?"

She nervously nodded yes.

"Now...I can trust you, right?" he asked a second time to be sure.

"Y-ye...y-yes. I swear on my..."

Boom just looked at her with piercing eyes. She wisely decided to rephrase her sentence.

"I promise."

"Okay, hope you don't see me again, miss. Have a good night."

He got up and walked right past the living room, where Germ was already busy at work on Travis, and went into the hallway. There, he lit up another cigarette and breathed the smoke in deeply. He was feeling so much better now. The next time he saw his comrade, he'd have a present for him. Something to make *him* feel better, too.

After a few more minutes, Germ was exiting the apartment. He had a brown paper bag in hand. When Boom looked at it close, he noticed that it was soaking wet, about to fall apart completely. It looked like there was blood dripping from the bottom, and its contents would soon be falling right through it.

"Nigga, what the fuck is that?" asked Boom.

"Wha?"

"What you mean *'wha?'* nigga? That!!! What the fuck you got in that bag?"

"Oh, it's the boy's heart, I thought *you* wanted it…for a souvenir or somethin', I don't know. I thought that's why you…"

"Are you crazy??" asked Boom, cutting him off. "I don't want that nigga's heart; put it back! And hurry up so we can get the fuck outta here…stupid muthafucka!"

CHAPTER 3

WHAT A RUSH! Boom was on top of the world now. He couldn't remember the last time he took so much enjoyment from bringing someone pain, especially someone this deserving of it. He felt like his blood was really pumping through his veins again. He was alive.

Boom didn't go straight home. He couldn't. He wasn't ready to hit the sack yet. He felt too good. He found himself driving the streets of North Philly with no direction...aimlessly.

Before long, he found the irony in it. He was finally able to take a step back, and look at himself from the outside in. Although he felt like he was alive again for the first time in years, still, he lived without cause, without direction. Thus far, his journey through life showed no clear path, no goal set to accomplish. He didn't know where he was going.

It reminded him of something his father once told him, when he was way too young to remember. But that's how it is; you remember the shit you're not supposed to, or the shit that you don't know you're supposed to anyway. He didn't know why he remembered it, until now.

He remembered driving through the slums of the South Bronx, sitting in the passenger seat of his father's old Cadillac Coupe DeVille. He remembered the buildings his father pointed out to him. He remembered because they took this tour of the slums on a regular basis.

He could see, with horrifying detail, every broken window, every walking-dead crack-fiend, and every car sitting on four bricks with all of the windows smashed in and the entire engine ripped out. He remembered wondering how the buildings, or what was left of them, could even stand up in the shape they were in.

Burnt, dirty, abandoned. Hurt, forgotten, lost...that was his vision of the Bronx in the mid-to-late '80s. His mind was not painting this picture incorrectly at all. He was actually seeing everything in front of his face again, clear as day.

"See that, son," his father told him as he leaned over to point out of the passenger side window. "That there's where you're from...remember it! NEVER forget it. You hear me?"

Young Sylvester could only nod to please his old man. He didn't know why, not yet.

"I don't want you to ever forget where you came from, Sylvester," he ordered. "Or else, how you gon' know where you goin'?"

It was that simple. If you could sum up the street life in one sentence, it would be: *"If ya don't know where ya came from, then ya damn sure don't know where ya goin'!"*

Boom was starting to see this more clearly now. He'd grown to be a man that only lived in the day. He had no idea where his life was going, because he had no idea where his life came from. To live in the day is fine, so long as you plan for the future, and NEVER forget the past.

Boom found himself in front of his building now. He was staring up the structure through the window, with a probing look on his face. He saw it differently now than he'd ever seen it before. There was a familiarity about it now, like he'd been there before...when he was young.

What Boom was actually seeing was that the building where he called home was actually very reminiscent of the funeral home where the service was held following his father's death. He had never noticed before, but the resemblance was striking. He wasn't even putting forth any effort; his mind just went back to that day on its own. His subconscious was trying to tell him something, so he did what came naturally. He shut the fuck up and listened.

Boom's recollection began now where it had left off from earlier that day. He saw his mother yelling at a woman that had just walked in to pay her respect. She must've been an unwanted guest, because she was yelling at the top of her lungs at the woman.

The other woman, afraid of being attacked and embarrassed, sought the protection of her man. She jumped backward away from Grace and took her position behind her knight in a shining wife-beater.

That's when someone else interjected. A man, dressed in a black suit with a black turtleneck shirt, came walking over, seemingly from out of nowhere. He stood between Grace and the short stocky fellow. With his face hidden below a black cabdriver hat, his dark shades didn't allow for any eye to eye, but the stocky guy just knew that he was staring him down from behind his shades.

The man dressed in black tilted his head to one side and lifted his jaw with pride. Then he threw out his arms, as if inviting the little man to do whatever came naturally to him. If he wanted to jump off, well he was gon' have to go through him before he could ever lay a hand on Grace. When the guy noticed the holster beneath the man's blazer, he reconsidered advancing. The sun was gleaming off the butt of the stainless steel gun, reflecting light into his face. He squinted for half a second, and that's all it took. The man dressed all in black saw his opportunity. He immediately took advantage, and...

"Alright, guy," said a policeman knocking on Boom's car window, waking him from yet another climactic point in his remembrance, as he shined his flashlight into Boom's face.

Damn, thought Boom as he tried not to lose the vision, not even paying the cop any mind. It was too late now. It was gone...again.

Boom winded down the window enough for him to say, "What the fuck is it?"

The cop didn't even acknowledge Boom's blatant disrespect. He simply went into the usual bullshit. "Alright, fella, watch yourself now, okay? Unless you wanna take a ride down to the PD, and I know you don't want that, do ya?" He paused for a response, and when he got none, he continued, "So, what ya doin' in there? Shootin' dope or smokin' crack; which is it?"

"Fuck you, man," replied Boom plainly.

"Feisty one, huh?" the cop said with a chuckle to himself. He was way too tired to dig too deeply into their exchange. "Fuck me?" he said. Any other time, he would've taken Boom for a long ride until he found somewhere to beat the disrespect out of him. But for now, he was just too damn tired. "Junkie, prick bastard! Take your fucking dope, or your dust, or whatever the fuck it is you're getting' high on, up to your shack to OD. Just take that shit off of my streets. And make sure not to shoot that last killer load up for another hour or two, could ya? That's when my shift's over." The corny copper was laughing out loud now. He turned his flashlight off and left Boom to his thoughts, or lack thereof, thanks to him.

Boom was starting to get tired now, too, so he decided to leave the catching up until tomorrow, when he had that talk with Black. He retired to the comfort of his apartment.

Upon entering, he heard a mumbled sound come from the living room, just to the left of the front door. That automatically put him on the defensive. He had his pistol drawn now, ready to let some unfortunate soul have the entire clip. He shut the door quietly and locked it, then entered with caution. The darkness that consumed the room made it hard for him to see, but all he needed was a moving target. Then he'd make it stop moving.

He opened the living room door with a fierce anger written all over his face. When he pointed his weapon, to his surprise…

"Boom, no!" Shonda managed to blurt out. "It's just me…Shonda!"

Boom let out a gasp and lowered his cannon. He shut his eyes for a second to come back to his senses. "What the fuck am I thinking?" he asked himself. He'd completely forgotten that he invited Shonda over for the night. He was so anxious to make his prior engagement on time that everything else just faded away. He was coming back to reality now.

"I'm sorry, Shonda; that's my fault," he admitted. "That's me just used to being alone here. It would take a bit of time for me to get used to coming home, and having someone already there. I usually got the crib all to myself."

Shonda was beginning to feel bad. Not only because she felt like she was invading Boom's space, but also because she wished that he could experience a real relationship like she had with Ivan. She knew that he was a rare breed. He didn't care much about the things that usually blind a young man's eyes to what's really important. He had a clear mind state, not fluttered with the urge to be the man, with the big jewels, and he the big car with the big wheels, and the nice expensive crib. None of that stuff meant much to Boom. He was simpler than that. That was the only reason he didn't attract the opposite sex to his fullest ability; he wasn't flashy enough.

"I'm sorry, Boom. I didn't mean to be an intruder. I promise I'll be out of your way as soon as possible."

She went back to couch, where she had made her bed for the night. Boom followed.

"You don't have to be sorry, Shonda. I ain't mean it like that. You know you ain't no burden or anything; it's just not what I'm used to, that's all. It ain't nothin' though; trust me, I just ain't want you thinkin' I was some fuckin' maniac or some shit."

As Boom took a seat at the end of the couch, Shonda moved her feet over a bit to make room for him. She was lying underneath a quilt and wearing a long T-shirt and socks.

"What you doin' in here anyway?" Boom asked, changing the subject. "I thought I told you that you could have my bed. You all the way out here, all curled up on this couch, for what?"

"Oh come on now, Boom. It's bad enough I'm in here invading your privacy. I didn't wanna be in your way. Besides," she said after thinking a bit more. "Imagine if I'd have been in there instead of in here. You would have blown me away for sure!"

She and Boom took a moment to share a laugh. The tone had definitely lightened up from a minute ago.

"Thanks for letting me stay here tonight, though," said Shonda. "And thanks for the ride home yesterday."

"Oh, come on. It ain't nothin'. How've you been dealin' so far?"

"Not too good," admitted Shonda. "But better. I know I wouldn't have been able to stand being in that place too much longer, so it's a good thing you came when you did. I never felt so vulnerable, Boom. It was crazy. I felt like my whole body was just turned inside out. It was so scary, just sitting there, lookin' at him like that. And no bullshit, I ain't the type to scare easy. But it was just too much for me." She paused as the visions consumed her, and then continued, "Besides that, them heels were tearin' my feet up, boy!"

They shared another little laugh to lighten things up again. Then Shonda asked the question that she'd been waiting all night to ask.

"So... Ya'll get him?"

Boom quickly looked up at her. She couldn't even hide that she was hanging on to his response. She could almost already feel the excitement she'd get if he replied, *'YES!!!'* She was all ready to jump for joy.

Boom didn't answer right away. He wasn't being at all quick enough for Shonda; she was sitting straight up now, waiting to hear the words.

"Hmm," he said with a hint of happiness peeking from his own face. He still had the vision of Travis crying out, from the pain he felt in his head. "Yeah, we got him."

"Oh, thank you!!!" Shonda said as she pulled Boom closer for a hug. She held on to him as tight as she could, and he returned her advance by wrapping his arms around her and squeezing. "Thank you! Thank you!" Shonda spat over and over again.

When her eyes met with Boom's, she said, "I love you so much!"

Boom was amazed to hear those words coming out of her mouth. He'd never even heard her say that to Ivan, not that she didn't love him; she just made it a point never to express those emotions in front of others. She was protective like that of her feelings. She was a soldier.

She was really happy. Shonda had a look of genuine love in her eyes, and Boom still carried a look of amazement. Suddenly, they both leaned in nearer to each other. The closer they got to one another, the slower time seemed to be moving. Shonda's huge grin began to fade as she wet her lips. They could both feel themselves getting closer and closer, but neither one of them could stop. They shut their eyes. Their lips met. It was completely unexpected, but it felt oh so good. Their lips tapped in short intervals at first, then their mouths opened. That's when Shonda's tongue met with Boom's. Then she gently sucked on his bottom lip as he did her upper. Their eyes remained shut the whole time as they sunk deeper and deeper into each other's mouth. Boom had never felt such passion. He'd never once kissed a woman, and felt fireworks exploding inside of his body. It was as exhilarating as he'd imagined it would be.

Boom pulled Shonda closer, and she didn't resist one bit. As he sat straight up, she straddled his lap, never disengaging their kiss. His arms were still wrapped around her and hers around him. As their kiss grew more and more intense, her hands traveled from the back of his head, around to his neck, then from there down to his chest. She was searching lower and lower, and Boom could already feel himself growing erect. Anticipating her next movement only made her touches all the more satisfying. When she reached his stomach, she lifted his shirt and threw her hand underneath. She slid her hand down his abs, until she felt something hard and stiff waiting for her safely tucked away inside of Boom's jeans. It was his nine-millimeter Glock. She felt the handle, and Boom's mind finally caught up to his body. He put his hand on hers to stop her from advancing any further. Their kiss came to a halt, but their eyes remained shut. They just sat there, neither one of them wanting to speak first.

After a long awkward silence, Boom finally said, "What are we doing, Shonda?"

She could only cover her face with her hands. Her body started to shake now. Without a response, she simply broke into tears as a flood spewed from her eyes and down her face. She was so embarrassed. She threw herself from Boom's lap and curled up on the other side of the sofa. She wanted to have an explanation, but she had none. Nothing she could say could justify what had just happened.

"I am so sorry, Boom," she managed to spit out between the sniffles and moans. "I am so, so, so sorry…please, I don't want you to think I'm some kind of slut. I would never do him dirty like that. You believe me, right? I just don't know what came over me."

Boom closed the gap between them to console her by rubbing her back. He also felt some embarrassment. Neither one of them had any idea how this happened.

"Nah, Shonda, I'm the one that should be sorry. I'm fuckin' up. I don't even know how that shit just happened. But it's my fault more than it is yours. I know what you're dealing with right now, and now I feel like I'm taking advantage of that. Shit is just wrong. I'm sorry, Shonda. I know how much you've lost, and…"

Pausing in the middle of his sentence made Shonda take notice. She lifted her head out of her lap to see if he was okay. He wasn't. His eyes grew wide, his lips frowned, and his chin was twitching now as he fought. He put up a great fight at that, but for long enough. He was ready. A single tear, slowly trickling down his cheek, brought a waterfall of emotions out of Boom that had been buried deep inside. He was letting all of those emotions go now. He could no longer hold back. His deeply obscured cries seemed to have no end.

Shonda let go of her shame and held onto Boom tightly, and he did the same to her. They remained clenched to each other for the entire night. They fell asleep just like that.

★★★

When the doorbell rang, it was eight a.m. Boom lifted his head and started rubbing the sleep off of his face. Shonda must've gotten up before him, because she was nowhere to be found. He got up as the doorbell rang again. He stretched out his joints and went to see who it was.

"Who that?" he yelled as he yawned.

"Me," said Black. "Rise and shine, lil' nigga!"

"Uncle Black?" said a surprised Boom as he opened the door. "What you doin' here?"

As he opened the door to let Black in, Shonda came from the back out of the bathroom. She was wrapped in one towel as she dried her hair with another.

"Boom, somebody's at the door!" she yelled before looking up. "Want me to see who it..." That's all she managed to get out before she lifted her head from beneath the towel. "Oh," she simply said. "I see you already got it."

Black looked from Boom to Shonda, then back to Boom. Complete and utter confusion filled the inside of his head. He wanted to say, '*What the fuck???*' But he didn't. He bit down on his tongue, and managed to keep his jaw locked.

"Hey, Black," said Shonda nonchalantly before walking back into the bathroom. She didn't even give the misrepresentation a thought.

Nah, he thought. *Jr. wouldn't do that...would he? Is that even possible?* Black shook off the thought, and followed Boom into the kitchen, where he was pouring himself a glass of orange juice to go with his breakfast cigarette.

"So what's up, Unc'?" asked Boom. "What *you* doin' here so early? I know you don't like burials and all; I ain't expect to see you until later tonight."

"Well, I knew you would be busy for most of the afternoon and maybe into the evening, so I decided to stop by early. Hmmm, seems like you got busy earlier than I thought you would," said Black sarcastically.

Boom looked at him up and down with a chiseled stare. "What's that about, Uncle? You comin' at *me* like that?" Boom thought about what he was implying, then the vision of what he let happen last night flew through his head. He took a long pull from the cancer-stick as the thought of him and Shonda... together...that *way*. Black was actually on point with the comment that he made, but it was *still* fucked up. He didn't know enough to jump to that conclusion. *Who the fuck did he think he was?* "It ain't like that, man," he said as his head lowered to the ground with shame. "I can't believe you'd even...awe, fuckin' forget it. I don't even wanna go that route."

"Listen, Jr.," said Black, trying to fix the ill mood that he'd set. "I ain't mean it like that. You know..."

"Yeah, I know," said Boom. "Don't even trip. It ain't nuthin'."

"Well, what I originally came here for was to fill up those blanks in ya head, boy. You've waited long enough. I guess I haven't really noticed how much you've grown over the years, and...you a man now, and...I guess I owe you that much. In a way, it was my own selfishness that kept us from having this conversation earlier. I just didn't want to relive that day...the worse day of my whole life." Black paused to look into Boom's eyes. He had the same look on his face that Shonda did last night before Boom told her about Travis. Hunger... emptiness...desperation. "You ready?"

Boom thought for about a half-second. He took the seat beside Black and blew another cloud of cigarette smoke into the air. "Shit yeah."

CHAPTER 4

"Beast??" yelled Pam through the bathroom door. "Can you hear me??"

"Yeah," Beast replied in his deep, raspy voice. "Of course I could hear you, bitch; you screamin' ain't you? What the fuck do you want??"

"You got a call; it's Bingham. He said it's important!"

"Well, tell that nigga I'm in the shower then," Beast replied. "What the fuck? I'm supposed to just jump out of the damn tub with soap drippin' from my dick to chit-chat???? You tell him—"

"I know," Pam replied before Beast got a chance to reiterate. "You'll call him back."

"Stupid ass bitch," he said to himself.

Beast never had a problem with expressing himself. He always said what he thought. His motto was simple...FUCK EVERYBODY! If he couldn't benefit from a situation, then there was no business to discuss. He didn't dress anything up, or paint colors on a picture that weren't there to begin with. Everything was either black or white.

Beast was the major player in the dope and coke business in the Philadelphia area: North and South Philly, plus all the neighboring cities alike. They all knew Beast. His name could definitely ring some bells.

But Beast, he wasn't your run-of-the-mill big-time hustler. He wasn't quick-witted, clever, or even smooth with his approach. His shit was much simpler: he saw something he wanted, he took it! He'd already strong-armed his way from South to North Broad Street, taking out each and every independent dealer or crew that posed any kind of threat. Now, he was even expanding his empire west as far as Harrisburg and east into New Jersey. But with all of the respect he got in the streets—add to that the fear he put into the hearts of so many men, women and children—he still couldn't take a fuckin' peaceful shower in his own home without this dumb-ass broad bothering him about some bullshit telephone call!

Beast stepped out of the shower feeling somewhat refreshed. He draped his huge frame in his plush, hooded, Tresaro bathrobe, and slipped into his flip-flop sandals. He grabbed a towel to dry his face, and then threw it over his shoulder to dry his long, silky hair. His face was cleanly shaven, and his skin complexion was light. He was obviously a mixed breed; half Black and half Sicilian...a mean-ass thug muthafuckin' Negro...with a hint of John Gotti's bravado.

One thing everyone knew, you didn't want this nigga Beast agitated. That's just asking for trouble. Now, he was already a little on edge from the fuss while he was in the shower; now he was standing in the middle of his kitchen in complete awe. *Where the fuck is my hash and eggs?* he thought. He looked around a second time, and still found nothing. He was dumbfounded at first, but that—mixed with the frustration from the previous disturbance—formed a nice blend of pissed off.

"Pam??" he yelled out. "Pam, where the fuck you at, woman??"

"Right here," she yelled from upstairs. As she walked down the stairs of his rich duplex apartment, she sucked her teeth, anticipating the bullshit that Beast was complaining about now. "What is it, Beast?" she asked, not even trying to hide her apparent attitude.

"The fuck you mean, Pam? Where's my goddamn hash and eggs?"

Pam simply rolled her eyes. She'd been used to Beast and his moods by now. It had been some years now since she had started staying there with him, but she was way too stubborn to break.

"Well," she began in an unusual, pouting tone. "I was just upstairs ironing *your* clothes. You think it's fair to chew my ass out for doing what I'm told?" She paused to see if Beast caught her intentional double-meaning. She smiled and batted her eyes.

"You is one nasty bitch, you know that?" said Beast with a telling grin now overthrowing the anger that had once consumed his facial expression. "You know how I am before I get something to...*eat*."

"Oh yeah," replied Pam, as her natural juices began to puddle in her silk, thong panties. "Mmm, I know exactly what you mean," she said while untying the belt that was keeping her robe together. "I'm so sorry, daddy."

Her dark skin was oiled just enough for the reflecting light to capture Beast's attention. He squinted his eyes a bit to get a clearer look. Up and down, he scanned her from the top of her head—with her hair flowing wavy and long – down to her pretty little French manicured toes. He began licking his lips, already feeling his blood racing to his lower region.

He beckoned her nearer with a nod and she quickly came to him. His grin now larger, he leaned in for a kiss. Pam decided that she was gon' play it tuff though. She wasn't about to just let him have it that easily, not after the bitch session he was just trying to conduct. He needed to suffer a bit. She leaned away. He leaned in closer even, and she weaved another advance with a turn of her head. Beast was relentless though. If he had one distinguishing character trait, it would be his relentlessness. He saw an opening and went full speed ahead. His tongue flew out of his mouth and went straight into Pam's unsuspecting ear. He then gripped the back of her neck with his huge rough hand and forcefully turned her head toward him. She wasn't at all turned off by his vigorousness. She couldn't help but show her excitement by giving a wet, passionate kiss. They kissed passionately for a minute, but then Beast was cutting the exchange short. He grabbed her by the neck and spun her around, bending her over the kitchen counter. With her head planted firmly between the blender and the toaster, she felt Beast searching for her penetration point. She was loving every minute of it, but she just couldn't stand waiting any longer. As he hardened, her wanting lips got more and more moistened…all four of them! When she couldn't take the anticipation anymore, she got her hands free of his grasp and reached around for his dick. When she got her hands on it, thick and hard, she hurriedly found her wet spot with his head. She then grabbed onto his ass with both hands and forced him into her hole. She let out a cry, but begged him not to stop. Beast was as hard as steel now, loving every thrust into her wet pussy, digging deeper and deeper into her stomach. He gripped her ass with both hands and gave it to her long and hard, just how she wanted it. She wanted him all the way inside of her. She wanted him deeper than he'd ever been. She wanted him to change the way she fuckin' walked!

If anyone could hear them from the hall, her cries would have definitely warranted a 911 emergency call. She sounded like she was being savagely tortured, and that every bit of her chocolate frame was in unimaginable pain. When, in fact, it was the complete opposite. This was the best feeling in the world for her. She was like a typical guy in that sense; she wanted it morning, noon and night. She wasn't happy unless she had a stiff one in her—in, out, back, forth, and sideways.

Pam was about to cum now, and Beast wasn't far behind her. His fingers sunk deeper into her soft, plump ass. Every stroke brought them closer and closer to ecstasy. He couldn't wait. His invasions became quicker and sharper once he found her hot spot. If he knew her like he thought he did, she wasn't far from orgasm. He stabbed her with his pipe faster even, abusing that nice little soft spot deep inside of her.

"Here it come!" he managed to yell between short, brief breaths. "Here it go; now get it wit me!" He coached her through it, when in actuality, it wasn't at all necessary. "Get it wit the boy, baby. Cum wit me!"

Simultaneously, they were climaxing. "Aaaaahhhhh!" said Beast, while Pam let out a high-pitched holler. One last plunge left Pam's leg shaking and Beast out of breath. They stayed there, just like that, until Beast got weak. He backed himself out of her slowly, and made his way up the stairs to his bedroom where a fresh pack of cigarettes was waiting for him. As soon as he entered the room, the telephone started to ring. Shit, he wasn't about to let that shit fuck his plans up. He intended on blowing that cigarette smoke into the air, and do absolutely nothing but enjoy his numbness. He collapsed on the bed, and tore the cigarette box open to get one. The phone had stopped ringing by the time he got it lit. He inhaled the smoke and exhaled it slow. That was all he needed, and he was happy with the world. Nothing could fuck that up now...yeah right!

He heard Pam climbing the steps and just knew that his pleasant feeling would be ruined. She stopped in the doorway with the cordless phone in her hand waving it at Beast. She still couldn't even open her eyes all the way yet. She looked like a dope-fiend on a marvelous high. Her body was swaying back and forth, and she didn't even know it.

"Beast?" she slurred, as if she were talking in her sleep. "Pick up the phone; it's Bingham. He say it's important, or whatever."

She walked over to Beast and handed him the phone. He reluctantly accepted.

"What, nigga?" Beast said with the same dope-like slur. "What you want?"

"We gotta talk, Beast," said Bingham, one of Beast's most loyal lieutenants. "The boy Strong…he dead. Somebody sent that nigga off, in the worst kinda way. Niggas did that man dirty as hell."

Beast's eyes were opened up real wide now, and his lips were pressed together. There was no concealing his anger and aggravation. Now, *no* piece of pussy could have an effect on his foul mood.

"Somebody?" he said.

"We on that now," replied Bingham, knowing exactly where Beast's train of thought was going.

"Oh, don't even bother," Beast replied after a second thought. "I already know."

He hung up the phone as Pam was about to lie down beside him. "What's wrong?" she asked, reaching for his cigarette.

He pulled it away looking up at her now like she was a stranger. "What, bitch?" he spat. "You know what? You just worry yourself with this one thing…get my motherfuckin' hash and eggs cooked!"

★★★

After a long recollection of memories that Black had buried deep inside of his past, he was finally ready to tell Boom just what he wanted so badly to know. For the first time, he was about to rehash that day. If there was only one thing that could force him to do so, it was Boom's need to know what happened to his parents, and why they couldn't be there with him as he grew into manhood.

"When I tell you that this was the one day of my life that I wish I could go back in time to fix," began Black. "I mean that shit with every ounce of my being.

"Now, Sylvester," he said, using a name that only he could. "It ain't pretty, and I ain't gon' make it sound no more sweet than it was. If you sure—"

"Fuck it, Unc'," Boom plainly stated. "Let's just get into it."

Black began the story with the killing of Boom's father, Vester. He spoke of the brutality and savageness it was carried out with. With dreadful detail, he told of how his father's body was found, near a dumpster behind an abandoned building just about where Prospect Avenue met with Southern Boulevard. He was left with his throat slit, and multiple stab wounds in his torso. He remembered a police officer telling them that he had already died from the stabs before his neck was slit. At that point, Black knew that it had to have been personal. If a nigga put that much time and effort in, he had some shit on his mind. It definitely wasn't just some random occurrence. Sure enough, the streets had an idea of what went down.

In fact, everybody claimed to know what transpired, but that's how it is in the hood. Everybody knows everybody, and they were all talking. That whole week, all anyone talked about was why Vester got done in the way he did.

"With all the different versions of the story I heard," admitted Black, "only one name popped every last time; this muthafucka named Carl Winchester. People called him Winch. He was just a little dude...physically, I mean. But that was before he got sent up. When he came home, he had the build of intimidation, and the scarred ice-grill to complement his muscular figure. He only did about four years in, but in those four short years, a whole heap of shit had changed. Just so happens, your father used to date his wife, back in the day before Winch got with her. One of the rumors say they hadn't completely ended that."

"You tryin' to tell me that my pops got murdered over a bitch?" stated Boom with the fire growing in his body.

Black didn't know how to respond right away. His face expressed no clue, just blankness. He looked as if he had just completely lost touch with his surroundings for a second. What Boom said just echoed in his ear over and over again. *'For a bitch, bitch, bitch...For a bitch, bitch, bitch...'*

When Boom continued, Black was brought back to reality. "That's what it is, Unc'?" Boom pleaded. "Huh, Uncle Black? Is that what it is?"

"I'm not saying that, Jr. Remember, I'm not speaking from first-hand knowledge. All I can describe is the picture that the street painted for me, son. If you really want to know, just let me get through it. This ain't the easiest thing for me either; you know what I mean?"

"Yeah, I know how you feel. Go ahead and finish. I ain't gon' say shit else." He was still boiling inside, but for now, he would maintain his frustration.

"Now, the streets wasn't always exactly on the mark, but there has been some times when it was right on point. Just don't be takin' what I'm sayin' as no cosign, alright?"

Boom agreed and Black continued.

Black brought the story up until the day of the wake. As soon as he began, Boom's brain was registering the data and filling in the blanks that his childhood mind had let go of so long ago. Finally, they were at the point in the story when one of Vester's partners started singing, "It's So Hard." The doors flew open and it slowly grew darker as silence fell over the room.

"Bitch, you got some fucking nerve!!!" yelled Grace at Patrice, the fur-coated woman that had just barged in with her man, Carl. "You must be out yo rabbit-ass mind comin' up in here...and with that sleaze you call a husband. If ya'll triflin' bastards ain't gon' leave *right* this motherfucking minute, I'ma wrap both my hands 'round your tiny little throat and squeeze 'til you stop movin', bitch!"

Patrice jumped backwards in defense. She comforted behind the shield of her man. Now his chest was poking straight out as his ice-grill got colder and fiercer.

"I ain't here for you, Grace," said Patrice from behind her man. "I'm here for Vester, and I ain't havin' you tryin' to stop me from saying goodbye to him. You know, we had our shit we went through, but I still loved him!"

"Just ease back, little lady," added Winch. "You know we ain't come here for no trouble. Once she pay her respect, we gon' be outtie."

Grace didn't budge an inch. She looked at Winch up and down. Her chest poking out now too and she had her chin lifted and her lips tight. "I ain't havin' it."

Winch would cease to be civil. "Oh yeah?" he asked, like he was pleased with her resistance. "Listen, cunt, you don't be getting' from out my way, you gon' be joinin' yo faggot-ass husband. I ain't playin' not a bit either."

Out of nowhere appeared Black by Grace's side. He had his head down with his hat pulled low. He stepped between Grace and Winch. He lifted his head to look him in the face. Through pitch-black shades, their eyes still penetrated each other's soul. Nothing was left hidden, but now Black saw that Mr. Winchester had no fear in his heart either. He was ready, just as ready as Black, if not more.

As it was apparently about to go down, Vester's old friend approached from the podium. He didn't have the same intentions as everyone else at this point. His only concern was to shield young Sylvester from what was about to happen. No one even saw him grab Lil' Silly and carry him out of the building. They occupied a stoop next door. There, they waited...Sylvester, unknowing of what was happening, and Vester's friend, not even *wanting* to know! He could only hope things wouldn't escalate too much, but he couldn't have even imagined how severe of a shit-storm was being created.

★★★

Back inside the funeral home, Vester's proceedings were about to turn into a slugfest. Not even giving it a second thought, Black lifted his arms, as if he was welcoming Winch to attack. That's when the chrome butt of his gun reflected a gleam of sunlight into his eye, and for a split second, he was vulnerable, as his eyes blinked to block the gleaming reflection. Black quickly attacked, throwing a left jab, followed by a right across his chin. He then grabbed him by the head with both hands and forced him downward as his knee lifted into his forehead. He repeated this motion over and over again, savagely digging blows into the head of Winch. He was so engulfed in this savage beat-down, that he didn't see the wide-body dread coming straight for him. He also didn't see Winch reaching for the blade he had inside of his coat.

A sharp poke to Black's side stung him. He was caught completely off guard. His arms flew up and his torso curled over to the one side. Another poke from Winch's blade made Black react. He grabbed onto Winch's arm, stopping him from pulling the blade back out of his side. He swung a wild elbow around, and it landed directly on Winch's jaw. By now he'd let go of the shank, and fell to the ground. But that's when the dread finally got a hold of Black. He grabbed him from the back and gave him a bear hug that dug the blade even deeper into the hole it had already made, as well as cutting off his air supply. When the blade finally fell out, Patrice saw an opening to deliver an attack of her own. Her man was still on the floor holding his head. She grabbed the blade and swung it around in Black's direction. But when the blade sunk in, it wasn't Black who got struck. It was Grace who caught the sharp thump to the chest, as she jumped in the way to protect Black, just as he'd done for her.

Patrice was shocked. She had never done anything like that ever in her whole life. Now, there was blood pouring out of Grace's chest, and Patrice's fur was covered in it. She backed up from Grace's body, now on the floor jerking back and forth. She looked at the blood on her hands. Her eyes were bulging out of her head now. She couldn't contain herself anymore; she began crying uncontrollably. Attempts to wipe her hands clear of the deep-red liquid all failed. It only spread the stains, as she tried rubbing her hands through her coat to clean them. She collapsed to the ground as the shock consumed her.

When the dread realized that things had gone way too far and so quickly, he let go of Black's body. Black fell to the ground lifelessly. The dread got Winch to his feet and helped him up and out of the building. They fled from the building, leaving Patrice on the floor going crazy, Grace on the floor with blood flowing freely from her frame, and Black on the ground unconscious. They even bumped young Sylvester to the side as they made their getaway in an uncaring haste.

Even now, as Boom heard the rest of the story, the holes in his memory were beginning to fill. He even remembered Winch and the dread running past him, as they left his mommy and Uncle Black on the floor for dead.

Now that Winch was gone, and all of the commotion quieted down, the few scared people that had been in the funeral home started coming out of their hiding places. Patrice's raving had been lowered to a segmenting hum as tears still ran down her traumatized facial expression.

By the time someone got where Grace was lying, she had already stopped moving. By now, a crowd had formed around Grace and Black while they lay. Then Black started to get his consciousness back. He lifted his head to feel the striking pain in his head get ten times worse. He was still leaking from his side, and his chest hurt like hell. Even with that, it couldn't amount to the hurt he was about to feel. He turned over to see Grace's dead eyes staring up at him. The look on her face was permanently burnt onto his brain. This was evident, as his words began to crack when he got to this part of the story. All he saw was the blood that was all over the floor. With all of himself, he tried to wake her, but to no avail. His cries grew louder and louder, but of course, she couldn't hear him.

He could only yell at the top of his lungs, "SOMEBODY CALL 9-1-1!!!"

CHAPTER 5

The meeting was set promptly for this morning. Once the news was brought to the attention of the boss man, he quickly organized to discuss what was to be done...what needed to be done.

All of the lieutenants were to sit down for this emergency exchange. Of course Bingham was there. The boy Dogg was there, and so was Bop. Them, plus another half-dozen cats in attendance all occupied seats around the huge dining room table for a...*board meeting,* if you will. War was coming, and you could almost get a whiff of the stench in the air.

They were all keeping themselves calm as best they could, while they waited for Beast. Some were smoking cigarettes or cigars to calm their nerves; others were as far gone as sniffing small sprinkles of cocaine right off that little space between their thumb and index finger. It was a tense time and everyone just needed to be cool.

When Beast walked in, of course everyone just stared with anticipation. All they needed was the word, and the wheels of death would be rolling sooner than later. He only had to deliver the directive, and his orders would be carried out to the tee.

He took his seat at the head of the table. With an uncaring expression on his face, he scanned the room to make certain everyone was there. When he knew he had their undivided attention, he spoke.

"This boy, Boom?" he simply asked. "Dead or alive?"

***

"I gotta ask..." stated Boom once Black was done with his story. "This nigga Winch? He still breathin' or no?"

"Well, last I heard..."

"Last you heard??" Boom said, raising his voice. "What, you don't know? You mean you ain't see this muthafucka and..."

"Listen here, lil' nigga," said Black, cutting into Boom's questioning. "Don't you ever trump *me* on no bullshit like I'm some kinda square or somethin', ya hear?? The only reason I told you what I did was so you could sleep at night... so that you could breathe easy. This ain't about you opening this wound, son. I put it behind me, long ago. I put it behind us!! That shit was the past. Let the past be the past, lil' nigga."

"Wait, fall back a second Unc'. The past?" Boom asked. "My mom's...my pop's...murdered, and it's just 'the past?' That's it, huh? You can't be serious, Unc'. That can't be all they meant to you."

"You don't even know the half of what she meant to me...what they both did!" After a sigh, he continued, "They meant so much to me that I chose this path instead of the one that might've led to more blood and death. You couldn't even *begin* to grasp what it took for me to leave that place, those people, alive, and breathing. You know what the difference is, kid. I'm here...with you. Don't hate me 'cause I chose you...don't just cut me off like I'm some kinda sucker. It ain't nothin' like ya thinkin', lil' nigga. Just wonder, what help would I be to you dead and buried alongside your father? What if I *did* go after Winch, him and that whore of his? What good would it do? I thought about all of that shit, and then I made my move. I needed to be there for you, Sylvester...for *you!* I made a promise that I'd look after you if *anything* happened. I'm a piece of shit without my word...I'm nothing!

"You know I ain't afraid of shit, but maybe one thing. And it ain't losing my own worthless life neither. Only thing that could ever scare me was the thought that you'd grow up without someone in this world to look up to...like a father-figure, even if it *is* just some old crook. I mean, you could be a lot better off, but you could've been a whole hell of a lot worse than having me as a pops. Don't you *ever* forget that!"

Boom was beginning to realize some things about Black that he couldn't see before. He knew he wasn't scared of nothin'; that's for damn sure. But he also knew now, for the first time, how different they really were. Boom wasn't scared of shit either. Call it courage, call it ignorance; call it whatever the fuck you want! There's such a thin line between the two that it doesn't even make a difference. But he would've still taken them out—shit he still might—but he definitely wouldn't have turned his back and forgot all about them that easily, no way!

Now what animosity was growing in his stomach once Black had caught him up on his past was tripled. He could forgive Black for not taking care of those muthafuckas, but he couldn't forgive himself if he turned the other cheek. He was a man now, all grown up. Things were different. His mind was already made up.

While Boom and Black had been talking in the kitchen, Shonda kept to the background. She didn't want to disturb them, but she also didn't want to be late. It was finally time for her to say her last and final goodbyes to Ivan. She came to the kitchen entrance and looked at Boom worriedly. "I'm sorry to interrupt ya'll, but..."

"Yeah, I know," he said. "It's about that time, huh?"

Black stood up to make his way out. Before he left, he made sure Boom was okay. "You gon' be cool, Sylvester?"

"Yeah," he quickly answered without any feeling or sincerity. "I'm alright."

"Just don't disappoint me, son...please don't. Bury your friend, and move on. Look forward, into the future. Think about that little girl. Handle yourself responsibly. Please, I don't ever want to hear about you goin'..."

"I got it, Unc'," stated Boom in the same monotone voice. He looked at him in his eye. "I understand...don't worry."

***

With that, Black was off. He felt as if this whole thing couldn't have gone any better. He was worried before he got there, right up until he sat down and began this memory lane trip. But he was feeling a hundred percent better now. Things didn't have to get as ugly as he'd thought they might.

***

Unfortunately, Boom couldn't share in Black's uplifting spirit. He knew now that things would be getting a whole lot darker before he saw any light again. He couldn't nor did he even want to fight it. Of course, he'd wait until after the funeral, and once Shonda and Sabra were doing fine again. Then, he would do what came naturally; he would find the muthafucka that caused his life so much hardship and pain, and settle this shit once and for all.

★★★

Today was different for Boom. He wouldn't be in rare form, as he was yesterday. For his final goodbyes, he would present himself to his comrade as he knew him. Shit, Ivan wouldn't have even recognized Boom in a damn suit and tie, not unless he was goin' to court or somethin'. No phony suits and ties, and shiny shoes and shit today though. Nah, grimey season was back in full swing. Once out of the shower, Boom dressed himself in a pair of Gortex boots, some black jeans, a black hoody sweater, and a black bandana hung neatly from his back pocket. The only thing that would be tied was the du-rag that covered his head. He was ready now, more than ever, to give his boy a final *"one love."*

★★★

The funeral was just as crowded as the wake was, if not more. People from all over Philly came through to show support. Most were welcomed, others...well, we'll get to that.

Above all, Boom was feeling so much better about today as opposed to yesterday. He almost had a bright outlook on things. Mostly, he was excited to be there with a parting gift for Ivan. He almost wished he was alive just so that he could see his face when he presented it. He's sure Ivan's face would be just as lit up as his. That's what made it easier for him. He knew that his efforts would be appreciated, whether Ivan could show them or not.

He waited until the casket was being lowered into the ground. That's when he pulled that neatly folded black bandana from his pocket, which was acting as his gift-wrapping of sorts. He approached the edge, where everyone stood to toss roses. His offer would have much more meaning than mere rose petals. He was allowing Ivan a true peaceful resting place. He could know with certainty that his murderer was gone now, too.

Boom tossed the bandana into the grave, which wrapped Travis' bloody trigger-finger, then said a prayer. *"In the name of the Father, the Son, and the Holy Spirit... Amen,"* he said to himself. "Rest in peace, brother."

Boom turned around to see Shonda over by his car. She was holding Sabra in her arms extremely tightly. Almost so tight, that her little chest was starting to hurt. Boom immediately came to their side. He rubbed Shonda's shoulders and she quickly turned to embrace him. He took Sabra from her and held on to her tightly as he returned Shonda's hug.

"Let it go," he said. "We can leave now, if you're ready. My nigga Ivan is gon' be good now."

Just as he was about to put them in the car, a black limousine pulled up beside them slowly. The back window came a quarter of the way down, just enough for Beast to get a good look at his enemy. The limo' slowed down more even while Beast squinted his eyes to get a better look. Boom didn't even see him; he was caught dead to right, completely off guard if it was about to go down. He had Sabra in one arm, embracing Shonda with the other. Nothing could've stopped Beast from taking him out right then and there. Luckily for Boom, Beast had common courtesy. This wasn't at all an attack on his part. He simply wanted a visual of this mean-ass bad muthafucka they call Boom, that's all. He knew he had the drop on him, but it wasn't that kind of visit...not the time or the place. This was just what he needed to know if the trouble was even worth it. He'd finally come to a decision. Now, he knew exactly what he needed to do.

***

The next few days were torture for Boom. He knew what he *wanted* to do, but he also knew what he was *obligated* to do. His responsibility lay with Shonda and Sabra before anything else, no doubt about it. But it was killing him staying in Philly when he knew there was so much unfinished business waiting for him back in the South Bronx. After a week, he said, "Fuck it!" He went by Shonda's place first, just to let her know that he was gon' be out of town for a few days. When he arrived at the apartment, he rang the downstairs buzzer. No answer. He rang it again, and still nothing.

"What the fuck?" he asked himself. "Where could she be?"

He thought for a second, but a second turned into a minute. A minute felt like an hour. He immediately lit up a cigarette. He called her on the house phone, but got no answer. Shonda knew to let him know if she was going anywhere. She definitely knew the deal. She was well-aware of the strong possibility that someone may be constructing a plan to counter what happened to Travis. Everyone had to have known who sent him back to his maker, shit, except for the police. Street-level cats definitely knew what was up, and Shonda knew that shit. What harm would it be for her to drop a line to Boom, just to be on the safe side? He called her cell phone next, and got more of the same; it simply kept ringing. It was bugging the shit out of him. In haste, he called Ivan's mother next. Maybe she knew where he could find Shonda.

"Hello," Ivan's mom answered.

"Hey, Ms. Loretta."

"How have you been, baby?" she asked before he got a chance to question her of Shonda's and Sabra's whereabouts.

"Much better now," he quickly responded.

"That's good, because you know my boy is in a better place now, right? He's still with us, in spirit. He'll always be by our sides, watching over us, making sure we're doing what's right. You are doing the right thing, aren't you?"

Boom was stuck. He took another long pull from his cigarette. "Yes, ma'am," he responded. "Listen, have you spoke to—"

"That's good, baby," she said, cutting him off. "I was just thinking about you the other day, too. You know, if you ever need anyone to talk to, I'll be here for you. I was just on the phone with Shonda and told her the same—"

"You spoke to Shonda?" he asked excitedly. "When'd you speak to her? Was it recently?"

"Well, I only just hung up the phone with her when you called. She told me that she was about to give you a call, something about seeing your number in her phone."

Boom took a deep breath. He would definitely be going out of his mind if anything happened to Shonda or Sabra. "She tell you where she was at?" he asked.

"Yeah, she said she was in the playground across the street from her building with Sabra."

"Alright, Ms. Loretta." Boom took a deep breath to ease his nerves. "I have to go, but I'll speak to you soon."

"Okay, honey. Don't be a stranger."

"That's cool. I won't. Bye-bye now."

Boom simply flicked the cigarette from his hand and made his way toward the playground across the street. Upon hitting the curb, he saw the most beautiful thing he'd ever seen in his life. He stopped at the fence and just stood there... watching Shonda on the swings with Sabra on her lap. They really looked happy. It was genuine. He almost wanted to run over and act like a kid again, too. His dark thoughts prevented him. He quickly got a flash of Winch running past him, worrying about nothing but saving his own ass. He had business to take care of. He only came to make sure that Shonda and Sabra were okay. He'd accomplished that; now the time had come for him to bring that part of his life to a close. He would make only one more stop before he was off.

★★★

He arrived at Black's house next. His place was a small, two-bedroom spot in the outskirts of Philly. The only thing even halfway inviting about it was the huge backyard. But that was Black, though. He wasn't an attractive kinda guy. This was the house that Boom remembered most from his childhood. It was fitting that it would be the last he saw of Philadelphia before he returned home... to his first home, that is.

Unfortunately, Black didn't answer the bell after four rings. Boom quickly felt the uneasiness from earlier coming back. Just as he was about to start vigorously punching numbers into his phone, he remembered that he had the key to the lock. He fumbled through his pocket and rushed his key in. A twist of the knob and he was inside. He looked around and saw no signs of Black, until the corner of his eye caught a glimpse of something in the living room. After investigating further, he saw that it was Black.

"Unc'??" he yelled to get his attention. "What's up, man?"

He approached closer to find Black, with his body stretched out on the couch in a wife-beater and briefs. His face was planted firmly in the cushion, and he didn't budge a bit when Boom called to him.

"Uncle Black??" he said again, even louder than before. "Uncle Black, you asleep?"

Boom walked over and nudged at his shoulder, but Black gave no response. Boom gave a harder shove at his side, but to no avail. He quickly began worrying. He began searching the room for clues as to what might've happened to his uncle. He needed some kind of indication if something went down, but that was Boom, always assuming the worse. He was a true pessimist, always jumping to the most dreadful conclusion. But another good look at Black made sense of the whole scenario. That's when he saw just what he needed to know exactly what was going on. As Black's arm hung lifelessly from the couch, in his hand was the key factor in his coma-like state. Even as he lay there, with no signs of life, his hand kept a tight grip on an empty bottle of Dewar's Reserve Finest Scotch whisky. Although relieved, Boom was still a bit concerned at the sight of Black like this. It wasn't like he didn't have a drink once in a while, but this was extensive. He rarely saw him drunk; tipsy was one thing, but drop-down, piss-drunk? Nah, something must've been really fuckin' with his head. He thought twice, and then decided against probing any further. Knowing Black, he was probably just stressin' over a woman. He could do that from time to time. He'd get all stressed out 'cause some birdie didn't meet his expectations of them. That's what normally happened. He'd meet a nice lady and things would be going good and then something would fuck it all up.

Boom decided that he would just leave what he came to deliver, and be out. Not that he was uncaring; he just couldn't deal with all of that right now. He had his own issues that he had to work out for himself. When that happened, he could go back to being the caring and sensitive person that everyone knew and loved...yeah right!

He pulled a small black box from his pocket, and opened it to take one last good look at it. He rubbed the silver clean with his shirt and read the engraving to himself: *"I won't ever cut you off, Unc'...ONE."*

He placed the brand-new shiny cigar-cutter on the coffee table with a note attached: *I had to do it. Don't worry. I'll be back soon!*

CHAPTER 6

During the drive up I-95, Boom found himself imagining all the things he could do to Winch once he caught up with him. He was trying to finish off a burger he had gotten a few rest areas back, but all he kept doing was trying to vision torturing that poor bastard to death and loving every minute of it. The thought of making him squirm gave him great excitement. "Muthafucka's gon' let out noises he didn't know he could make," he said to himself aloud. *Whew*…it gave him shivers. He tried to imagine the look on Winch's face when he finally realized who Boom was, and that he was all grown up now. Ain't no telling what all of those years could do to an adolescent, but he would know exactly what he was there for, no doubt about it. His life would definitely be flashing in front of his face by then…that is what they say happens to people before they meet their maker, right? Yup, he'd be going down that trip sooner than later. Boom couldn't wait. He was so anxious.

In fact, it had been quite some time since Boom felt so much anxiety before a hit. By now, so many had died at the hands of this cold-hearted young man that there ceased to be any feelings involved. He definitely put some numbers up in his murder game. Shit, just went down like it was a regular day now. It was nothing like that the first time though. The first body he caught was different, a lot different. Don't get it twisted though; it *was* difficult, but well…it was kind of easy, too—if that makes any sense. Fuck it; you'll understand better once you know that whole story.

***

Back before Boom was Boom, and he was still Sylvester, he attended Benjamin Franklin Middle School in Philly just like any other regular kid. He wasn't too big on his studies, but he kinda slid through without making too much noise. He kept a crew of three, maybe four cats, nothing heavy. That character trait stayed with him. In fact, he never really liked to roll too deep. He didn't see the need.

Of course he'd already met Ivan by then, but Germ didn't click until later on. He and Ivan used to roll with a dude named Paul. He was a pudgy kid, dark skin with an Afro and big lips. He was from Philly, born and raised...a real hustler type; always tryin' to figure up ways to get some paper. He was actually the one connection young Sylvester made that set his life in the path of a professional hit-man. Fuckin' junior high school kids, huh?

"Yo, Sylvester," said Paul as they ate lunch in the school cafeteria. "Can I ask you somethin'?"

"What the fuck? You need permission or somethin'?" Sylvester replied while munching on a chicken sandwich. "Go ahead."

"You got a dad?" he asked.

"What?" Sylvester was looking at Paul with a fierce glare in his eye.

"Do you got a dad, nigga?" he asked for the second time as if there wasn't anything wrong.

"What the fuck kind of question is that, B?" Sylvester replied as he looked deeper into Paul's eyes to illustrate how much he wasn't feeling his line of questioning. "You tryin' to be funny or some shit?"

"Yo, Paul," interjected Ivan with a word of advice. "His pops passed a while back, so that's probably a sensitive topic. If you don't want this crazy mutha-fucka to jump across this table at ya fat ass, ya best be gettin' to a point."

Paul quickly took heed. "Oh shit," he said, realizing why his friend was staring with a look like he was imagining tearing his head off. "My bad, man. I ain't mean it like that. My fault, I just...I mean I just..."

"Spit it out, nigga," darted Ivan as his time was fading too quickly for him to recover.

"Well, you know that nigga Mark, right?" he finally spit out. "He's that quiet kid that sits in front of me in homeroom. Well, that nigga told me some foul shit about his pops today, and...you know he got a little sister and shit, right? So we just talkin' and shit, you know about nothing, right? Then this start goin' into all this heavy shit about his father, and that he's doing these things, and he don't know what to do. Finally this nigga tells me—"

Sylvester cut him off right there dead center of his sentence. He could anticipate this conversation taking a turn that wasn't suitable for the time or the place. He said they could wait until after school, and he proceeded to finish his sandwich.

★★★

They met in front when school let out. Paul brought Mark with him, so that he could tell the story himself. They all went to the park to drink some beers and talk—Sylvester, Ivan, Paul and Mark. Mark looked nervous though, like he desperately needed to get something off of his chest. He couldn't contain himself much longer.

Mark was the privileged kid compared to Sylvester, Ivan and Paul, but he wasn't rich. He definitely didn't need for as much as the others. But of course where his life lacked financial despair, he made up in other areas. Things were about to change though, if for the better was anyone's guess.

They got settled in the park and began drinking. It wasn't a minute before Mark blurted out, "Yo, I wanna kill my dad…wait, no…*I* don't wanna kill him…I mean—"

"What the fuck *do* you mean?" darted Sylvester. He quickly began to get disgusted with Mark, and he was starting to wonder what the hell this was all about. "How could you even say some shit like that outta ya mouth, B? That's some crazy shit!"

"Hold up," said Paul. "Let the boy explain…just hold up a minute."

Mark took a deep breath and continued. "You can think I'm crazy if you want, but all I know is…" His voice dropped to a low tone. "…I want my dad dead."

"Why?" asked Ivan. "What the fuck you gon' get out of killin' ya own pops?"

"It's not for me," replied Mark. "It's for my baby sister…"

It turns out that Mark's father, some up-and-coming lawyer, was molesting his own eight-year-old daughter, and had been doing so for some years now. Mark sort of always knew, but never once spoke to anyone about it until recently. He could no longer fight off the truth; it was hitting him too hard now. He'd finally decided that the only way to stop this man from continuing to traumatize his little sister was to murder him. He knew that if he went to his mother that she wouldn't believe that about her husband, or even worse, would give him another chance. He also knew that he couldn't go to the police, especially if his mother would be standing by her man's side. He had put some real long hard thought into what his options were, and when it came down to it, the only way to stop him would be to get rid of him for good.

Although Mark knew what he wanted, he also knew that he didn't have the balls to do it. That's why he chose to confide in Paul. He told Paul of the situation for only one reason; he would help pick someone they could trust to do the job. That's when Sylvester came to mind.

By this time, if he hadn't already, the entire school knew that if anyone was capable of the ultimate crime, it was Sylvester. This general consensus was only multiplied by his actions, such as taking on whole crews by himself, extorting people that ranged from crack-heads in his neighborhood to teachers in his own school, and openly showing blatant disrespect for the police—or any authority figure for that matter. He was the perfect person for the job.

When Mark was done, Sylvester wanted some time alone with him. He wanted to make absolutely certain that his mind was made up, and that he wouldn't be getting any second thoughts once it all went down. They walked over to some benches a bit further down to have some privacy.

"Ay man, you sure this is what you wanna do?" asked Sylvester. "Ain't no turning back from death; you know that, right? Once he's gone, he's gone for good. I mean, it's one thing to murder some random dude, but ya own pops? I don't know."

"Lemme tell you like this," said Mark as he confided in Sylvester. "I don't know you all that well, but I *do* know of you. I wouldn't just trust any-old-body with this, but I got respect for you. Shit, as far as Benjamin Junior High...you *that* muthafucka!" Mark's tone took a sharp turn in the serious direction again. His eyes started to well up before he went on to say, "I just can't...I don't know, man. She's only eight, man. Eight years old? I can't allow that shit." After another long pause, he continued, "Besides, it ain't just my sister no more. That fuckin' bastard!" Mark was about to crack. "He even started ..."

"Enough said, Mark," said Sylvester when he'd heard enough. He was positive now that Mark wouldn't be talking to too many more people about this. He had too much to lose. All of his chips were on the table, and he was bluffing. He was fully prepared.

After talking some more about how it would all go down, Mark and Sylvester walked back to where the rest of them were; now sitting in silence. When they were altogether, Sylvester gave a telling nod to Ivan. He looked over to Paul and gave him the same. Following a few more minutes of silence, Mark got up to leave. He could almost breathe easy now. They all exchanged pounds and Mark was off. As soon as he left, Ivan and Paul couldn't wait until they were able to ask Sylvester what they had talked about.

"So what's up, man?" asked Ivan. "You really gon' do it?"

"I'ma have to now," replied Sylvester. "Ain't no turning back."

"See why I was coming at you like that earlier, now?" asked Paul, still explaining the misunderstanding from the cafeteria. "I ain't mean nothin' by it, but that shit was fuckin' my head up, too. I mean, ya own father?"

"Yeah, well that muthafucka would've ceased to be my dad had he wilded out like that! You know muthafuckas call *me* a crazy nigga and I ain't scared of nothin' and all that, but I don't know if I would've been able to do this shit if it was a different situation. I did some niggas dirty, but I ain't never take no life, you know? You know what though; this coward is makin' it easy. Shit, I always wondered if I had it in me to take a body anyway…feel me?"

"Hmm," said Paul, with his heart now filling with even more fear regarding Sylvester and his abilities. "I hear that!" as if he could identify.

"So, it's all set up?" asked Ivan.

"Yeah, he supposed to be getting' a burner from that nigga Loddie…a little three-eighty or some shit. He had it all worked out like you wouldn't believe. Son is for real, yo."

***

It wouldn't be long now. Sylvester would be taking a big jump into his future with this shit he got himself into. And he was a hundred percent right, too; there was no turning back now.

Mark's plan was set up to be executed the following weekend. For the rest of that week, he and Sylvester cut out of school and went over their plans. They went through every detail over and over again.

It was supposed to go like this: Thanksgiving was nearing, and Mark's mother was taking him and his sister to Chicago to spend the holiday with family. Mark's father was supposed to go, but Mark was sure he would be pulling out at the last minute like he always did. Something always came up. He would take on a new case, or something would develop in a case that was already open. Whatever it was, Mark was positive that it would only be him, his sister and his mom going away, leaving his father home all alone. And just like he predicted, Mark's father told them Thursday night that he'd have to work through the holidays and that he wouldn't be able to go. That was all Mark needed to give Sylvester the word that the plan was a go.

When the time came, Sylvester was ready...or as ready as he'd ever be. He was to be at Mark's house shortly after they left for the airport. They were to catch a six-thirty flight so they would on their way around five p.m. His father would be dropping them off, he'd come home, and that would be it for him. Sylvester would be waiting, ready to put his ass down for good.

Just like clockwork, Sylvester could see from down the block that Mark and his family were right on schedule. They packed their luggage into the back of the Mercedes wagon and they were off. They pulled right past Sylvester as he covered his face behind a black hooded sweater. He peeked from behind his masking to make sure nothing was out of the ordinary. *Toof!* He spit as he made his way over to the house.

Just as planned, the door in the back was left open. Through the rear he entered through the kitchen. He went straight upstairs to the master bedroom to find a suitable hiding place. The best he could do was the closet. He sat down inside and waited...and waited...and waited.

He could've been in that closet for damn near three hours. The sun had been long gone. Now the moon lit the night, and Sylvester could get a glimpse of it through the shutter-style closet doors. It was a beautiful full moon. It looked close enough to touch.

"The fuck is takin' this nigga so long?" he asked himself with frustration. "Goddamn!"

It was too quiet. Sylvester's mind was running away. *Something must've gone wrong,* he thought. *No way it takes this long to run to the airport and back…no fuckin' way.*

His frustration led to drowsiness as he rocked back and forth and stomped his feet to keep awake. His eyelids still grew heavy and he could feel himself about to doze off, and he couldn't help it. Every blink was longer than the previous one. His head would lean to one side, and then he'd catch himself and try shaking it off. He would have definitely fallen asleep right there in that closet had this nigga not come home when he did.

Just as Sylvester was about to collapse, something caught his eye. The light was bright enough to fully wake him and force him to squint his eyes to see. It was what he'd been waiting for. Mark's father came to a halt in the driveway and shut the ignition off. This is when Sylvester grew anxious. There was some fear buried deep inside of him, but he didn't care. He just wanted to hurry up and get it over with.

The key entered the lock, and the doors opened up making a squeaking sound. Sylvester could hear Mark's father downstairs flipping the locks back on the door. He didn't come straight upstairs as he hoped though. He went into the kitchen first. He could hear the clinging of glasses. Then Sylvester heard a sound that scared the shit out of him. He heard a female voice downstairs with Mark's father.

"Shit!" he spat aloud. "What the fuck is he doing down there with a bitch? Mark ain't say shit about no bitch. Somethin's wrong wit this; man, I could feel it."

Still, Sylvester had no choice but to get ready for the hit. He reluctantly checked the pistol to make certain he was fully loaded with a slug chambered. He pulled the ski mask over his face and threw the hood over his head. Just like this, he sat there and rocked back and forth grinding his teeth. Now he couldn't even shut his eyes long enough to blink; he just stared at the bedroom entrance through the closet door.

"Come on…come on," he whispered to himself. "Let's get it over wit' already, nigga…come on."

After only five minutes, Sylvester couldn't take it anymore. His nerves got the best of him, and he had to see what the fuck was going on. He slowly slid the closet door to the side and crept out, making sure to listen closely if the voices were in motion. They weren't; they were still coming from the same area downstairs. Sylvester bit his lip with uneasiness and twisted the door knob just enough to crack the door open. The door was facing the staircase that led downstairs to the front of the house. To get to the kitchen you would have to make a U-turn once at the bottom of the steps. Sylvester knew he couldn't go that far without being seen. Still, he couldn't force himself to sit in that closet for any longer. He had to at least get a peek at what the hell was going on downstairs. He leaned over the banister at the top of the stairs until he could see something. He saw the woman's boots, a pair of red high-heeled stilettos. He leaned over more and got a glimpse of her legs. She had pale white skin and was wearing black fishnet stockings. Sylvester started to put two and two together. But just as his brain started calculating, he heard them walking towards him. He looked over the banister again, and they were right below him, almost at the foot of the stairs. One of them only needed to glance upward, and he would be spotted. He slid. Just as they turned the corner to climb the steps, he hopped back into the bedroom just in the nick of time. Sylvester was in such haste that he almost fell as he tried to make it back to the closet. He had to settle for underneath the bed or they would've caught up to him for sure. His body was under the bed just as the door was opening.

"Whew," he whispered. That was too close. Things could've gotten way messier than he wanted had they seen him at the top of the steps dipped head to toe in black and wearing a ski mask. He needed a controlled environment and that would not have qualified. Shit, what happens if this all falls apart? Fuckin' Mark denies everything and Sylvester gets a nice six-by-eight underneath a fuckin' jail? He wasn't havin' that.

He could hear Mark's dad and his company being all playful and giggly now. All he had to do was wait until they got into it and then he'd strike.

"So, how do ya like it, baby?" she asked him. "You wanna get right to the fuckin', or you want me to suck it first? I give awesome head. Wanna see?"

"No-no-no," he answered as she went straight for his zipper. "Not like that... how we spoke about before, you know?" He took her hands and put them back at her side. "Don't act all slutty and shit. That's not how *I* get off," he said. "Call me your dad; say it like I told you."

The light bulb went on in the young lady's head like it was complex mathematics she was calculating, and then she went into character as best she could.

"Ooh, big daddy, I've been a very bad girl. You're gon' have to spank my ass like I deserve until I learn my lesson. Take it easy on me; please, big daddy. I didn't mean it."

He wasn't pleased at all with her mediocre performance. As she approached him, he just rolled his eyes at her. She lay over his lap and lifted her skirt enough so that her little ass in her pink cotton panties was hanging out. She poked her bottom up and hungrily awaited her punishment. Unfortunately, it wouldn't be coming as she expected. He pushed her from his lap onto the floor and came down on her back with his boot. Then he delivered another blow to the back of her head. Her head popped up like it was weightless and turned over. She was face-to-face with Sylvester now as he stared at her with his eyes bugging out of his head. But she kept her eyes closed. She was confused and frightened at the sudden turn of events and didn't know what do. Sylvester as well; all he could do was lay there staring, anticipating the look on her face if she opened her eyes. That's when Mark's father came plowing down with another vicious blow to her head. She opened her eyes and saw Sylvester staring at her with his eyes bulging and his mouth wide open. If she could've gotten any more scared at that point, Sylvester had just accomplished that. Her eyes were bulging now, too, and she could hardly breathe. It wasn't until Mark's father bent down and lifted her up by the head before she showed some sign of life. He pressed her against the wall opposite the bed with his hands tightly gripping her around her neck. All she could do was point and moan.

By now, she thought that she could somehow be safer with the madman that had just started relentlessly beating her out of nowhere. Shit, talk about a muthafuckin' dilemma, right?

Unfortunately for him, he didn't take heed to her alerts. He saw something in her now that he didn't see before...what he was actually looking for. He saw the fear in her heart, and that's the kind of look he needed to get aroused.

"Yeah, you little slut, that's how you make your daddy happy," he said. "You know how I like it, don't you? Why you gotta make me teach you over and over again how it's done? You must like it when I force you, huh? Stop playing innocent with me and give me what you know I want!"

By now the girl was crying hysterically. Her eyes were turning red and her face was turning blue. She could hardly breathe, let alone warn this filthy bastard that there was someone dressed all in black behind him with a pistol aimed at the back of his head.

This fool didn't even see it coming. Sylvester took one deep breath and shut his eyes tightly. After another deep breath he squeezed the trigger...*BOOM!*

All it took was that one shot and everything else went silent. Sylvester opened his eyes in time to see blood flying through the air. When Mark's father's lifeless body collapsed to the ground, standing in front of Sylvester all covered with splattered blood and bits of flesh was a girl no older than thirteen years old. She had a look on her innocent little face like she had seen the devil himself before her. And in her lifetime, this was close enough to it.

For a while, Sylvester couldn't even bring himself to say anything. He just stood there staring; while she stared back anticipating her own death. She could've shit herself when Sylvester finally spoke...

"Clean yaself up and get the fuck outta here before somebody calls the police," he instructed before turning around to leave. He stopped when he reached the door. He turned and said, "You might not wanna be tellin' nobody about all of this, understand?"

With that he was gone. He left out the same way he came in shedding pieces of his disguise along the way as he fled. He didn't even feel as bad about it as he thought he would. Shit, after he raped this little girl, that bastard would've probably found some little boy to traumatize next. He was better off dead.

CHAPTER 7

Finally, Boom was about to hit the GW Bridge. He could almost feel NYC already. But that's probably because he'd spent the last few hours basically tasting the numerous stenches you hit traveling up the New Jersey Turnpike. He was just that much happier to be near New York now.

After what seemed like forever, he finally pulled past the toll booth to get over the bridge and into the Bronx. He knew he was in the BX as soon as he came off the other side, as he was immediately slowed down by the potholes in the expressway. He didn't mind. He could take his time and roll through the hood taking in the sights. Besides the potholes, the burners (graffiti) will also let a nigga know just exactly where they are in the world. The shit was beautiful.

As Boom eased up the highway puffing on a freshly lit Newport, he lost himself in the scenery. It was a lot different here than how he remembered it, of course, but something about it was still the same. It was familiar. It gave him a different feeling than Philly did somehow. It was almost like he didn't have anything to worry about...like the calm before the storm.

Maybe it was the fact that no one knew who he was, like he didn't have to live up to anything. He could just do him. There was no pressure. But that feeling wouldn't last too much longer. Boom realized again just what had brought him back to this place. The pulls from his cigarette got longer and deeper. He had to put his game face back on and get focused. He knew where he was gon' start; now all he had to do was get there. If only he'd have concentrated a bit earlier, he could've dipped out of the way of a huge crater in the street that practically ate his whole front left tire.

"Fuck!" He fought to keep control of the car. He flipped on the hazard lights and hit the brakes to slow down. As the tire deflated, he managed to steer off the highway at the Jerome Avenue exit. When he came to a halt at a stop sign, he hopped out to see the damage.

"Damn, this is some bullshit." He bent to take a closer look. The tire was in shreds barely clinging to the rim. "Goddamn, look at that," he said to himself.

Lucky for Boom, he stood to find that he had pulled up right around the corner from a Speedy's Flat-Fix. That was the good news. The flip side to that coin was the shop didn't have his tire in stock and needed to order it.

With a name like "Speedy's"... he thought. But it was what it was. He had three options at this point: either wait the four or five hours for someone to bring it from another site in Brooklyn; or leave it and come back for it. The other option was driving around on a damn donut. He didn't wanna risk it though. No telling what those streets would do to a defenseless little donut. He left that shit there and asked where he could find the nearest subway.

The train ride was just what he needed to relax a little. He went to the first car and stared out of the window, just as he remembered doing as a kid. The BX was definitely cleaner-looking than he remembered, especially the trains. Now the static-ridden voices that used to announce the stops were replaced with nice, clear and concise, robotic-sounding words giving the rider a warm, pleasant experience. Not like back in the days, when the loud obnoxious guy would get on the horn and scare the shit out of you...nah, now it was all neat and cute.

From the elevated train's height though, you could still see the burners that signified the hood with colorful pieces of artwork for the whole world to see. That was the love in the heart of the city. It wasn't shit else. Boom saw it for real. This new mask only concealed its true essence, what it was and always will be...the ghetto.

When his train ride came to an end, so did his trip down memory lane. He got off at Prospect Avenue. If Boom was gon' find out the truth, he would start where his pops ended: *where Prospect Avenue met with Southern Boulevard.* He took one more gaze at the clear blue sky. The sun was just starting to go down, but he was way ahead of it. It was already dark in Boom's eyes, and fuck if it wasn't about to get darker.

As soon as Boom hit the street, he scanned the avenue. It was like some sort of animal instinct working overdrive. His foot hit the sidewalk and he transformed. He stood in front of the train station stairs looking from the left to the right and up and down the blocks. It wasn't even something that he was doing consciously. It was uncontrollable. He didn't even know what he was looking for at first, but it came to him once he found it. It was right across the street, unsuspecting, completely oblivious to the fact that it was being sized up. One thing Boom could always tell...was a hustler. He looked at them as cattle, like a pile of cash just waiting to get taken. It was in his nature; he enjoyed the act of robbing more than the money, and who better? It was nothin' for them. But now it was more than that; he just couldn't help himself. Boom could see the transaction before it even happened.

The young hustler saw the custee when he hit the corner. Of course, Boom saw him from all the way down the block and could already see the picture taking form by now. The addict was in customary garments, wearing a pair of dinged sweat pants, a brown sweat shirt with a gray T-shirt on top of it—that could've possibly been white at some point in time—and dirty sneakers to match. He walked up and mumbled a couple of words when he got close enough to the dealer and was directed into the Chinese food restaurant.

"Order you an egg-roll or somethin'," he instructed. "Then take a seat at the table by the window."

The customer obeyed. He entered the restaurant and the hustler followed after giving a minute grace. He was also in traditional gear for his occupation, a pair of dark blue denim pants, a blue hood sweater, and a pair of crispy white Air Force Ones. On his head he wore an "oversized-fitted" Yankees cap. His gaudy jewelry only accented his demeanor: a shiny pinky-ring; a long Cuban-linked chain, at the end of which held a Jesus pendant flooded with diamonds, and his snarled lip revealed his gold fronts. He sat across the table and made the exchange underneath. The hustler then stayed there while the fiend got up to get his food and leave. After another minute or so, he also got up to make his way. It all took maybe three minutes, *tops*, and the dealer was now ninety dollars richer. He even gave the custie one for free to make it an even ten jacks. This kind of gratitude wouldn't go unforgotten the next time around. With this sale, he was done with his afternoon package and it was time to re-up. He walked to the side of the restaurant where an alley separated it and a Hollywood Video store. After giving a courtesy look over his shoulder for anyone watching, he picked up a Coca-Cola cup that was sitting on the floor by the dumpster, lifted the lid and stuffed the wad of cash inside with the rest of his take for the day. He came out of the alley and walked down the block, cup in hand with a straw hanging out of it as if there was Sprite in that shit or somethin', still giving a paranoid look over his shoulder every few steps.

"Mmmm," Boom said to himself almost as if his hunger was about to get the best of him. "So far from my house...but so close to home." He seriously considered following the boy where he was going, waiting for that perfect opportunity to present itself, then pouncing on him like the sheep he was. He shook those thoughts off though; it wasn't the right time or the place. But that's just how his mind worked, and he didn't fight it either. He wasn't ashamed of it or nothin', but he definitely had to stop taking his work home with him—so to speak.

The fact is he was really only searching for a suitable place to start asking questions. He had to know that it wouldn't get him that far, but it was better than nothing. He walked over to the alley where the hustler just left. Investigating the block further made him come to the realization that this was actually the spot. It had to be. There weren't any other alleys that he could see, so this must've been it. This is where his father's body was found. He could picture him lying there, dead eyes staring aimlessly with a blank look on his face, all drenched in blood. He felt his chest starting to get tighter. His rage, which he had done a good job at keeping under control until this point, was fueled by his own horrific imagination. His mind started to delve deeper and deeper into it, only causing him to get more and more vexed. If he didn't stop himself now, he would surely flip. He could easily have just grabbed the first person that walked by and popped their head off of their shoulders. He was that volatile. Luckily for Boom, or the poor soul that would see the barrel of his pistol, he saw a sign right across the street that seemed to be calling him. It read: Virginia's Lounge. It was just what he needed.

Upon entering, he found that the place was fairly empty, which was understandable given the time of day. He took a seat at the bar at first. He ordered a scotch and soda, and then took his drink to a table in the back. He threw the drink back in one shot and got the waitress' attention to order another. She brought it over to him with a peculiar look on her face. She wasn't used to seeing new faces; usually it was the same alcoholic losers forcing cheap booze down their throats vigorously attempting to alleviate their troubles while trying not to vomit all over the place. She couldn't help but stare at Boom perplexed. Boom didn't even realize. He was only concerned with the drink she came over with. He didn't even take his eyes off of it; he just grabbed it and threw it back.

"Lemme get another one of these and a Heineken, shorty," he said as he reached into his pocket for his cigarettes. "Good lookin'."

The woman wasn't going to fulfill his order quick enough though. He paused with the cigarette in his mouth about to light it, and looked up at her with a furious look in his eyes.

"Ain't no smokin' in here," she said, pointing to the "NO SMOKING" sign.

Boom simply sucked his teeth as he snatched the cigarette from his lips. *This is a bar, ain't it?* he thought. *What's this 'no smoking' shit?* For about a second and a half, he seriously considered going out front to chief his stogie, but then he looked around. Besides a fat guy sitting all the way at the other end of the bar fighting to keep his eyes open, he was the only one in there. He looked up at her again before pulling a crispy hundred-dollar bill from his pocket. He made sure to notice the look on her face when she saw it; then he sat back in his chair.

"I don't think anybody's gon' mind, you feel me?" he asked.

The woman looked from the C-note to Boom, then back to the bill. Boom lit up the cigarette and blew the smoke in the air. She had no response, just a blank look on her face. "I'd appreciate those drinks now, ma."

She simply rolled her eyes and walked away. "Good lookin' out," he said.

Now with every pull Boom took from the cigarette, the liquor was starting to take effect. He could feel himself getting a little tipsy, but just kept taking deep pulls to speed up the process. He had a nice buzz going by the time the woman came back with his drinks. As she laid the drinks down and turned to leave, Boom stopped her to ask her a question. The words were out of his mouth before he realized he was saying anything.

"Shorty, you wouldn't happen to know how I get at a cat by the name Winch, do ya?"

The woman turned back with a confused look on her face. "Who you said you lookin' for?" she asked. "Wrench? Is that somebody's name or somethin'?"

"Winch," Boom corrected. "Not Wrench...Winch! Know what, you just never mind. Forget I asked, but thanks for the drinks though, ma. Appreciate it."

The girl simply sucked her teeth with a roll of her eyes and a nod of her head and walked away. As she got back to the bar, the hustler from earlier entered. He must've been all re'd up by now, ready for his evening hustle. After a quick scan of the bar's interior, he took a seat on a stool and ordered himself a Corona.

"This shit ain't gon' be the least bit simple," Boom said to himself as he took a paced swig from his drink. But, in the corner of his eye, he did notice that the waitress went back and had a brief exchange with the woman at the bar, Virginia. She was a short stocky woman with a long blonde weave running down her back, brown-skin complexion, and her cumbersome boobies were damn near about to fall out of her top. She must've said something that made more sense to her, because it prompted her to immediately get on the horn. She spoke quietly and briefly, trying to make sure that Boom was paying her no attention. What she didn't pay any attention to was that now the hustler was interested in the conversation as well. He took small sips from his beer and paid close attention to what was going on.

When Virginia hung up, she still attempted to be aware of Boom's actions, peeking at him through her beady eyes. Her lips got tight and pressed, accentuating her light mustache, and she stood at attention with her arms crossed. She didn't have much to watch though. All Boom did was sit there smoking and drinking, seeming uncaring. He was just working everything out in his head. The answers weren't apparent yet, but he was on to something. The shit could mean absolutely nothing. But in his head, he knew that it could also mean everything. If something was gon' go down though, he would rather it be when he had his car with him just in case. Boom was never the type to run into a dark room without knowing where the light switch was. He knew exactly how to play it, but it would have to wait until tomorrow when he got his whip back. Since he was somewhat satisfied with his findings thus far, it was time to make scarce for the night. He hurriedly finished his drinks and waved over the waitress.

"What I owe you, shorty?" he asked as he reached in his pocket.

"Well, it's twelve for the mixed drinks and six for the beer," she replied. "That comes out to about forty-two bucks..." She looked at that crispy hundred still sitting on the table and reached out for it. "...but this should cover you for sure, playa."

Boom quickly beat her to the bill and replaced it with a fifty. "Thanks," he said before getting up to leave. He left her standing there grilling him with a *"No he didn't"* look on her face. He could feel her stare but he didn't care. No fuckin' way was he about to give her a Benjamin just for the luxury of smoking indoors... *yeah right!*

Boom chuckled to himself, now feeling a whole lot better than he did a little earlier. He walked right past the bartender and the hustler without even turning his head and giving them a second thought. He went straight for the door and threw it open to breeze from the spot, not even paying enough attention to the street to see a woman standing right in front of the door. They collided and her purse dropped, spilling all of its contents onto the ground. He quickly bent down to help her.

"Awe shit, my bad, ma," he said in a sincere apologetic tone. "I ain't even see you. That was my fault." Boom looked up to see if the young lady was angry at all, and his eyes met with hers. She had light brown eyes that contrasted her dark chocolate brown skin nicely. She was staring at him like she wasn't conscious of it. He couldn't help but be distracted by her curious glare, not to mention her beauty. She had luscious wet lips and a real slick short hairstyle. His eyes went from her beautiful eyes down to nice round breasts, slim waist, and wide hips. She was put together quite well. Boom held out a tube of lipstick to try and shift her attention. "My bad."

The woman finally came to her senses and realized that she was staring. "Oh, thanks," she said, taking the lipstick from Boom. "Uh...that's okay. Don't worry yaself about it." They both got back to their feet when all of her things were safely tucked back in her bag. She laughed and said, "At least you helped me with my stuff; most fellas would've knocked me flat on my ass and just kept it movin', you know?"

Boom shared in her humor. "That's fucked up...niggas ain't shit like that, huh?"

If it was up to her, they would've stood there gazing at each other for the hours to come, but Boom had to go. He wanted to think through some shit and had some time to kill before putting in some work later. He turned to leave but she called to him.

"Wait!" she blurted.

Boom turned back around, and just as the young lady was about to speak, the bar doors opened up again and interrupted her. It was the hustler. He, too, came out in a hurry, but obviously didn't expect to see people standing in front of the door.

"Pardon me," he said before sliding between them and walking down the block.

Boom didn't like the look in his eye when they came face to face. He was trying to hide something. He wasn't feeling that not one bit. He made sure to pay close attention to him as he walked away. When he caught him looking over his shoulder at Boom, he knew he had him. "Cocksucker," he said aloud.

"What you say?" the woman asked.

Boom had forgotten she was even standing there. "Oh, nothin'," he said, recovering from his outburst, and then changing the subject. "You had somethin' you wanted to tell me?"

"Yeah, I feel like I know you from somewhere."

"Oh, yeah, I don't think so, ma. I ain't from 'round here. You sure you got the right cat?"

"I don't know, but it's just there's something real familiar about you. Where you from?"

"Not here," Boom said being evasive. "I *was* born here, but it's been some time now since I been back, feel me? So unless you talkin' fifteen years ago or better, you got the wrong dude; sorry."

Once more, Boom attempted to get on his way, but once again he was stopped short.

"Sylvester!" she said. "That's it, right? Sylvester?"

Boom had no choice but to turn around. He had a perplexed look now. *Is this shit even possible?* he thought. *Where you know that name from?*

"You don't remember me? It's Phylecia! Remember your mother used to watch me when we were kids."

"Phylecia? Does sound kinda familiar," Boom said, but he was lying his ass off. He didn't know her from Adam. He just couldn't break her heart; she was so excited and shit.

"Yeah, I know it was a really long time ago, right?"

"Shit yeah!"

"We were just kids, but for some reason I saw you and knew I knew you from somewhere."

"Photographic memory-type shit. That's what's up!"

Phylecia giggled as she remembered more. "We used to play house and stuff like that. You remember that, too?"

Boom's face had *'I have no idea what the fuck you're talking about'* written all over it, but he humored her. "Yeah, that's crazy, right?"

"I had a crush on you; I bet you never knew, huh?"

"Nope."

"Yeah, you couldn't have known, but everyone else did."

"Yeah, I bet. Anyway, what you been up to?"

"Oh, me? I'm tryin' to do me right about now. I'm doin' some modeling, getting my portfolio tight and shit. But modeling isn't gonna be where I stop. I really wanna be a fashion designer. I'm about to get it poppin' in a minute, too!"

"That's good," Boom said uncaringly. His mind was wandering now. He wasn't at all interested in continuing this conversation. He was getting his focus back now; there was shit he needed to do. It didn't help that she brought up his mother after it'd been so long since what happened. It probably would've been different if those feelings weren't so fresh and new to him. She ain't know that, but that didn't matter. The damage was done though, and Boom was looking for the exit out of the discussion.

"Yeah, so I'm about to blow. I gotta find me a room in a telly before these niggas get on some shit about no vacancies. It was nice seeing you..."

"I can show you where you can find a nice room," she said.

Hmm, Boom thought. *Could this be*...naaah. *She couldn't be. Could she?*

"Come on, it's only a couple of stops on the train. It'll give us a chance to catch up on old times."

Boom thought about where this might be going and said, "Fuck it, let's hop in a cab then."

They caught a taxi and were on their way. It wasn't a long ride, but it was enough for Boom to get the distinct impression that Phylecia was coming on to him. He was looking at her through suspecting eyes now. This was just *too* convenient. Mostly, all he did was listen to her talk about herself and her promising career as a model. *"Model"*...Boom cringed every time he heard her refer to her career with that title once he found out what she was *really* talking about. For the most part, Phylecia was a video ho, but she had done a couple of magazine covers also. Nothing as huge as you would think from how proud of it she was;

it was the kind of magazine that has centerfolds. To her that shit could've been *Essence* when in actuality it was *Black Tale.*

When they pulled up to the motel, Boom knew how serious she was when she hopped out of the cab with him without him even asking or anything. They weren't in the room for two seconds before she was making herself comfortable, flipping her shoes off and stretching out on the king-size bed. Beneath her short denim skirt, Boom could get a glimpse of her white lace panties as she lay. She knew exactly what she was doing. Boom just stared in amazement. Nothing like this had ever happened to him before. He was still trying to take it all in, but he didn't want to give the impression that he was nervous or anything. He went into the bathroom first; just in case something popped off he needed to stash his pistol. He wrapped it in a towel and hid it behind the toilet bowl. When he returned, he took a seat at the table across from the bed and had himself a cigarette to relax. They were silent for a little while after that, until Phylecia spoke her mind to make a request.

"Sylvester, you think you could do me a favor? I mean, I figured since we're here and all…"

"What's that?"

She sat up on the bed and looked at him with pleading eyes. "You think you could give me a little foot massage? I been on these heels all day running around, and my damn feet are so worn and…"

Boom didn't even wait for her to finish her sentence. He was up and heading in her direction. He wasn't planning on stopping to bullshit with her feet either. By the time he got to the bed, his belt was already undone and he was bending down to get a taste of her juicy wet lips. She didn't hesitate either and she was biting her bottom lip waiting for him to get in close enough. When he did, she returned his advance by throwing her tongue down his throat and pulling him onto the bed with her. When he was on top of her, she clung to his him and wrapped her legs around him. Boom had a handful of her breasts by now, trying to force his hands under her bra. He could feel her swollen nipples through the cup, and he could hardly wait to get to them. In two snaps, her bra was loose enough for Boom to get hands below them. She was unbuttoning her blouse for him now, so that he could get a better grasp. When her shirt was finally off, the most wonderful tits Boom had ever seen came bursting out. He threw one in his mouth while he fondled the other with his free hand. Phylecia's eyes were rolling up into the back of her head now. She arched her back giving Boom even more assistance. He was playing with her nipples with the tip of his tongue, taking them in his mouth to suck on from time to time. By now, Phylecia's pussy was dripping wet, and she could feel it throbbing with every beat of her heart. Boom was as hard as he'd ever gotten as well. He was poking her through his pants. She couldn't help it anymore; she grabbed onto his dick and ran her hand up and down the shaft like it was a beast that needed to be tamed. She was ready and willing. She turned him over on his back and straddled him. His dick was throbbing now, and she could feel it jumping through his jeans. When she went reaching for it, Boom stopped her.

"Damn, I don't think I got rubbers."

Phylecia simply looked down at him. He was disappointed in himself for not thinking of this earlier, but she didn't care one bit. She got up and started going through her bag on the floor. When she turned around, she was holding just what they needed to keep the party going. Boom was thanking God at this point. Phylecia took her time, removing every piece of clothing slowly until all that remained were her knee-high stockings. Boom matched her every advance by removing his own clothes. Phylecia waited for Boom to look at her in her face, and then put the condom in her mouth and held it with her lips. She crawled across the bed to him where he was waiting with his dick pointing straight up in the air. She shut her eyes and lowered her head to his crotch and found the tip of his dick with her lips. Moving ever so slowly she went lower and lower, sinking Boom deeper and deeper down her throat. When he thought she couldn't go any farther, she took the last couple of inches in one gulp, and then held it there for a few seconds while Boom let out uncontrollable appreciative gestures. When Phylecia felt as though she'd teased Boom enough, she mounted his lap. As she injected herself with his vein, she felt her back jerking without her control. She was breathing in short gasps and letting out small high-pitch moans. As she rode him faster, her breaths and moans sped up to the same tempo. They continued like this for the twenty or so minutes to come. When she finally opened her eyes, she smiled at the sight of Boom about to explode. She could tell he wasn't far from climaxing, but she didn't want him to get that easily. When she stopped, his mouth opened up widely but he couldn't bring himself to speak a word. She had a devious smile on her face now, and she had more planned for him before she was done with him. Without ever once letting him loose from the inside of her trap, she slowly spun around and turned her back to him. Then she continued slowly up and down on his penis as it begged to be hollowed out. She would next get into a squatting position before letting Boom release himself. Up and down, back and forth, she rammed it in and out of her stomach. She was ready for Boom to bust now, and he was willing to comply. She could feel his body tensing, and she knew he was coming. She didn't hold back any intensity still, not until every drop was gone. Even then, she kept on even after he had already let go all he could muster. It wasn't until she felt him softening inside her when she finally came to a halt. She jumped to her feet feeling proud. She looked back at Boom, and the look on his face was priceless. He was all numb and incoherent. She was loving every minute of it.

She went over to where he'd left his pack of cigarettes laying on the table and took one out. She lit it up, took one long pull and blew out a cloud of smoke. The rest of it was for Boom; she put it to his lips and he started pulling on it immediately. Next, she went into the bathroom. Boom lay there puffing away on a nice well-deserved Newport. When she came back, she had some toilet paper and a warm washcloth. Boom simply sat there watching as she removed the condom with the tissue, and cleaned him up with the towel. He was definitely impressed. When the cigarette was done, he rolled over to take a nap. When he woke, the beginning of his quest would begin. What he didn't realize is that it had begun already, and he just didn't know it.

CHAPTER 8

It was about midnight when Boom's eyes opened back up. To his right, Phylecia was sleeping soundly. He eased his way out of the bed making sure not to disturb her. He stretched his arms and snapped his spine back into place, and then he began getting dressed. When he was fully dressed, he went for the door.

"Damn, the fuck I'm thinkin'?" he asked himself aloud. His mind caught up to him as soon as he twisted the doorknob, and he remembered that his burner was still stashed in the bathroom. He came out of the bathroom tucking the 9-milly in the back of his pants; and to his surprise, Phylecia was sitting straight up awake.

"Where are you going?" she asked.

"I just have to make a run right quick, that's all. Go back to sleep." Boom went about his exit as if what he did was nothing out of the ordinary. He proceeded to the door before Phylecia called to him.

"Wait, don't go," she pleaded. "I mean…wouldn't you rather just stay here with me? I mean I'm pretty sure we can find something to do." She let the sheets drop uncovering her breasts and looked up at Boom with an inviting look.

Boom simply bit his lip. He gave the impression that he was actually considering her offer, but that was bullshit. He was way too focused at this point. He just figured he'd spare her feelings, seeing as though she had just gotten through putting in so much work. "Sounds tempting, ma, but I need to make this move right now. No matter how much I just wanna play the cut here with you, I gotta do what I gotta do, feel me?"

Phylecia put her head down and looked up at Boom with her bottom lip poking out. She jumped to her feet and stood there completely naked. She slowly made her way to Boom, and when she got close enough, she leaned in for a kiss. When their lips met, she forced her hand down his pants to fondle his soldier. Boom wasn't the only one focused!

"You still wanna leave?" Phylecia asked with a big smile.

"Nah," Boom answered. "But I still am...one!"

Phylecia's pride had just taken a sharp kick to the mid-section, but she still pursued.

"You comin' right back, right?" she asked Boom as he fled.

"Yeah!" he yelled over his shoulder as his aggravation started to take over his tone. "Come on, what the fuck?"

Phylecia's questioning ended there. She just stood at the door with her tits and ass hanging out and not caring.

Boom jetted from the telly and quickly jumped on the train and after two stops, he was back on Prospect Avenue. When he got to the stairs, he took a peep around the corner to scan the street...jackpot!

"How you want it, jack? I got nicks—five for twenty, and dimes—takin' no shorts but they fat as a muthafucka. Let's get it crackin'! Yeah, keep it moving; let's go!" The hustler was on his job, for real. It wouldn't be long now before he'd be out; then he could call it a night. He made seamless transactions with the fiends that could only be noticed by a trained eye. He was shaking and moving with grace and poise like a ballerina. Everything had to go down right on the Ave now, since the Chinese restaurant was already closed. This is where the new jacks would be set apart from the seasoned veterans. He had it down pat, but Boom could pick up on all the mannerisms. He was waiting for him to go back to that stash spot so he could make his move. As soon as the hustler took that nervous look around, Boom started down the steps across the street from where the hustler was posted up. By the time he got to the alley, he was standing face-to-face with the hustler as he was coming back out to the street. Although Boom was the last person he thought he'd see when he turned around, he still managed to play it cool. He sized him up, looking from his eyes to his feet, then back to his eyes.

"Fuck you lookin' at, jack?" he spat. "Want somethin'?"

"Whoa...easy, dog," Boom replied in a non-threatening tone. "I just thought you'd be able to help me out. You mind if I ask you somethin', homeboy?"

His eyes squinted. His lip curled up revealing a small gleam off of his 14K choppers. He didn't know quite how to respond at first. When his mouth finally formed words, they weren't at all what Boom wanted to hear. "I don't know you, nigga! I ain't ya homeboy! I don't know where you come from or who you wit. Muthafucka, I ain't got shit to say to you!"

"Damn, dog," said Boom, still in non-defensive mode. "Why it gotta be that? All I need..."

"What you *need* is to be gettin' the fuck out my face, jack!" He started to reach, but he wasn't at all quick enough. "You gon' make me dish yo punk ass if you don't..."

That's all he managed to get out before Boom had his cannon drawn and pressed up against the hustler's forehead. Now he looked cross-eyed as he stared up at the nozzle of the 9-milly. He was probably regretting the words he spoke already.

"Before you WHAT???" Boom asked.

The hustler had no response. That was probably the best decision he'd made all day.

After looking to the left and right, Boom nodded for him to go deeper into the dark alley where they could have some privacy. The hustler, still not taking his eyes off of the pistol, pointed at his cranium, backed his way into the alley until Boom told him to stop.

"Alright, that's far enough, nigga," he directed. "Let me ask you now; ain't you hopin' you were a bit more muthafuckin' cooperative, you fool-ass nigga?"

Again, no response.

"What's ya name, homey?"

"I ain't ya boy, jack! We ain't friends; why the fuck you wanna know my name for?" His heart was coming back to him now, but he still didn't know if it would be to his advantage or not. One thing was for sure, if Boom was gon' cap him, no way in hell he was about to let him talk himself out of it. He had nothing to lose.

Boom didn't even blink at the boy's obvious disobedience and said, "I like to get to know niggas before I merc 'em, that's all. It's all the same to me though. I don't need to know ya name, but you can make things a whole lot muthafuckin' easier on yaself if you just be easy and give me what I want. You feel me?" Boom didn't wait for an answer. He just cocked his weapon to emphasize his point. "Should I ask again, nigga?" he yelled.

"Branson, nigga!" the hustler spat. "My muthafuckin' name is Branson. Nice to meet you, too!"

Boom smiled at Branson's response. It was amusing, to say the least. "Hee-hee," Boom laughed aloud. "Let's do this quick then, Branson. Let's not make it harder than it need to be, feel me? What I'ma need you to do is get down on ya knees, and before you get cute, I saw you reachin' for that whistle. Just pull it out slow and throw that shit over there."

Branson complied. He slowly pulled his 38-Special from his belt and tossed it. He even voluntarily put his hands on his head for good measure.

"Aight cool, Branson," Boom said. "Now I only got one question before I decide what to do with ya bitch ass. I'm in town lookin' for a cat that go by the name Winch. You know who that is, right? Before you answer, I know you know the dude, so I don't wanna hear none of that bullshit, ya hear? This information may be valuable enough for me to spare ya life, dog. You hear me? You can still live after all of this shit. You give me what I need, and I'm just gon' have a talk wit the cat. After that, I'm out and you won't ever see my ass again...guaranteed! He don't even have to know how I got at him, ya know?"

"So I'm supposed to be a snitch or somethin'? Fuck you think you talkin' to, nigga?"

"Whoa," Boom said. "You stupid muthafucka! I don't hate nothin' more than that bullshit you talkin' right now, nigga! Look, you could label that shit whatever you want, but it's gon' come down to life or death...which one? Fuck being a snitch; you'd rather be in a box somewhere pushin' up daisies? What kind of dumb muthafucka you gotta be?"

Boom swung the pistol around, connecting a vicious blow to the back of Branson's head with a loud thump. As Branson's body was rocked to one side, Boom landed another crack to his skull before he hit the floor. Now he stood over Branson, with the burner pointed directly between his eyes.

"Muthafucka, you gon' gimme what I want or I'ma make it *real* hard on you," said Boom as he looked around to make sure no one was watching. "You hear me?? It ain't a game, nigga!" Boom lifted the pistol again, and came straight down on the bridge of Branson's nose. His skin split open to the white meat and blood immediately started gushing from the fresh gash in his face. Boom wasn't done yet though. He kept swinging the pistol around landing fierce blows to Branson's face and sending blood everywhere until he was ready to speak.

"Alright, stop fuckin' hittin' me, man! Alright, I'll tell you what I know, please!" he pleaded as blood pumped generously out of his mouth and nose.

Boom paused with a fire in his face. Even though he should've been pleased that his hard work was about to pay off, he was upset that he had to stop so soon. He wanted to pound out some more of Branson's facial features before he really gave in. He would have to just settle for what he was given though.

"So talk, nigga," Boom spat with his face twisted. "I'm waitin'!"

"I'm workin' for him out here!"

"Winch?" Boom said, thinking out loud. "He's in the drug game?"

"Yeah, man. This his block right here, but I never see him. That's my word on everything, B; I only seen this dude one time in my life. And I been pumpin' here for a whole year now, B. I can't help you find him, man!"

"What about the connection, nigga? Don't try and play me like I'm some kind of square or some shit! What the fuck, he sendin' you the packages UPS or some shit? How you get the dope, and how he get that bread? Answer me, nigga!"

"It's never him directly. It's always through a shorty. He don't touch none of this street-level shit, man; I'm tellin' you. All the transactions go through a broad!"

"What's her name, nigga? Spit it out!!!"

"Patrice!" he yelled. "It's Patrice alright!"

That name definitely rang a bell in Boom's head. He heard it ringing over and over in between his ears and he couldn't hear anything else. The next question out of Boom's mouth was where he could find her. Once again, Branson complied. He was getting really good at being a snitch by now. He had no more reservations about the act; now the information just slid out like nothing.

"It don't make no nevermind, jack," said Branson with a nervous giggle. "You ain't never gon' get next to Winch. Apollo gon' damn sure make certain of that, hee-hee. You don't know what the fuck you just got yaself into, homey. You might as well call it quits now, jack. Quit while you're ahead."

"Apollo, huh?" Boom asked. "I'm 'posed to be scared of a nigga named Apollo?" Boom laughed aloud. "Fuck is you, crazy? You don't know how close you are to your death right now??? You better start worrying about that! Listen, fuck Winch, Patrice and this Apollo muthafucka alright. Worry about Branson right now, nigga. If I don't get to them, remember I already to got you, you bitch ass coward!"

"Whatever, homey."

"I ain't ya muthafuckin' homey, nigga!" Boom spat. "And don't talk unless I say you can."

When Boom got enough information out of Branson, he thought to himself. For about half a second, he was actually a bit conflicted about whether or not he should kill him right there. Of course he came to the realization that if he let him live, then he'd most likely go running straight to Winch and announce Boom's arrival. That wouldn't be good at all. On the other hand, he probably already knew that *somebody* was looking for him if he called that whole scene in the bar correctly. Still, Winch would have no idea how serious it was until after this. Shit, let Branson tell it, Winch would probably hear a story about ten niggas, all three hundred pounds or better waving huge Mossberg shotguns. He didn't need that much heat. Fuck it!

"Sorry, *jack*," Boom said before putting his hand in front of Branson's face to shield the blood that would be splattering. "I was just starting to like you."

Just as the trigger was about to click, over came the same fiend from just a little earlier.

"Yo, you got five more of them..."

He saw Branson laid out with Boom hovering over him with the burner pointed at his face and paused. He couldn't move. His eyes grew wide while he stood there not even able to close them long enough to blink. Boom was a little startled. He pointed his pistol before he noticed who it was, and then he hesitated.

"Damn, get the fuck outta here, muthafucka!"

That was the opportunity that Branson needed. He swung his arm around and caught Boom in the jaw with his elbow, sending him flying. He quickly got to his feet and went for his burner. Boom let off a shot, *BOOM*, that sent the customer fleeing. It also changed Branson's outlook; no longer did he plan on getting to his gun to put up some kind of fight. He was fine with running for his life at this point. He zoomed out of the alley as Boom let off two more shots. *BOOM, BOOM!*

By the time Boom got to his feet and out of the alley, Branson had already launched himself up the train station stairs. Boom started to follow him, but then he heard the downtown train pulling up. He knew he wouldn't be able to catch it. He looked left, then right. Then he just took off running.

Branson was safely in the train just as the doors closed. He saw no one else in the car. He looked through to the other cars to see if Boom had made it onto the train, too. Then he got low behind the door and peeked out of the window to see if he was able to get to his feet quick enough to follow him this far. He figured Boom didn't get up in time to see which way he ran, but he was still looking around like a nervous wreck. He couldn't stay still. The train pulled off, and he could breathe just a little easier. He tried sitting down, but that didn't last too long before he was back to his feet and pacing back and forth. He was sweating profusely, repeatedly wiping his brow with the sleeve of his sweater. Finally, he got hold of the pack of cigarettes he had in his pocket. With the cigarette in his mouth, he struck match after match, trying desperately to light it. A minute passed and the train pulled into Jackson Avenue. Branson thought, *Oh shit, what if this nigga got here before me!* He was giving Boom way too much credit.

The doors opened, and Branson's heart rate sped up to a thousand beats a second. He was still breathing hard even though he wasn't out of breath. His eyes couldn't stay on one thing for more than a second. That's when a light bulb went on in his head. He quickly fumbled through his pockets, looking for his cell phone. He needed to get word to Winch that someone was after him quickly. He found his phone just as the doors closed, and Branson calmed down just a little bit more. After looking around a couple more times, he was sure that Boom couldn't have gotten on the train before the doors closed. He stood up against the door that separated the cars as he dialed the emergency number to get at Winch. As the phone rang, he finally got the match lit for the cigarette he had still hanging from his mouth as his jaw twitched with uncontrollable nervousness. When the train pulled off, Branson realized that this was the last stop before it went underground.

"Fuck," he said nervously taking pull after pull from his cigarette. "Hurry up and answer! Answer the fuckin' phone, goddamit!!!"

"You know I hear muthafuckas ask for those right before they die."

Branson heard a voice from behind him and froze. It was Boom standing in the little space between the cars. Branson couldn't even breathe anymore. He leaned forward off of the door in an attempt to make a subtle getaway. His body was moving, and he wanted to be going a whole lot faster, but he couldn't. Boom opened the door just enough to stick his arm through.

"Hello," said the person on the other line of the phone.

Branson never got a chance to utter a word...

BOOM!!! The bullet went through the back of his head and came out through his mouth, sending bloody gold teeth flying all over the inside of the train as it descended below ground. It was fitting; he was just that much closer to his final resting place. Now he didn't have that far to travel. Unknowingly, Boom had done him a service.

When the train pulled in to Third Avenue and 149th Street, Boom exited the same way he came by hopping over the chain that connected both cars. He landed on the platform and checked his person for any obvious indications that he'd just murdered a guy, and when he was satisfied, he hurriedly walked toward the turnstiles. He left Branson stretched out on the train in a bloody mess. He looked over his shoulder and Branson's eyes were staring directly at him. He simply sucked his teeth and kept walking.

Boom noticed that this would've been the stop he needed to get off anyway. *Shit, couldn'tve got any more convenient,* he thought. Now he was one step closer to Winch. Also, now he knew that he and Patrice were still together, making it that much easier to find them both and handle them accordingly. She was already sized up properly. All Boom had to do was figure how to get at Winch through her. For the most part, Boom had made a shit-load of progress for his first night in NYC. Things were falling together pretty nicely. The only thing that was baffling Boom was the fact that Patrice was still on the street, and still with Winch at that. How in the hell did she beat a murder case?

★★★

When he got back to the room, the sound of the door woke Phylecia. He had forgotten that she was even there. Or maybe he had just hoped she was gone by the time he got back, but oh well.

"What happened, Sylvester?" she immediately asked as he entered. "You don't look good. Are you okay?"

"Listen," he said before she got a chance to ask him another question. "I don't mean to snap at you or be mean or nothin', but I got a lot on my mind right now so I'ma need you to shut the fuck up for a minute! Please don't take that the wrong way, but I just need it to be silent in here right about now."

"Well damn, maybe I should just leave then."

Boom didn't answer. In his head he was saying, *'Well then go ahead and leave, BITCH!'* But he'd shitted on her enough for the night. It wasn't even in his character, but he was just used to the women being there when he wanted them to be, and then they'd disappear when they needed to. It was never any of this hanging around and shit. Boom was never really into relationships.

He went into the bathroom to put his pistol away. While he was in there, he washed his face and took a shit, thinking that Phylecia would be gone by the time he got back out. Of course, that wasn't the case. She was still in the bed sitting straight up, staring. The shit was almost pathetic.

Boom paid her no mind. He simply started getting undressed to jump back in the bed. He'd have another long day tomorrow and he really couldn't wait to get it started. When he hopped in the bed, Phylecia was still staring at him, waiting for him to acknowledge that she was there. He could do nothing of the sort. The first thing he did was grab his cell to make a call. When he found the number he was looking for, he dialed it from a land line.

"Yo," said Germ on the other end of the line.

"You was sleep?" Boom asked.

"Yeah, why? What's good?"

"Nothin', just wanted to holla at you right quick to let you know I'm probably gon' need you to come up to New York."

"What the fuck you doin' in New York?"

"I can't go into all of that right now, but I'm probably gonna need ya help. So if I call and say, *'come through,'* I need you to be ready to make that move, hear me?"

"Alright, you obviously talkin' business? So talk to me. Who's the mark?"

"Some old school cat," Boom responded. He paused to look over at Phylecia, who was still all in his face hanging on his every word. He beckoned her closer with a nod of his head. She immediately accepted his invitation. She began kissing him on the cheek, and then she worked her way down to his neck. Boom only needed lift the covers to let her know where her love would be the most appreciated. Once again, she didn't hesitate for a second before she went under the sheets. She started out stroking him, and then led into kissing, licking and eventually sucking. Boom just closed his eyes and let his head lean back.

"You still there, homey?" asked Germ.

"Oh yeah," Boom replied, still loving Phylecia's head game. "So, we got this boy and his bitch Patrice. I'm up on the broad though. I'ma be on that bitch hard tomorrow. I'll know a whole lot more then. If I need you to come through, you'll know by tomorrow evening at the latest; then we can do us. Ya na'mean, I'm tryin' to tear into these muthafuckas...*for real!*"

"I'm good with that, dog. You know how I do it."

"Yeah, and that's what's up," replied Boom, confident that Germ would be more than ready to buss his gun. "Listen," he said, changing the subject. "You saw or spoke to Black today?"

"Nah, I don't never see that cat. You know that. Why, what's up? Somethin' wrong?"

"Nah, don't worry about it." Boom knew it was a long-shot the second the question came out. That's when he realized that leaving Black in the condition he was in had bothered more than he knew. "He just looked bad before I left, like he was stressin' on somethin'."

"Why don't you just call him?"

"That's another long story. I'ma have to holla at him when I get back off this shit here. Won't be long though, feel me? This shit should wrap itself up, and I'll be back home in Philly in no time."

"Alright then, no doubt."

"Yeah, I'll holla, brother. Oh, and make sure you check in on Shonda and Sabra for me, too. Make sure they good. I'll speak to you tomorrow."

"One."

"One."

When Boom hung up the phone, the sheets lifted up. "I thought you were going to be on the phone all night or somethin'."

"Don't stop," Boom spat, directing Phylecia's head back to his lap. "Yeah, keep doin' it like that. Mmm..."

CHAPTER 9

"Wake up, baby," said Shonda to Sabra. "It's time for school, honey."

Sabra lifted her head with a nice long yawn and a stretch of her little arms. She rubbed her eyes in an attempt to wake up faster. When she looked up, she saw her mom staring down at her with unconditional love in her eyes.

"You ready to get up and get in the bath?"

Sabra nodded reluctantly. What kind of a question was that? She wanted to roll over and go back to sleep. But that option was laid out there for her to decide. It wasn't a multiple-choice question.

Sabra got out of the bed and found her Princess slippers with her feet before following her mom into the bathroom where she was running a nice warm bath for her. She got out of her Dora the Explorer jammies and hopped in. The water was perfect.

"Don't forget to clean inside your belly button and behind your ears," instructed Sabra before walking into the kitchen to fix breakfast. She gave a holler when the food was almost ready. "You ready to get out of the tub, baby?" she asked.

Of course she wasn't ready to get out, now that she was having all kinds of fun playing with her family of rubber duckies.

"Hmm," Shonda said to herself. "Okay, well look at your hands...are they all wrinkly like raisins?"

"Yyyeeesss," Sabra reluctantly moaned.

"Okay, then rinse off, honey, so you can eat your breakfast!"

By the time she returned, Sabra was rinsing the soap out of her hair. Shonda scooped her out of the tub and brought her back into the bedroom to dry her off. When she was dressed, she took her downstairs into the kitchen where her cornmeal was warming. Inside of fifteen minutes, she was done and they were ready to go.

Shonda called a cab to be ready outside by the time they got downstairs, but noticed Germ pulling up just as she was about to hop in.

"Ay what's up, Shonda?" Germ said after jumping out of his black '95 Q45. "You headed over to the school to drop Shorty off? I'll bring you over; it ain't nothin'."

"Thanks, Germ!" Shonda said curiously. She waved off the cabby and walked toward Germ. "What you doin' here anyway?" she asked. "Shit, I didn't even know you got up this early in the mornin', hee-hee."

"You ain't even bullshittin' neither," Germ said, taking part in Shonda's playful banter. "Shit, I'm one of those night people, dig? I was just stoppin' through to check on ya'll, you and Shorty, ya know? Makin' sure it's all good in the hood."

Shonda quickly put two and two together. "Did Boom send you over here to check up on me or somethin'?" she asked with piercing eyes. "Why ain't he just come over himself? He too busy nowadays, huh?"

"Nah, it ain't nothin' like that; come on now, Shonda. He just out of town on business right now and he wanted to make sure you didn't need anything."

"Out of town on business?" Shonda asked. Even though Germ seemed to be telling the truth, she still worried. "Out of town where?"

Germ thought before he responded. Just the obvious hesitation made Shonda reconsider whether or not she wanted to know the answer.

"Never mind," she said before Germ even got a chance to speak. "Forget I asked."

"Well...I spoke to him last night if you worried. He's alright; he just had some moves he needed to make, and then he'll be back home in no time. He was just in a hurry, so he dropped a line to me to make sure I connected with everybody, that's all."

"Everybody?" Shonda asked, showing a little bit of jealousness that he didn't call himself to check on her.

"Yeah," replied Germ. "You, Shorty, and Black."

Shonda felt a little better that she wasn't the only one he didn't call directly. She didn't know it until just now, but she kind of missed him these last few days. The thought gave her the chills. She quickly nodded it off.

"Come on, hop in," Germ said. "We outta here, or what?"

Shonda got in the backseat with Sabra. After their seatbelts were securely fastened, Germ was off.

"So when do you think he'll be back?" Shonda asked.

"I ain't exactly sure of that, but...it shouldn't be too long."

★★★

The drive to the school was quick. They didn't speak much about anything the whole way there. Germ's mission was complete. He just needed to drop a line to her to make sure that she was doing okay. He also conveyed Boom's concern without him having to call himself. When Boom was done in New York, they could have all the time in the world to figure out where their relationship was gonna go from this point. For now, business before pleasure.

When they pulled up to the school, Shonda hopped out. "You gonna call if anything happens, right?"

"No doubt!" Germ quickly responded.

"You promise?"

Germ burst with laughter at Shonda's request. At first he thought, *What the hell does she think is gonna happen?* Then he realized what had already happened. He also realized just who he was talking about. This wasn't a regular nine-to-five cat here; this was Boom. "My bad, I ain't mean to laugh. There ain't no need to worry though, Ma. Boom got his situation all under control. But, just in case something does happen, you'll be the first I call."

"You promise?" Shonda asked again.

"Yeah, I promise."

"Alright, Germ, I'll see you later. Enjoy the morning hours for once, okay?"

"Alright, I hear you, Shonda. I'll do that...holla at ya boy!"

★★★

Boom woke up at about seven a.m., and Phylecia was already in the shower. He was just now realizing that he didn't get any of his personal things out of the bag before he left the flat-fix. He tried rinsing away his morning breath with a mouthful of some cheap mouthwash that was on the sink next to the bathroom, but that shit didn't work out well at all. He was about to knock on the bathroom door to let Phylecia know that he was gonna run out to get a toothbrush right quick, but his thought process was thrown by the sound of her voice on the other side. He could hear the shower running, but below that in a really low tone just above a whisper, he could hear Phylecia talking.

What the hell could she be in there talkin' about on the phone that couldn't wait until she got done washin' her ass? Boom thought. He thought a bit further and came to the realization that she might've only turned the shower on to drown out the sound of her voice. Now he was beginning to believe that she was trying to hide something. He pressed his ear up against the door to get a better listen.

"...but from what I heard, he ain't far off. This boy is sharp." Phylecia paused to listen if Boom was up yet. She didn't hear anything and continued, "Yeah, I know that's what you thought, but what now? I heard him mention Patrice while he was the phone last night. I played it off but I was listening to him the whole time. I did good, right?" She waited for a response and then continued, "Alright, you don't have to remind me, but I'm just sayin'...okay, whatever! I gotta go before he get up, speak to you later..."

Boom had heard enough. What killed him the most was that he had just gone through all of that shit last night to make certain his arrival was not announced. Now, all of that effort went to shit. His body was burning so hot he could almost feel his blood boiling inside his veins. His upper lip curled up below his nose as he bit down on the bottom one. His fists were balled up, and he was breathing extremely hard. He pounded on the door repeatedly before yelling at the top of his lungs, "Bitch, who the fuck you in there talkin' to???"

Phylecia got so scared at the sound of this animal trying to take the door completely off the hinges that her cell phone slid from her grasp and dropped right in the tub. She didn't even get a chance to holler for help. Her eyes grew as she searched for a possible escape. Her whole body began to twitch.

It only took a few seconds—and some well-placed kicks—and Boom had the door open. Phylecia simply stood there, completely nude and dripping wet, peeking at him from the other side of the shower curtain. She was already feeling herself about to cry. She couldn't even bring herself to lie or make an attempt at covering up what she was doing.

Boom threw the curtain to the side, looked her up and down and said, "You tryin' to play me or somethin', you fuckin' slut???" He gave her a swift back-hand slap that left her in a daze. She was helpless against the blows to follow as she couldn't even see them coming anymore. All she felt was her head getting numb, and it flew back and forth from the continuous slaps Boom let fly at her. "Answer me, bitch!!!" he yelled. "Oh, you can't talk now, huh? You was talkin' fine just a minute ago, wasn't you? What's the matter now, you shy or some-thin'? It's just a bit too late for that shit!!!"

Boom grabbed her by the throat and dragged her naked body out of the bath-room as she kicked and screamed to get free. "Shut up, bitch!" he spat at her before throwing her to the bed. He quickly went back into the bathroom to get his gun. He snatched up her cell, too. When he got back to her, she was on the floor on the other side of the bed, making her way to the door. He grabbed her by her hair, lifted her to her feet, and threw her back to the bed. In one hand he had the burner; in the other he was holding her cell phone. She didn't know which one she could take her eyes off of. She just looked from one to the other. Of course she knew what the gun could do to her, but the information in that phone could very easily compound the problem. Then she didn't know what to expect.

"Who was you talkin' to?" he asked in a calm voice which was actually more menacing than the yelling he'd just got through doing.

He flipped open the cell to take a look at the last call, but all he caught was the area code before the phone started to blank out. It was a 718 number. The phone was soaking wet and the screen faded away into a blur just before it went off completely. It only fueled his rage. He quickly abandoned his calm and col-lected tone, and resorted back to the violence that filled his frame. He threw the phone to the ground and leapt at Phylecia. She lay on the bed covering her face with her eyes shut tightly. She couldn't bring herself to open them. She was deathly afraid of what she might see. If she would've opened them, she would only see the barrel of Boom's gun. He held her down with the weight of his body to prepare her for questioning. He wrapped his free hand around her neck until she opened her eyes to beg for her life.

"Please..." she murmured. "...don't...kill...me...please!"

"What the fuck you know???" spat Boom as he moved his Glock from between her eyes, just so that she could see the fury in his eyes. "Who the fuck sent you?!!" He yelled before thinking to himself. He was able to find the answer to his own questions before long. "What am I saying? It was that filthy mutha-fucka, Winch, right? Yeah, ain't no doubt about that. But how did you know who I was and where to find me??? I only just got back to the Bronx!" After another brief thought, Boom answered his own questions again. "It was that bitch in the bar; I see now…she put you on me, huh? FUCKIN' ANSWER ME!!!"

Of course, with his hand still wringing her neck, she wasn't even able to respond even if she wanted to. It was all beginning to make perfect sense now though. As soon as he dropped the name in Virginia's, she jumped on the horn. Ten minutes later, up walks Phylecia. He didn't realize it before, but she must've been on her way into the bar when he ran into her.

"Yeah, that's it!" he thought to himself aloud with his hand still firmly wrapped around Phylecia's defenseless little neck. "So you just his little whore, huh? I wonder how many others you laid down for him…"

Phylecia's face was beginning to turn blue. There were veins bulging out of her forehead, and her eyes were bloodshot red. Tears ran freely down her face and she desperately wanted to breathe, that's all…nothing more, nothing less. Boom finally granted her that luxury. He remained on top of her, watching while she choked and gasped for air.

"…how many before me?" he asked rhetorically. Again, he didn't wait for an answer. His mind was already preparing the perfect punishment for her deceit-fulness.

★★★

When Boom left the motel, he was feeling a whole lot better about himself. There was no time to waste now. He didn't have much time to get to Winch, now that he was aware of his presence. Although he got the urge, he didn't even have the time to stop by the bar to pay that bitch Virginia a nice visit. Nope, he only had time for one thing…get to Patrice before someone got to him first. He'd definitely need his car for the job, so that was his first stop. From there, he hit I-95 North, and he didn't have far to travel at all. By the time he reached 172nd Street and Elder Avenue, his leg was shaking with unmanageable nervous energy. He drove down the block slowly, analyzing each house until he got the one that matched Branson's description. He could almost still hear him yelling,

"It's the green house on the corner!" He pulled past the house and halfway into the next block before he made a U-turn and parked so that he could see the house in front of him. There, he sat and waited for *something* to happen. He could've just run up in the house with his pistol drawn, but if Winch had gotten as huge as it seemed thus far, there'd be security up in there with Patrice for sure. He expected two thugs with her at the very least, but there could've easily been more. Obviously he wasn't afraid to bust his gun, but you can only squeeze one shot at a time. For the time being, he kept a close eye on the house and tried to figure out all options.

"Two-family house, most likely with a basement," he said aloud. "Probably about six bedrooms total, plus kitchens, bathrooms and living rooms. There should be access from the back to the main floor and the basement. That may be the best way to go." He looked up and down the block and was pleased with his discovery. At the sight of numerous abandoned buildings and the lack of children playing in the area, Boom was that much more confident about his ability to execute his mission with as little fuck-ups as possible. He continued his conversation with himself, "Not too many neighbors, huh? Nobody to call time-out. It's lookin' good!"

Boom went through his plan over and over in his head, changing it around until it started to look right to him. The first couple of hours went by like nothing. The next two felt like it took a bit longer…still nothing. Boom was chain-smoking Newport after Newport now, and a pile of butts was accumulating outside his car. There was no activity whatsoever. Boom knew that the luck he'd had so far would run out sooner or later. Everything had just gone smoothly, a little too smoothly at that. He was due for a brick wall to jump in front of him and obstruct his progress.

By the time the sixth hour came and went, he was beginning to get a little jumpy. It wasn't the first time he had to sit around and wait on a mark to open up a window of opportunity for him, but this time definitely held more meaning than the others. This wasn't just business. This was personal. It couldn't get any more personal.

Finally, eight hours later, a black Ford Excursion pulled up and stopped in front of Patrice's house. The driver, a tall dark man wearing dark shades, exited the vehicle continually looking over his shoulder. As his head spun back and forth, his long dreads swayed from side to side. Boom instantly placed the old face with the new name he'd just learned.

"Hmm," he said to himself. "Apollo...and that's gotta mean *guess who* is in the muthafuckin' back."

His luck was definitely starting to look up again, but it started to look too good to be true when Apollo started toward the house, leaving the truck unguarded.

"What the fuck?" Boom asked himself. "This is supposed to be head of security fittin' to hold me down? This is gonna be too fuckin' easy, man."

Boom jumped out of his car as Apollo entered the house. Boom was wearing a black fatigue jacket with his hands in the chest pockets. In one pocket was his trusty Glock 9, and in the other was a back-up .38 revolver. Both weapons were loaded, cocked and ready to ignite. From where he stood it was impossible to tell whether or not there was someone else in the truck. He crossed the street to come up on the passenger side. Even from the front viewpoint, Boom couldn't get a clear view inside due to the dark tints. He was still a block-length away walking up to where the truck was parked. Just as he was about to cross the street at the corner, he got a sudden change of heart. He didn't have enough advantage just walking up like that. He caught himself being just a bit too apprehensive. He even surprised himself at times; he had the perfect plan for a quick hit and an even quicker getaway. He called it *The Nudge.*

When Boom got back to his car, he sped to the next corner and made a sharp left. Three more right turns left him exactly where he needed to be. He was pulling right up behind the Excursion now. He came to a halt when they were side by side. It was killing him not to look over and get a glimpse of his enemy before he put him out. He wanted to be face to face with him. He wanted to look into his eyes, and as soon as Winch knew who he was, send a flaming hot slug through his skull. The blood would trickle slowly down his forehead letting him know that he was about to die. Everything would go silent as his life flashed before him. The only thing that would ring out over and over in his head would be the last sound he heard...*BOOM...BOOM...BOOM...*

He put the car in reverse and began backing into the free space behind the Excursion. When he was halfway into the spot, he put the car back in drive. Before he hit the gas, he made sure there was slug chambered in the 9 and then laid it down on his lap. Then, he let the brakes go and stomped down on the gas.

KABOOM...the force of the collision rocked the big truck from its position, and it swayed back and forth until it stopped. Eager and anxious, Boom waited for Winch to exit the car to examine the damage. Hopefully, he would make some kind of noise and talk some shit. That would make killing him even more pleasurable. He'd definitely show him who was boss. Boom was so excited, a smile started to creep out from beneath his freezing cold ice-grill. "Come on, you cocksucker," he said to himself. "Jump out and get what's comin' to ya." But nothing happened. "Maybe he saw the set-up from a mile away," Boom thought to himself. Then, he realized he was giving Winch a whole lot more credit than he probably deserved. It wasn't that serious at all. It took a minute, but Boom finally came to the realization that there couldn't have been anyone inside of the truck. It was obvious now. He defaulted to Plan B. He had to move quickly to get it in gear. Just as he was about to hop out of the car his phone rang; it was Shonda.

"What's up, Shonda?" Boom quickly said. "I can't talk right now. Lemme give you a call right back, ma. I'm busy right now. That's cool?"

"Boom, you need to come home now. I need you!"

"Huh?" Boom replied. "What you mean? You okay?"

"Boom, you just really need to be here! Somebody got her!"

"Got who? What you talkin' about, Shonda?" Confusion overwhelmed Boom's facial expression. He was completely lost. He was way too focused right now and she was just babbling like she was crazy. In addition, his focal point was quickly shifted when Patrice's front door opened. Boom tucked his toast under his leg when he saw Apollo at the door, looking right in his direction. His lips got tight as his jaw locked. His breaths got shorter and faster. His eyes bulged from his head and his brows met just above the bridge of his nose.

"Ay, what the fuck you doin', boy?" yelled Apollo in a deep monstrous voice. "I'm talkin' to you, muthafucka! You don't hear me?"

Boom bit down on his lip as Apollo neared his car from the passenger side. His sweaty palm gripped the handle of his hammer even tighter now. The closer Apollo got to him, the tighter he gripped the 9. Apollo would be the first casualty in this quest for vengeance. He'd get it, and then Patrice would get it. Then all he had to do was figure out how to bring Winch to him, and then he'd get it, too!

"Oh, it's a game or somethin', muthafucka? You actin' like you don't hear me talkin' to you. I'll tell ya now, I find a scratch on my truck and that's ya ass, boy!"

Boom was jumping for joy inside. He wanted so badly for Apollo to provoke him. He was quietly cheering him on. That's when Shonda spoke three words that forced Boom to listen to her and understand the seriousness of why she'd called.

"Somebody got Sabra," she said as she was no longer able to conceal her hurt. All Boom could hear from the other side of the phone was Shonda crying. As if her eyes weren't red enough...she must've cried two gallons of tears since she found out. There was nothing else she could do but cry.

"What you just say?" said Boom to Shonda.

"You heard me, muthafucka!" Apollo yelled as he stood not even three feet from Boom bent over on the passenger side of his car. He was virtually in arm's reach. All it would take was a quick extension of his hand and a swift pull of the trigger. In addition, Boom's attention was somehow shifted from this beast-like man standing in front of him when he saw Patrice peeking over from the doorway. Seeing her face made the images from that day flash in front of his eyes till he could see nothing else. He desperately had to fight off the urge to empty out a clip in her face. He needed to do the same with Apollo. It took all of his power and strength, but he had more important matters to deal with now.

"My bad, boss," said Boom to Apollo. "Any damage? Don't worry, I got you."

"Oh, you damn right you got me, nigga!" Apollo replied.

"Don't worry, Shonda," Boom said as Apollo went to check his bumper. "I'll be right there."

Then he hung up as Apollo frustratingly checked his truck for damage. Boom just sat there fighting back the temptations. With this news, he felt like a murder-spree was just what the doctor ordered. He could only peek over at Patrice from time to time. He knew that if he looked for any longer than that, he'd lose it and twist her wig backwards. That wasn't important anymore though. A minute ago, his life didn't mean shit to him. The only thing he was concerned with was removing these people from existence. Now, his life still didn't mean anything to him, but it meant the world to that little girl. It was the difference between life and death. He couldn't let her go that easily, not only to fill a void in his own being.

"You good over there, brother?" asked Boom to Apollo. "See anything?"

"Muthafucka, I ain't ya brother, first of all..." replied Apollo, sustaining his vicious attitude. "...and you's a lucky nigga I just got this grille put on my shit. If not, you'd be coming out ya pocket for sure. But everything is cool though."

Hmm, Boom thought. *Yeah, I'd be comin' outta my pocket alright...with the cannon to put ya ass down for good. Anyway, in due time.*

Boom pulled off with a pleasant wave and a fraudulent smile. As he turned the corner, tears began forming in his eyes. He just knew that something he'd done had caused whatever had happened to Sabra. He couldn't even bring himself to call Shonda back to get the details. He had a three-hour drive ahead of him, and the wrong thing would make him really flip out. For now, he had to maintain. When he got back to Philly, that's when he'd know how to respond if a response was warranted—and it most certainly would be. Until then, he blew down cigarette after cigarette, and tried to settle down as much as possible.

CHAPTER 10

"Why me, Germ?" Shonda cried. "Why *my* little girl? *What the fuck did I do... what did she do to deserve this???"*

Germ couldn't answer. He simply sat there next to her staring off at the wall, trying his absolute best not to make eye contact. He wasn't prepared for this. His thing wasn't relieving pain and despair. His thing was causing it. Germ really couldn't grasp this grieving and consoling shit one bit.

"I can't believe this is happening to me," Shonda continued. "I mean, it ain't even been a month since Ivan passed, and now this shit! I can't cope. I was just starting to get my strength back from losing my husband. Germ, I don't know what I'd do if I lost Sabra...if I lost my baby-girl. I'm gonna fuck around and lose it. You hear me, right??? Mark my words, I'm gonna completely lose my mind if something happens to Sabra!"

Damn, Germ thought. *Boom better hurry the fuck up and get back. Shit, talk about losin' my mind. I'm about ready to take it to somebody chest*...hard!

***

The drive back down was worse than the drive up. It was pure torture, especially because Boom had to wait until he got all the way to Philly before he found out all the details. It was critical that he remained focused for the ride, and this was how he kept his composure. In his own mind, he was sure that he'd flip out before he even reached Philly if he knew for a fact something horrible had happened, and that there was nothing he could do about it now. Keeping those visions out of his head was getting more and more difficult though. He saw little Sabra tied up in some cold, dark basement somewhere in the middle of nowhere. She was probably scared and hungry. She was probably crying her pretty little eyes out. She wouldn't even know why she was there. Her sufferance would come, not for something that she'd done or someone that she'd wronged in her short lifetime, but due to someone else's actions…someone else's decisions. There was no way to predict that things would come this far, that it would escalate this much. But now it was what it was, and there wasn't anything else anyone could do. The source for someone else's vengeance, Sabra was merely a pawn in the big chess game of life.

As for Boom, he couldn't get down I-95 fast enough. He'd passed a buck a long time ago and was at a steady hundred and ten miles per hour by now. The objects he passed along the way ceased to be anything but a blur of lights and lines in his eyes. Nothing else existed. His focus was so strong that it almost felt like he was traveling down a one-way pipeline or tunnel that would leave him right where he needed to be.

By the time Boom was getting off of I-676, his heart was pounding hard and fast. Every twenty seconds he would have to wipe the sweat from his brow while making sure not to drop cigarette ashes in his lap again. Before he knew it, he was mumbling to himself.

"Wait 'til I get there, muthafucka…it ain't gon' be sweet at all, just wait. Whatever it takes 'til I get Sabe…'til I'm holding her in my arms. Shit, if that don't happen, I'm turning Philly upside-muthafuckin'-down!"

Boom would repeat these words over and over again to himself for the better part of the ride down. He didn't stop until he was at Shonda's doorstep.

"Boom!!!" she yelled upon opening the door to find her only hope for ever getting her daughter back. She threw herself at Boom and collapsed in his arms. "You have to help me get Sabra back! You have to help me bring my little girl home! I just can't stop thinking about where she is and why anyone would wanna hurt her…why anyone would have this much darkness in their heart. What did *I* do…huh???"

"Nothing, Shonda," Boom said, holding her tightly in his arms. He rubbed her back to console her and continued, "You ain't do nothing. Don't blame yourself. This shit ain't got nothin' to do with you…or Sabe. This is my problem to solve, and when I tell you that you don't have to worry...I mean that shit one hundred percent. She *will* be coming home soon, no matter what. If it kills me, I won't stop until all of Philly is burnt to the ground. I'll leave this whole fuckin' city in a pile of ashes before I let something happen to baby-girl. I mean it, Shonda." He positioned her so that she could see the look in his eyes. The pure severity in his face spoke louder than his words. There wasn't even a hint of fraudulence in his tone. She didn't get the feeling that he was saying these things just to make her feel better, or to calm her down. She truly believed him. After a long glare, he pulled her in close and held on tight. She returned his embrace.

When Germ came to the door, Boom lifted his head to look at him. He saw a look in Boom's face that was incredibly scary, even for a fearless muthafucka like him. His ice-grill sent a chill up his spine. His eyes were so red and filled with fury that he could almost feel the steam rising off his head. If he ever worried about anybody in his life, he was worried for the sorry bastard that was responsible for this shit. He knew, before they even spoke, that Boom was gonna stop at nothing to rectify this situation.

"Listen, Shonda," Boom said in a soft tone. It was horribly obvious that his voice could crack at any moment. "I want you to go in the bedroom and lay down for a while. Calm ya nerves and try to rest for me." Boom saw the look of unwillingness in Shonda's face when he spoke, but he proceeded. "Please, Shonda, I'm begging you. I don't need to be worrying about your well-being, too. I just need to know that you're safe and that you're not gonna do anything crazy. I'm gonna handle this shit."

"Fuck that, Boom!" she spat. "Whatever you gonna do, I'm gonna be right there every step of the way. Now you done already sat me down once. I can't sit this one out, Boom!"

"Listen to me. I can tell you with all sincerity, I could give a fuck I live or die! I don't care what happen to me, 'cause my life ain't worth a damn anyway. But what happens if I take you with me and you don't make it back. What the fuck am I gonna tell Sabe??? I made the promise to look after her like she was my own daughter, and I'll honor that if it means my life. But what is there to bring her home once I get her? How's she gonna understand that her father *and* mother is gone now, and they ain't never coming back? I ain't havin' that shit, Shonda!

So yeah, I sat you down the last time, and you gonna have to sit this one out, too. That's jus how it gotta be."

Although Shonda was still shaking her head back and forth, she knew that Boom was right. She was just being selfish. She didn't wanna be involved because she thought they would be a stronger.team with her, but so she could take some enjoyment in torturing whoever was responsible into a slow and painful death. She was just too much of a gangstress for her own good.

When Boom was sure that Shonda knew that this was the only way things could go down, he put his arm around her to rub her shoulders. Then he led her upstairs where she could calm down in the bedroom. As soon as he came back downstairs, the questions started.

"So what the fuck happened?"

"They ain't talkin' about shit up at the school, son," replied Germ. "All they said was that some fiend or somethin' fell out and started having a seizure or some shit right outside the gate where all the kids was playing at. Of course they jumped on that shit to get the nigga some help, and inside of all the excitement and shit, little Sabra end up disappearing. They don't know what the fuck happened. They talked to all the kids and they don't know shit either."

"What happened to the fiend?"

"I don't know. The nigga rode the ambo to the hospital, but they never checked him in. He just disappeared."

"So ya'll ain't hear nothin' from nobody? Ain't no ransom demands, or no requests, huh?"

"Nah, Boom...nothin'!"

Germ paused for a second as what he said sunk into Boom's mind, and then he continued, "Yo the shit is all fucked up! I mean, of course the police is investigatin' but what the fuck does that really change, ya na'mean?"

"Fuck that, homey," responded Boom with a focused look on his face. "Ain't no mystery or nothin', dog. This shit here about one man and one man only. Do me a favor and call Black. We gon' need a third man for this if it's goin' down tonight, and we gotta be on point like a muthafucka. Tell him we comin' through to talk."

Boom went back upstairs to make sure Shonda was doing better. He stood at the doorway and stared at her. Her eyes were closed, but she wasn't asleep. He could see them twitching. Maybe she just didn't want Boom worrying about her. Maybe she knew with all he was already dealing with, that he didn't need her to deal with as well. That showed a lot of smarts. Boom admired her strength and commended her loyalty. If anyone didn't deserve for all of these horrible things to happen to them, it was her. That made it that much more imperative that he bring Sabra home.

He sat beside Sabra and gazed out of the window at the moon. When he looked back at Shonda, she was staring up at him with her eyes glossy. She had a worried look that she couldn't find it inside of herself to hide. That's when Boom made a vow to Shonda that he would honor if it meant his own death.

"Those muthafuckas ain't gon' see another moonlit night…not one!"

When Boom leaned over to give her a kiss, her eyes immediately shut tightly, still discharging tears while her lips twitched.

"Yo, Boom!" yelled Germ as he banged on the door. "Yo, Boom, I spoke to Black! He said he gon' just come through and meet us here. He said he don't wanna just sit around waiting all night."

After a short pause, Boom proceeded to lean in to deliver his kiss. His lips landed brief and innocently on Shonda's forehead, and then he left. Shonda's eyes didn't open back up right away. She kept them closed for a while, until Boom was out of the room. When she knew that he was gone, she helplessly wept. She couldn't muster the strength to do anything else.

★★★

Black arrived to find that Boom and Germ had already filled the living room with weed smoke. He'd been drinking heavily and on edge ever since he got the call. He had no idea what was in store for him when he got to Boom. He was consumed with nervous energy.

He entered and lit up a cigar, blowing the smoke in the air as he leaned back into the couch. On the coffee table in front of them were the weapons they needed for the night, cleaned and fully loaded. They sat there, not making a move or uttering a word. Black didn't say one thing either. He sat and waited for some kind of indication as to what was gonna happen. For Boom, it was like they were speaking without words. To him, he was engaged in a complex conversation in his head. He looked from Germ to Black, and then took a deep pull from the blunt. When he leaned forward to address them, the smoke eased out of his mouth and nostrils with every word he spoke. He didn't talk long. He was straight to the point.

"We 'bout to tear into this muthafucka here...no two ways about the shit. We know where he at...right now! Let's go get him."

With that they were off. Boom didn't even have to say the name, Beast. They automatically knew who he was talking about. They were officially at war. But this wasn't that regular type of shit, where niggas would just go around dumping on ya boys. They wasn't talking about shortening the nigga numbers to drag out the bloodshed. Nope. One calculated hit would put an end to all of their problems. They were gonna go straight to the top...*fuck it!* Ain't no rules involved when you fuck around and take someone's child. What they did to each other was one thing. It was another thing to go into family where innocent bystanders come in, just guilty by association. The worse code to break is *'no women and children.'*

***

They proceeded to Shampoo, a nightclub that Beast used to launder his drug money. For the most part it was a successful establishment, but that was all extra where Beast was concerned. He only needed a high potential cash business to use as a front for his enterprise, and it worked out perfectly in that fact.

One thing about the spot was that anytime you needed to find him that would be the best place to start looking. He'd be cooped up in the plush office upstairs with the huge windows that looked down on the main dance floor. From behind his huge L-shaped glass desk, he could lean back in his nice executive chair and watch everything going on. He knew that niggas could find him there if they wanted to, but not too many niggas wanted to find Beast. Nobody ever brought it to him directly. The issues cats had with Beast never exceeded the street level. He was one of those dudes you didn't want it with. In the past, Boom and Beast had had their small quarrels, but it was almost always indirect; "eye for an eye"; you take one of mines and I take one of yours; you hit one of my spots and I strip one of your boys naked and beat the shit out of him in the middle of the street...you know, shit like that! It was a mutual respect. They only crossed paths on occasion and when they did, it wasn't ever anything too serious. All of that was about to change.

Now for Boom's plan to work, something dramatic had to happen first. It wasn't enough for a fight to break out or something small like that. Beast and his employees already had contingency plans set up for such things. There was a uniformed and undercover security staff, and all of them were carrying. Nah, some crazy shit had to pop off; something wild enough to force Beast to leave the club. It'd have to be something that would definitely draw the police, because no way is Beast gonna stick around and wait for the authorities to sort things out for him. Even though it was his club, he wasn't gonna give them a reason to connect him to anything. Once on the outside, he would be easy pickings.

Germ would handle the diversion, and Boom and Black would be waiting for him to drop into their hands outside. One thing was for sure; they couldn't just roll up in there with guns blazing like it was some kinda motion picture where a thousand slugs get sent and no one gets hit but the bad guys. It was mainly because everybody was *the bad guy* in this situation. This was gonna have to be a bit more intense.

It started out with Germ entering the club and getting a seat at the bar. The bar was also elevated from the dance floor, and eye level with the office that Beast would be in. The office was on one side and the bar was on the other, but from this vantage point, he could make sure that they weren't about to pop off for no reason. When the time was right, he'd put the plan in gear.

On the outside of the building, Boom and Black were slowly creeping up along both sides of a black Yukon Denali XL truck parked around the back entrance. It was a well-known fact that this truck had been costumed by the same cats that make the Secret Service vehicles that transport the Pres'. It was completely bullet/bomb proof from every angle. If a grenade went off underneath, it'd probably feel like a speed bump to the passengers. There was no way to penetrate it from the outside, so they'd have to already be inside to make the right move.

When Germ saw a fold in the blinds inside the office, he knew that Beast was there checking on things in his establishment. Germ quickly flipped out his two-way and sent a text message to Boom giving him the signal to move. At that point Germ ordered a bottle of Belvedere vodka. When the tall bottle arrived,

Germ quickly yanked it out of the cooler and turned to find a suitable victim. When he spotted a big, dark-skinned guy standing at the end of the bar, he immediately knew that he was security. He popped the bottle top off and made his way toward that end of the bar stumbling like he was drunk. He walked extra sloppy, spilling the vodka out of the bottle and fumbling on people. His head was swaying from side to side, and he had his arms out to feel his way around like he was blind. Even though he looked blind, Germ never once took his eyes off his target. When he knew he had his attention, he walked directly towards the security guard. When he got into arm's reach, he leaned on him as if he couldn't stand up by himself. The security guy wasn't at all amused. He helped Germ stand up, but he was mean-mugging him the whole time.

★★★

Outside, Boom gave Black the signal to approach the Denali from the driver's side while Boom came up on the passenger side. When Black got to the window, he gave it a knock to get the driver's attention. When he looked up, Black put a fresh cigar in his mouth.

"Got a light, brother?" he asked in a nice, calm tone.

The driver shook his head. "No."

"Come on, baby," Black insisted. "You gotta have a light in there, man."

"I don't fuckin' smoke, alright," he snapped. "Now get the fuck outta here before I get you the fuck outta here; you understand what I'm sayin', punk?"

"Huh?"

"You heard me, muthafucka!"

"What you just say to me, cocksucker?"

"Oh, okay, since you wanna play deaf," he said while rolling down the window to yell loud enough for Black to hear. His pale white face was turning red with frustration now. Not only was Black interrupting the man from the porno mag' he was occupied with; he was also disturbing his meatball sandwich dinner. "Can you hear me now, cocksucker??? Beat it!!!"

Just then, Boom knocked on the passenger side window. The unsuspecting driver looked over at him, taking his eyes off of Black like an idiot. Boom simply smiled at him and waved playfully. Now the driver was getting confused and scared. He didn't even have a chance to look back. Black swiftly wrapped a rope around his neck and tightened up the grip, squeezing harder and harder as the driver fought unsuccessfully to get his breath back. This continued for a few more seconds until the driver could no longer give any resistance. His body hung from Black's clutches lifelessly, and his eyes shut for good. Black quickly reached in the window and hit the button to unlock the doors. As soon as they unlocked, he threw the door open and grabbed the driver's body. He pushed him over to the passenger side and left him hanging off the seat with his head on the floor. He jumped in the driver's seat while Boom jumped in the back, staying low to the ground.

★★★

"Ay, dog," Germ slurred. "You know where the bathroom is, homey? I'm about to fuckin' vomit all over the place! Everything looks like it's spinning around, man. I can't see straight for shit."

As soon as the security guard turned his head to point Germ in the direction of the bathroom, Germ saw his opportunity. With one hand, he held the security guard's head. When he got a good enough grip, he lifted the other hand holding the huge Belvedere bottle. In a chopping motion, he landed a brutal blow to the huge man's head with the bottom of the bottle. He tried to grab onto Germ, but couldn't even see him, what with all the blood in his eyes from the gaping gash that Germ had just opened in his forehead. He almost got a good grip on Germ until he repeated this blow twice more, forcing him to lose his balance. That's when Germ flipped the bottle upside-down and hit him in the face with the side of it. The bottle shattered, splashing vodka all over the place. Now with him in a daze, he searched his person for his burner and swiftly relieved him of it when he found it tucked under his belt. In a snap, he had a match lit and tossed it. The guard didn't even know that his body was on fire at first. All he saw was blinding light when he tried to open his eyes. He kept blinking to get his sight back, but what he didn't know was that there wasn't anything wrong with his vision. The light that had consumed his sight was actually the flames rising off of his own boiling flesh. When he moved his arms and saw the light move with them, he realized that he in fact was the gleaming light. At first he started yelling hysterically, and then he ran frantically. It wasn't long until everyone in the club was pointing and staring in awe. His cries had now surpassed the loud sound of the club's state-of-the-art sound system. He let out a high-pitch, sustained scream that dug deep into the ears of everyone in the building. By the time he got to the stairs, he couldn't even stand anymore. He went tumbling down the steps in a ball of fire and stopped in the middle of the dance floor. To Germ's surprise, everyone just stood around gawking and pointing at this horrendous sight.

"Look at these muthafuckas," Germ said to himself. "Oh well..."

He lifted the burner into the air and started letting off shots...*BOW, BOW...BOW, BOW, BOW!!!* Everyone scrambled to flee the scene immediately. That's when the shades flew up from the offices. Astonishment and fury filled Beast's facial expression. He quickly went for the door. Not even a second went by before he was out of the office. Before he made his getaway, he directed two guards to come with him and another to go after Germ.

"Catch that muthafucka and put his ass out of commission. Throw him in a fuckin' bag or somethin' and bring him to me...but don't kill his ass." He wanted to take care of him personally.

By then Germ had already dipped out of the back way, and there was no catching up to him. But Beast couldn't have known that this wasn't just a freak occurrence. This was a well-orchestrated jack and it was going exactly as planned. His next main concern was getting as far away from this shit-storm as quickly, and as obscurely, as possible. Inside of a minute, he and his two armed thugs were outside of the club. Everyone was going crazy, and cars were flying out of there quick enough to travel through time to flee the scene. They made their way to his truck, planning on doing the same. The sirens could already be heard, and soon enough, they would be visible. There would be no way to explain everything that went down, and Beast had no intention on trying.

When they got to the truck, they jumped in without even giving it a second thought. First, one of Beast's henchmen; then he got in. The other guard squeezed in after him, putting Beast safely between them just in case the madness wasn't over yet. If he would've paid half the attention he was giving the street to the condition of his truck, then he might've not gotten caught so off guard when the shots started.

BOOM!!! Before Beast knew what was going on, a shot was fired, leaving the bodyguard to his left slumped over. It wasn't even a split second before another loud shot rang out...*BOOM!!!* A flaming hot slug pierced the other bodyguard's head from the back, leaving a small hole where it entered and taking half of his forehead off when it exited. Blood and human particles were everywhere, but good thing for Boom and Black that Beast opted to get his windows so darkly tinted. From the outside, it appeared to be a regular Denali. On the inside, it looked as though there was enough blood scattered all over the place to fill a bathtub. It was a slaughterhouse.

Beast wanted to react, but he was too late. He felt the pressure of a .44 caliber on the back of his head as Black pulled off. Boom was sitting in the trunk area low to the ground.

"Ya'll muthafuckas must not know who you fuckin' wit!" Beast blattered.

"Hmm..." Boom chuckled at his statement. "...why is that always the first thing niggas say when they about to get it? Why do muthafuckas always think they're somehow exempt from the streets? This is what it is, muthafucka! You ain't talkin' ya way outta this one here, dog. Should I even introduce myself, nigga? Do I even have to tell you who I am?"

"Fuck all that, young scrapper," Beast replied. "Ain't no need for no introductions. I *know* who you are...you a DEAD man, that's who. I don't need to be formally introduced to muthafuckas that are as good as dead!"

"Oh, we gon' play that game, huh?" Boom said matter-of-factly. "Me, I like getting to know the people I'm about to murder, but fuck it; let's do it your way for now. Lemme introduce you to somethin' else then."

With his free hand, he flipped out of a long folding knife with a serrated edge. He pressed the blade firmly against Beast's neck and tucked his pistol back inside of his pants. Beast still sat there with his face screwed up, not budging a bit. Boom quickly snatched a handful of Beast's long hair and tugged on it until he was facing straight up. The sharp edges of the blade were digging so deeply into his flesh now that small droplets of blood started trickling down his neck.

"You feel that?" Boom asked in a low, menacing monotone voice. "I ain't afraid of you. I should just put that out there right now, playa. Trust, you don't want me to show you how serious I am. We can end this my way, or we can end this your way. If you answer these questions I'm about to ask you without all of the bullshit, then we ain't got a problem, dig? It can be just that simple. We can both walk away from this with what we value the most in this world."

"Oh, yeah? What's that?"

"Well you, you can leave with your fuckin' life and I don't have to put an end to it."

"Hmm, and what about you then? What you leavin' wit?"

"This ain't a game, muthafucka! You know damn well what I'm doin' here. Now we can be civil and all of that, but if you second-guess that I'm dead-fuckin'-serious for even one second...then I'll just cut ya muthafuckin' head off. I won't stop 'til this ratchet is diggin' into ya spine, nigga! Lemme tell you, I'm already fightin' it; you ain't that far from never seein' the light of day ever again!"

"You did it to yaself, Boom," Beast uttered, now biting his lip with anticipation. He was so angry that his breaths started to get shorter and harder. He was fighting back the urge to turn around and snap Boom's neck with every bit of strength he could muster. "There wasn't no need for all of this, dog. *I* let *you* live."

"What???" Boom said, now digging the knife even further into Beast's neck. His eyes were bulging out of his head, and sweat was running freely down his face. He thought to himself that all he had to do was entertain Beast's ranting for just a bit longer and then he could chop a nice-sized chunk out of his neck. "You thought you was doin' *me* a favor? You thought that I wasn't gonna come after you? You thought that I was gonna pass up the chance to make you beg for forgiveness before I ended your life for all of this? Nigga, is you out ya muthafuckin' mind???"

"Take it how you want it, punk! The only reason you're still walking this earth is 'cause of me! You hear me? I gave you every beat your heart is making right now. I granted you every breath you takin'...*ME!!!*"

"Yo, if you don't shut the fuck up, I'm gon' show you power, muthafucka! I'm gonna show you who son's who at the end of this, Beast. Just give me the word and you could take ya *last* breath."

"Keep poppin' that shit, young'n. I ain't even studyin' none of that bullshit right now. You do what you gotta do."

Boom knew that he couldn't just kill Beast right then and there. He knew that Beast knew that, too, or else why would he be playin' so tuff. He'd have to be crazy, or maybe he was just *that* gangsta. This was chess and Beast had Boom in check. Boom was forced on the defensive or he'd be checkmated for sure.

"Let's just make this simple, man. Maybe ya life don't need to end right now. Maybe you can just tell me what I wanna know. You tell me where she at, and I'll take you with me to get her. If she's okay, then it can end with that. We can put all of this shit behind us and start over wit a clean slate. Of course if shit pop off behind some bullshit later on in the future, then we'll just have to get it on then. As of now, I only have one concern."

"I don't know what the fuck you talkin' about!"

"Come on, just tell me what I need to know, man," Boom pleaded. "Just tell me what I need to know."

All the while, Black drove the truck through the back blocks of the hood listening closely to everything that was said. It was definitely a nerve-wracking experience.

"Why you gon' make me do this, Beast??? I don't wanna kill you but I will! Stop playin' tuff and gimme Sabra back. I swear I let you live!"

"I ain't concerned wit all that shit, nigga. I don't give a fuck about dying, but I ain't got a fuckin' clue about the shit you talkin'. Who the fuck is Sabra?"

Boom was confused now. He didn't know how to respond at first. He just froze in that position, not knowing how to react. He almost believed him. *Why would he lie?* Boom thought to himself. The only reason would be if he was just trying to play tuff, and he wasn't coming across as that type. He truly didn't give a fuck! Now if he *was* scared, this wouldn't be the right way to secure his safety; it was in fact a sure way to get killed. *What the fuck was he doin' with this move?* he thought.

"Stop fuckin' lyin' to me, nigga!!!" he yelled when he couldn't think of anything else to say. Denial was starting to take over his mind-state. There was no logical choice but for him to believe that Beast had something to do with Sabra's disappearance. What other option was there?

"You gon' tell me where she is or I'm gonna end you and find her myself. If you can't give me that, then there ain't no reason for me to not kill you, nigga!"

"Then kill me, muthafucka! What you waitin' on??? Do what you gotta do, nigga, but I ain't got a clue to what the fuck you talkin' about right now! If you comin' at me like this behind some broad, then I should've taken ya ass out that day at ya boy's burial. Hmm…that's who this is about then, huh? Just some bitch that got ya fuckin' nose open?"

"You better watch ya muthafuckin' mouth when you talkin' about my goddaughter, muthafucka!!!" Boom could feel the blade digging even deeper into Beast's neck. If he continued along this route, he would kill Beast prematurely for sure. "And what the fuck was you doin' at Ivan's burial anyway…huh, nigga??? What, you came to pay ya respects or some shit??? Don't play me like I'm some fuckin' brain-dead coward. Jack the zipper-head, huh? Just open me up and put whatever the fuck you want in there? Nigga, I'm *not* Travis!"

"Fuck Travis!!! That nigga wasn't worth the drama that would be caused if I came at you. I figured one for one, and then everything could be said and done. Why drag this whole bullshit out longer than it needed to be? Them two niggas there just cancelled each other out. I'm a businessman."

"You ain't answer my question, nigga!!! If you ain't plan on makin' a move, then why the fuck would you be at Ivan's burial??"

Beast took his time answering. Boom was in too sensitive of a state and he needed to be spoken to like a child for him to fully understand. "I went there 'cause I knew that's where you would be at. If I wanted to lay you down, I could've done it then. I had you dead to right, baby. But nah, I let you live. I gave you a pass. I ain't see no benefit from dustin' ya little small-time ass off the face of the earth. There wasn't nothin' on the bottom-line for that shit. I'm startin' to regret that decision."

"Yeah, so what about Travis?"

"Nigga, you can't hear or somethin'? *FUCK TRAVIS*…and his little beefs over all that bullshit. That ain't have nothin' to do with me. Like I said, I'm a businessman. Every move I make is beneficial to me and the bottom-line…period! What would I get from laying you down?"

"Well, if all of this shit is just so small to you, why'd you send that bitch-made ass nigga, Travis, after Ivan to begin with? You must've known that that shit was gonna start a war. I know this is the first time you and me is meeting face to face, but I'm sure you heard about me before tonight. I don't think you'd consider us friends."

"Muthafucka, you got all of this shit twisted," Beast replied, trying to get things back into proper perspective. "I ain't make that call on ya boy. Like I said, that shit ain't have nothin' to do with me."

"Wait, but Travis did Ivan 'cause of that holdup. He got three bricks off ya boy, and that's what made him come after us. You tellin' me that that shit don't faze you, huh? You *that* large, right?"

"Nah, baby, it ain't go down like that at all. Travis found out that Ivan was bangin' his baby-mother. That's what had him feelin' some sorda way. You know, I don't really blame him. That shit just comes down to principles. What I ain't feelin' was all the shit that had to follow. If he would've done that shit right, it would be known why Ivan got it like he did. Muthafuckas would know that he ain't do that shit under my flag."

"This is some bullshit," Boom said, pulling his cannon back out from behind him. "What you take me for?"

"Listen, lil' nigga, I ain't do nothin' to this goddaughter of yours. You got it wrong. I ain't new to this shit here. *No women and children.*"

Boom finally had to come to terms with two serious realities. One being that Beast was in fact telling the truth about his involvement, or lack thereof, in the disappearance of his goddaughter, Sabra. The other, of course, was the fact that he was now back to square one.

★★★

"Whew!" Germ said as he slid out the back door and down the fire-escape of the Shampoo club. "That was close!"

Just before Beast's thug came bursting through the door, Germ was quickly around the corner and halfway down the block. The excitement was all over, but his blood was still rushing through his veins at ninety miles per hour. Calming down off a high like that was harder than a two-day crack binge. He lived for that kind of thrill. That's what made him feel alive. And until now, he hadn't been getting as much of it as he was used to. Things had slowed down so much since Boom decided that he was gonna organize the clique. Now that they were established thoroughbreds, Boom wanted to use the name they built as window-dressing for some new hired help. They were to build a family with

Boom, Ivan and Germ sitting at the head of the table. From then on, they'd be civil criminals—if such a thing even existed. All that came to a halt when Ivan got put down. Now it was back to old times and Germ was riding the wave.

From here his next stop would be Boom's crib, where he'd wait for his return. Hopefully, everything turned out as expected. First, he needed to make an important phone call to report their progress.

"Hello," said Germ. "Yeah, so we got his ass…and good!!! Boom wit that nigga Beast right now. Shit, that nigga probably beggin' Boom and Black to kill him quick. That muthafucka in for it now; I can guarantee you that. So you don't worry; this will all be over soon. Shorty gon' be home and shit's gon' be right the fuck back on track, ya heard…holla at ya boy!"

CHAPTER 11

"WHAT THE FUCK IS GOIN' ON???" Boom yelled at the top of his lungs. He didn't know what to make of all of this shit. He was stuck. He put all of his eggs in one basket when he fingered Beast for all of this madness, and now he was left without a clue. He felt helpless. He just sat on the ground in his living room with his hoodie pulled low over his face. His expression remained screwed while every pore in his face sprouted sweat. In one hand he kept a lit cigarette, twitching between his index and middle finger. In the other hand was his long .44 revolver, also twitching with nervous energy. He could do nothing but rock back and fourth on the floor while he inhaled Newport after Newport. Of course he couldn't bring himself to report the bad news to Shonda. She'd be devastated. His only option was to do exactly what he intended from the beginning: turn the whole city of Philadelphia upside-muthafuckin'-down until he found Sabe.

Just as Boom was about to lose his mind, he heard a knock at the door. His animal instinct immediately kicked in, and he stayed low to the ground. He made his way to the door without making a sound. He took one more pull from his cancer-stick and put it out under his boot. By the time there was another knock at the door Boom was cocking the hammer on his .44. He stood at the door sideways with the barrel pointed directly into the peephole.

"Who dat??" he yelled as he was about to pull the trigger. "Who is it?"

"Boom?? It's Germ, nigga, open up!"

"Oh shit," Boom said aloud, realizing that he was about to off the only partner he really had left in these streets. He quickly uncocked the banger and threw the door open.

"What the fuck happen, man?" Germ asked. "I ain't even expect you to be here already. Why so early? Where's that nigga Beast at? Ya'll got him, right??"

Boom didn't answer right away. He just walked back into the living room and took his place back on the floor. He lit up a fresh cigarette and rested his head on the wall as he blew the smoke into the air.

"Yo, what the fuck is up, man?" asked Germ once more. "Talk to me, baby."

"I let that nigga go," Boom simply replied. "I let him walk."

"What???"

"It wasn't him, dog. He ain't got her."

"Accordin' to who, Boom? What the fuck you mean 'he ain't got her'? What the fuck is goin' on here???"

"He ain't the one, nigga!!! Alright? He ain't the muthafuckin' one, man."

"Beast told you that?"

"Yeah, nigga, and I believed him."

"Are you serious?? He told you that shit and you believed him? What the fuck is you thinkin', dog?"

"Fuck what I'm thinkin', nigga! It ain't him and I'm positive about that shit!"

"Hold on, slow down a bit. All of this shit and you let him walk? How could you believe that? Besides, even if he ain't the one, you still let that nigga go. What happens when he comin' back for us, huh? You think *he* gon' just let shit slide?"

"I ain't worried about that shit, Germ. Fuck that nigga Beast, man. All I'm concerned with is getting Sabe back, that's it. Nothin' more…nothin' less."

"Yeah, I know but you can't leave that kinda liability just walkin' freely in the streets with a strong team of henchmen. Fuck that, you should've still just heated that nigga down. If for nothin' else, for good measure, ya na'mean? That shit was sloppy, bruh."

"That nigga can't hurt me no more, Germ. What you don't understand? I'm already dead!!!"

"I hear you, man, and I know we gotta get that little girl back to her mom, but you gotta think. It'll only be a matter of time before they ain't gon' have you to watch over them if you softenin' up like this."

That's when Boom jumped to his feet. There was only an inch of air between him and Germ now, and Boom was staring at him with the windows to his soul wide open. "You see soft in my eyes, nigga?" he asked.

Germ took a breath and swallowed the lump in his throat. He was starting to realize very quickly that he would have to choose his words more carefully from now on. Boom was showing him how much of an unstable creature he was at this point. Anything could've set him off.

"I ain't tryin' to son you, my nigga," Germ replied in a softer and lower tone than what his level had risen to just a second ago. "I'm just lookin' after you, that's all. We supposed to watch each other's backs and shit, right? We family, dog. I just don't think it was a good move leavin' that nigga walkin' around free right now. For all you know he got niggas schemin' on ya crib right now. They could be climbin' the muthafuckin' walls!"

Boom finally blinked his eyes and shook off his ice-grill. He lowered his head as he made his way over to the sofa. "You soundin' just like Black right about now, Germ. I had to listen to that nigga chop me down about playin' it safe the whole way goin' to drop him off. He said the same shit about just offin' that nigga Beast for good measure. Then he start goin' on about how now I should realize where my place is, and if I would've stayed there by their side...and blah, blah, blah. That's what really got me fucked up in the game right now. I was off bullshittin' when all of this popped off. If I was here, the shit may have went down different, ya know. I gotta start thinkin' about other people before I think of myself next time. I knew that it was a possibility that some cocksucker would try somethin'. Especially now that my righthand man, Ivan, is gone. Niggas might be lookin' at the kid like somethin' to eat right now. Shit, when you start thinkin' about all the niggas I've done dirty over the years, the suspect is like tryin' to find a needle in a haystack. Meanwhile, I'm up in NYC causin' havoc."

"What the fuck was that trip about anyway, dog? You said you was trackin' down some nigga and a bitch?"

"Yeah, just some unfinished business, that's all. I was just wrappin' up loose ends."

"So what happened?"

"Shit, nothin'! I was just about ready to blast off...when I got the call from Shonda. I couldn't keep those two goals in my head at the same time; one had to be put on the back-burner."

"So you say you was right on they heels and shit, huh?"

"Yeah, somethin' like that. But fuck that, man, I got shit to worry about before all that diggin' into my past bullshit. On the real, I'm 'bout to turn this muthafuckin' city inside out. You wit' me?"

"Oh yeah you know I'm wit you, killa, but let's back up a second though."

"We ain't got time for all of this, Germ, she still out there...I can feel it. We don't have the time."

"Nah, hold on and just run with me right quick on this. How far back does this beef go in NYC?"

"More than I can even remember."

"See, that's what I'm talkin' about right there. Don't you think it's kinda strange that this shit happens as soon as you about to catch up to these muthafuckas?"

"What you sayin'?"

"Well, these muthafuckas large, or they just pack-holders?"

"Definitely larger than I remember, but large the same. This nigga done came up and he got his bottom-bitch right there by his side."

"So, they probably deep as fuck, right?"

"Yeah, they might be. What the fuck this gotta do with anything, dog?"

"If what you sayin' is on point, then what's to say they ain't get wind of you comin' and set up some insurance for themselves? Who's to say they arms don't reach this long, ya na'mean?"

"You sayin' that they might've had somethin' to do with this shit?"

"Anything's possible, dog. If they as big-time as you say, it probably wouldn't have even been a thang for them to set somethin' up to snatch one of your most prized possessions out from underneath you."

"Yeah, but they would've had to been watchin' me from jump to get the drop like that. That ain't no shot in the dark, feel me?"

"I feel you. But look at it from their point of view. If you had beef wit a cat, and you ain't see no reason to heat him down 'cause the beef done damn near dried up, wouldn't you still keep tabs on the cat?"

"You may be on to somethin', Germ. That shit makes perfect sense. But we talkin' about some real aged shit, man. I mean ten years plus, know what I mean?"

"Yeah well shit, New York ain't but a few hours away, dog. How hard would it really be to find you? I'm for damn sure your name ringin' bells in more cities than Philly. I can tell you this much; if you was my enemy, I'd wanna keep close watch to ya. When the time comes and we gotta go at it, then I'm ready to do what I gotta do, feel me? You ain't a regular dude out here on these streets, baby, believe it or not. Trust me, I mean I done heard the stories niggas be tellin'. You infamous."

"Hmm," Boom said in amusement. It was almost laughable to him. He thought, *What the fuck! I ain't Keyser Soze and shit!*

"What you thinkin' about?"

"Huh, nothin'," Boom said before taking a nice long breath. When he spoke, his tone got just a bit darker. "You know what this shit mean, right?"

"Nigga, you know I know what *this* shit means."

"Wanna ride?"

"Ride or die, baby, it's whatever to me! Holla at ya boy!"

"Alright then, we gon' need some more hammers."

★★★

That was all that needed to be said between them. They were both ready and willing to see the last of their days on the planet as long as the directive was accomplished. It was obvious to Boom that he had a real soldier with him. He'd fit the position of his lieutenant nicely. In Boom's eyes, he was in no way near a replacement for his brother from another mother, Ivan. But at least now the hole in his heart didn't feel as big.

While Boom went digging through the hollow wall in his closet, Germ went into the kitchen to make an important phone call. When all of the burners were all laid out on the bed, Boom went to get Germ so that they could start cleaning and loading the weapons. As soon as Boom walked into the kitchen, Germ quickly hung up the phone, ready to get down to business. Boom didn't even give a second thought to Germ's behavior, and they proceeded back to the bedroom to the armory ready.

When they were just about done, they had all the means to bring a strong war to small country! They packed up and hit the street with enough fire-power to dust Winch, Apollo, Patrice, and any other muthafucka that dared stand in their way.

In the trunk of his LS sedan, he had a sawed-off shotgun that, at close range, could blow a hole in a nigga chest so big that you could run the 2 train straight through it. Besides that, they had a semi-automatic Tec-9mm, fully loaded with hollow-tip slugs. Boom gave Germ the Glock and kept his .44 revolver. And in his fatigue jacket lining, he had a fifty-round Calico M-960 submachine gun he was saving for a special occasion. This was exactly that type of occasion. The drive north consisted mostly of their entrance and exit strategy.

"Yeah, so we gon' just roll up in there and take heads, right?" blurted Germ, giving no thought to his plan's obvious lack of tact.

"Naw, nigga! Is you crazy?" replied Boom. "Remember why we goin' there. How they gon' tell us where they got Sabra if they dead, nigga?"

"I don't care how you wanna do it, nigga, I'm wit you! Here, nigga, hit that," he said, handing Boom a freshly lit blunt.

Boom inhaled the bud deeply and blew out the thick choke-smoke. His eyes were already bloodshot red and glossy. He looked at the road like he was in that tunnel from earlier in the night. Everything else just faded away and all he saw was the path.

"So what we gotta do is..." Boom said as he took another long hard pull from the trees. "...we gotta be slick about it. From what I already saw, it looks like there may be five or six bedrooms in the whole house. The front door is way too risky. We can most likely get in from the back way. We come up through the basement and *BOOM*, they won't know what hit 'em."

"You sure they'll be there?"

"Shit, I'm pretty sure the broad'll be there. I ain't too confident about the dude. We'll just have to see what we find when we get there."

"I'm just tryin' to figure out how many heads we lookin' to take, ya na'mean? I ain't tryin' to get blind-sided, especially 'cause we ain't trying to murder them muthafuckas right off the bat!"

"Yeah, I feel you, dog. But we ain't got but so much time." Boom's voice dropped to a monotone low pitch as his lip curled up on one side. "I got a promise to keep."

They talked for the few hours to come about every variable they could imagine. They felt like nothing could go wrong, but they were definitely mistaken. A few hours worth of planning could've never prepared them for what was gonna happen in the next twenty-four hours. This one would definitely be coming down to the wire.

CHAPTER 12

The bright stars that lit the night sky were about to fade as the color changed from midnight to royal blue. It was still a bit dark but just bright enough that it felt like morning was just a few blocks away from reaching you. The moon was diminishing and the sun was just about to come out. Now that dawn was here, Boom really felt the pressure to fulfill the promise he'd made the night before. It was only a matter of hours now, and time wasn't standing still for him at all.

Now it seemed as though Boom was right back where he started off only a few days ago. A lot had happened since then, but his main objective managed to remain the same: he had to find Winch and as soon as fuckin' possible! Even though now it wouldn't be for sport, or revenge, or closure. There was something much more important at stake now. When his search was over, he'd have Sabra safe and at home with her mother. Winch staring down the barrel of his fresh-out-the-box Calico would be a big plus, but that's all. If it came down to a choice, the selection would be obvious.

It seemed almost impossible to Boom that he could have an objective more important than avenging his father's murder. He was amazed that he had actually developed that type of bond with someone. It was ironic; the fact that he could love someone enough to die for made him feel alive. He knew that kind of love for Uncle Black. He later found that he had the same kind of love for his boy, Ivan. First of all though, he knew that unconditional love for his father. In the short time they did have together, Boom had no foul memories of him. He couldn't think of anything negative about him.

"He was a good dude," Boom said aloud.

Germ peeked over at his comrade briefly, but didn't engage him. He made like he didn't even hear him blurt that statement from out of nowhere.

Boom went on with his thoughts, not even realizing how insane he was beginning to look to Germ. It wasn't until he blurted out another random thought before Germ took it upon himself to comment. He felt his friend calling out, and he probably just had something he needed to get off his chest.

"They killed my pops for no reason," Boom said.

Germ looked over at him again and thought long and hard before he responded. He knew that he wasn't the type of person for consoling and understanding. Call it a flaw if you like; he was perfectly fine with that character trait. But it seemed like everybody else just wasn't getting that shit!

"What's up, man? You got somethin' on ya mind, Boom? I mean besides rockin' these jokers??"

Boom saw what Germ was trying to do from a mile away. He didn't notice he was being so blatant about his mind-state. He could get his focus after he aired out his thoughts just a bit.

"Nah, I was just thinkin' about my pops, dog," Boom replied, diving straight into the can of worms that Germ opened up for him. "He was a good dude, ya know? He ain't need to go out like he did."

"What you talkin' 'bout, homey? I ain't never heard you speakin' of ya pops before."

"Yeah, that's 'cause he dead. He been dead for a while now. Nigga got killed when I was real young and shit. I really ain't have too much to say about him, you know. Ain't no whole lot of years of memories to reflect on and shit. It's just recently...I been feelin' like it's coming back to me more and more every day. I don't know what the fuck is goin' on. Maybe it was the time I spent in the BX. Maybe it was that flashback from Ivan's wake. All I know is that shit fucked me up!"

"What you mean 'flashback'?"

"I caught an ill vision at the wake, when them dudes went up there and started singin'. It was crazy! I felt like I wasn't there anymore. I was back at my father's wake when I was a lil' young scrap. But the shit felt more like me sitting next to myself watchin' the whole shit go down. It bugged me out."

"Oh, for real? How'd he die?"

Boom simply nodded his head back and forth while briefly taking his hands off the steering wheel to rub them together. "Oh, this muthafucka we about to go see...," Boom said matter-of-factly. "...yeah, he the one that murdered him. That's why I came back up to this muthafucka in the first damn place. I was just a kid..."

Boom started to really understand what was the driving force behind his merciless Winch-hunt. Although he knew it wouldn't bring his father back, someone needed to be held responsible for what he had endured. Someone would have to see the other side of his gun and hear that *BOOM!* He'd suffered too much. He'd lost too much. It was payback time in Boom's eyes. But that still couldn't overshadow his main objective.

★★★

"Son, that's bugged out right there. You like muthafuckin' De Niro in *Godfather Part II* and shit."

Boom gave a small chuckle in response. "You ain't even bullshittin'. You know I was just gon' take that bitch-made coward apart with this Calico...but maybe I *will* just carve a hole in that nigga torso with a nice-sized blade."

"Plus you said he that nigga runnin' the show, right?"

"Somethin' like that."

"Yeah, so you know what that means, right?"

"What?"

"We could just take that nigga whole shit over and really be on top! Who the fuck in they right mind is gon' try and go up against us??? That shit would be ill, for real!"

Boom only pondered Germ's suggestion for a split-second. "Nah, that ain't what we came to do, nigga! Fuck that nigga, *and* his so-called empire! We here for Sabe...once she's safe, then it's whatever my nigga."

★★★

It was going on six a.m. when they were about to cross the G.W. Bridge. Now any appreciation Boom held on to for this place no longer existed. He couldn't love a place that was the backdrop for such horrific experiences. All of this shit was happening because he had come back to this place. And he only came back in an attempt to rectify some other horrible shit that happened there a long time ago. The Bronx was looking like a huge knot of bad luck to Boom now. Nothing good could come from this place, and he was the proof of that. Just the fact that he was born there made his life hard enough to break the regular cat. Of course it made him stronger, but no one needs to be *that* strong. He was ready to see the last of the Bronx…for good this time!

***

In a blink they were exiting the highway and Germ was noticeably excited to finally be there, ready to get it on. Boom, on the other hand, was feeling his stomach tightening with nervousness. There was a whole lot riding on the move he was about to make. He was already up to his knees in shit, and he was about to take a deep breath and dive straight into it. How low would he have to go? Shit, that was all dependent on how long he could hold his breath.

For the next ten to twenty minutes they drove through the blocks slowly to scan the area. They came down Bronx River Avenue and cut over 173rd, came down Stratford and spun around to Boynton. They covered every inch of the hood till they were comfortable enough with the vicinity to make a quick getaway without worrying about making a wrong turn.

They ended up parking on Elder Avenue—almost a full block away from the house. Just as Boom was putting the car in park, something unexpected happened.

"Awe shit!" Boom spat as his cell phone began ringing and lighting up. "We would've been fucked had this fuckin' thing started buzzin' while we was up in there tryin' to creep on these jokers!"

He looked at the name in the phone and it only brought more frustration. It was Shonda.

"Damn, I knew I should've just called her before we left. I really can't deal with this shit right now. I don't need more stress. I know if I would've called, it would've been some shit though, you know. She don't even know what happened. She'd have flipped out on a nigga. We really put all our eggs in one basket with that nigga Beast." He thought again if he should answer or not. His jaw stiffened as his grip on the phone got tighter. "Naw, fuck this, man," he said as he pressed the button to forward Shonda into his voicemail. "Not right now…not until I got somethin' good to tell her."

Germ wanted to comment, but he ended up biting his tongue. Maybe Boom was right. He didn't need more shit on his mind. Maybe it was best to put her off for a little while longer.

"Anyway, make sure put your shit on silent. Let's get it on!"

They jumped out of the LS as the clock struck seven a.m. Doing shit like this in the morning hours was usually a bit more risky than Boom liked to be, but fuck it; they didn't have a choice in the matter.

As they made their way to the rear of the car, they kept a hawk's eye to the street. Nothing looked out of the ordinary. They proceeded to the trunk and when Boom popped it open, they saw their arsenal staring them back in the face, begging to be squeezed off. Boom and Germ were just about ready to give them exactly what they wanted.

Boom grabbed the sawed-off shottie and tucked it down the side of his pants while Germ snatched up the Tec and hid it under his arm below his jacket. They both checked their handguns to make certain they were fully loaded and ready to blast off. When they were satisfied, they caught each other's eyes for a brief moment. Then Boom simply said, "Alright then, let's go ahead and dig into these niggas already!"

***

They went around the back as quietly as possible, making sure to watch for any signs of security. No cameras, no motion detectors, no visible alarm tape on any of the windows or doors. Just as Boom suspected, there was access into the house from the rear. It was looking a bit *too* easy now.

After careful inspection of the back door, Boom flipped out his shank to jimmy the lock. A few twists and turns later the door was open.

"Can you believe this shit?" Boom asked rhetorically. "Stay on point though."

In one hand, Boom clenched the handle of his .44 and cocked the hammer. In the other he kept a tight grip on his shank. When the door was open all the way they could hardly see three feet in front of their faces. They squinted to adjust their eyes to the pitch-black room. Taking each step gracefully on their heels, they crouched low to the ground to enter. Keeping their pistols aimed with their line of sight, they scanned what they could see in the room. Mostly, all they could see was old dusty furniture, tools, and black garbage bags. When Boom spotted the stairway on the other side of the basement toward the front of the house, he tapped Germ on his arm and pointed to direct him toward them. They proceeded even more slowly and carefully. Just as they were about to get to the stairs, they heard something moving on the right. First there was some crackling and scratching, and then it sounded like someone humming in a high pitch, like if they had tape covering their mouth. They immediately went to investigate. Just before they reached where the sound was coming from, the humming turned to growling. Out of the darkness emerged a huge Rottweiler. As this monstrosity of an animal leapt toward them, his legs stretched out making him look at least seven feet long. His jaw opened wide and saliva dripped from his tongue as it swung from the side of his mouth. It was indeed painfully obvious that he was hungry, and right about now Boom and Germ were looking like two juicy sirloin steaks. As he got closer, his eyes bulged out of his head more and more. When he could finally feel something in his mouth, he locked his jaw down and sunk his teeth into Germ's forearm.

"Aaah! Get this muthafucka off of me!"

"Shhh," Boom whispered looking toward the door to see if anyone was coming. "Shut the fuck up, nigga!"

First Boom lifted his cannon to take care of the dog but had second thoughts.

"The fuck you mean *'shhh,'* nigga? What you waitin' on???" Germ asked in a lower, but even more frantic voice. Boom was not moving fast enough for him at all! He began scrambling to shake the beast from its grip, but he wasn't succeeding in the least bit.

After a brief second, Boom's instincts came back to him. He knew that if he let a shot off prematurely, it'd be a wrap. Everybody in the house would hear it, and it would just be that much harder to get to Winch. Of course if he let Germ's panic attack continue, the conclusion would be the same. Instead of bussing his tool, he quickly began delivering stabs to the dog's mid-section with his blade. After five times the dog still hung on as Germ swung him around wildly. Boom grabbed the dog by the head and poked him four more times in the neck before he heard something else coming from behind him.

"Oh shit!!!" he said aloud.

Another Rottweiler came out from the back and leapt toward him. The force of the animal sent Boom to the ground face flat. By the time he turned over, the dog was already on top of him with his mouth wide open about to take a healthy chunk out of his jugular. Boom protected himself with his left arm, letting the gun fall to the ground, and swung his right hand around to the side of the dog's head. When his swing stopped, he must've put the entire blade—plus a part of the handle—in the dog's head. Still he yanked it out and delivered another blow to finish the job. The dog finally stopped moving completely, and he threw him off to find Germ still tussling on the floor with the other beast. He had lost some energy from the repeated stabs, but he was still focused on making a meal of Germ nonetheless. Before Boom could get to them, Germ accidentally knocked over a toolbox, spilling hammers, screwdrivers, and wrenches all over the place. Germ quickly searched the floor with his free arm until he found what he was looking for. He gripped the handle of a long flat-head screwdriver and drove right under the dog's chin. He forced it in with every bit of energy he had until it popped out the other side. His attacker finally stopped moving as well. Germ tossed him to the ground as blood still flowed from his wounds.

"You good?" asked Boom as he helped Germ back to his feet.

Germ simply gave him a *'what the fuck you think?'* look and said, "Yeah, I'm good." When he took off his jacket, all you could see were the tears in his sweater. He lifted his sleeve to reveal wounds down to his white meat. That's when the blood started to well up in his wounds and drip down his arm.

It was obvious now why there wasn't much keeping unwelcome guests from entering the house. They had all of their security on the inside to handle whoever was crazy enough to try anything. Boom and Germ both knew now that this wouldn't be as simple as they had originally assumed.

"Damn, you gon' be good, nigga?"

"Yeah, don't worry, I'll be cool." He simply tore a piece off a dropcloth covering some old furniture and wrapped his arm to stop the bleeding. It was all he had so it would have to do for now.

With that Boom retrieved his pistol and reverted focus back to the stairway while making sure to scan the entire area to be ready for any more surprises. Now, out of the quietness, they could hear another noise. It was deep and dragging. The closer they got to the stairs, the louder they heard rumbling coming from the other side of the door at the top of the steps. The louder the noise got the more it sounded like a running lawnmower, or an eighteen-wheeler revving the engine. They climbed the steps slowly not knowing what the hell to expect.

"What the fuck is that?" Germ whispered.

Boom's face described his response without him even saying anything. He thought to himself, *How the fuck am I supposed to know???*

When the rumbling stopped they heard a cough and then yawning.

"Somebody's sleeping behind there," Boom whispered with his ear pressed firmly against the door.

"Damn!" Germ blurted aloud.

"Shhh, nigga!" Boom whispered.

"That's a fuckin' human soundin' like that??"

Boom simply shook his head back forth. "Shut the fuck up. I got an idea."

They were crouched down at the top of the steps. There was a small landing, but basically the door was directly in front of them.

Boom took a peek through the small space between the bottom of the door and the floor. He saw exactly what he expected to see. "Perfect!"

"What's the plan?"

"Just hold the door. I'm gonna turn the knob, but don't let it open too fast. You got it?"

"No doubt! Let's do it."

With Germ putting resistance on the back of the door, Boom proceeded to twist the knob as slowly and quietly as possible. As soon as the knob was turned all the way, the door started opening too fast for Germ to hold it. On the other side was a heavyset man sitting in a chair leaning up against the door. From what Boom could tell someone was positioned against the door in a chair, but no way could he tell that he'd be so fuckin' humungous!

"Oh, yo what the fuck, man!" Germ spat as the force of the guy's weight pushed him backward. He was losing his balance and wouldn't be able to hold on much longer. "Hold it, hold it!!"

Boom's eyes bulged at the sight of this massive being waking from his sound hibernation. He panicked. The guy's first reaction was to grab onto the doorway to stop himself from falling, but he grabbed Boom instead. His face was stone blank when they were finally eye to eye. From his perspective he just woke up feeling like he was falling backwards, only to find a complete stranger staring him in the face. He felt like he was dreaming. Of course it would be more like a nightmare when Boom got done with him.

Luckily for Germ, Boom acted quickly. He knelt down and squeezed himself back up from underneath the guy's arm. With his trusty blade in hand, still dripping dog's blood, he made precision stabs and managed to poke the fat man four times before he knew what hit him. Boom would continue to pierce various parts of his torso until he stopped moving; no matter how many stabs it took. Every calculated incision made a thumping sound followed by a bubbling pop as blood started to pour freely out of his body. The unfortunate man could do nothing as his chest was consumed with sharp deep openings. His head went back as he started coughing up thick dark blood. Boom continued his brutal attack. Then the man's eyes rolled up into his head and his body slouched over. Now, all that remained was 350 pounds of dead weight, and Germ couldn't hold on any longer. He was slipping fast. Boom tried to reach back to help Germ pull the chair back up but he couldn't get a good enough grip in time. Germ's pivot was being forced further and further down the stairs. He took a step backward to get his balance back but his foot missed the step. He finally felt his body falling backwards and he couldn't do anything to hold on. Before he knew it, he went tumbling down the stairs while three hundred-fifty pounds of dead weight followed closely behind him. He landed at the bottom of the steps on his back. He opened his eyes just in time to see the large-sized man heading in his direction. The chair he was sitting in broke halfway down the stairs, and he finally landed right on top of Germ with a loud thump. The noise from him hitting the floor could've woken the entire neighborhood all by itself. On top of that, Germ started yelling and fighting to get the huge man off of him to open his breathing path back up.

Boom started down the steps to help Germ get back to his feet before the heat came, but it was already too late. He didn't even get halfway down the steps before he heard the rumbling of footsteps. As he turned to greet his guests, he quickly tucked his revolver back in his pants as he went for the sawed-off. As Boom pointed his large weapon, a figure appeared in the doorway...*BOOM!!!* The blazing buckshots landed squarely above the guy's right kneecap. The shot nearly separated the bottom half of his leg from the rest of his body. The only thing holding him together were strands of flesh and his denim pants. He started leaning to the right, as he was no longer able to keep balance with only one leg left. Then...*BOOM!!!* He was hit again. This shot blew his shoulder blade to pieces. He hit the wall when he realized he was hit, and that's when a nice little Baby-Uzi dropped from his clutches and tumbled down the steps. The wall stopped his fall and kept him up on his good foot. He could do nothing but just stand there and wait for his fate.

Boom saw the vulnerability of his victim and moved toward him to take advantage. Outside of the stairway, Boom first looked over the one-legged man's shoulder to see if there was anyone coming from the back of the house. It was still dark so he couldn't get a good look. But his attention was shifted when he heard shots coming from the steps that led to the second floor behind him. He reacted quickly as the first couple of shots missed him entirely. The shots continued as he grabbed onto the hobbling man and spun around to use him as a shield. He quickly dropped the shottie to use that arm to put the guy in a sleeper-hold. With one swift motion, his revolver was drawn with his free hand. The shots immediately followed. He started blasting off from his hip as he walked toward the man. A single shot to his right shoulder sent him backwards toward the front door. He still returned fire piercing his comrade's torso with slugs. Another shot from Boom's cannon fell upon his chest, and then another hit him in the neck. He was falling now and could no longer shoot back. Shit, by then he'd already sent his dismembered friend back to his essence. Boom let go of him when he realized that he wasn't fighting back anymore. They both hit the floor at the same time as Boom lifted his .44 to continue firing on his opponent for good measure. *BOOM! BOOM! BOOM!!!* The last three shots went into various parts of his chest, jerking his lifeless body from side to side. Boom didn't stop pulling the trigger until the hammer let out a clicking sound indicating that he was out of ammo.

As Boom emptied out the smoking shells to reload he heard, *"YOOO!!!"* Germ came flying out of the basement door with his Tec in one hand, and the Baby-

Uzi that dropped down the stairs in the other. All Boom could see were flashing lights as Germ lit up the dark hall leading toward the back of the house with his automatic weapons. It looked like strobe lights. With every flash, Boom could get a better glimpse of a figure creeping through the dark. When he looked a bit closer, he saw that it was a man holding a long .357 Magnum revolver in each hand.

Boom's jaw dropped at the sight. All twelve of those slugs could've easily gone into his back had Germ not gotten drop on him.

Now his body was being fluttered with shots. He literally looked like he was being electrocuted as all of those slugs made entrances into, and exits out of, his body. "Aaahhh," he cried as his body collapsed in slow motion. His trigger-finger started squeezing, but it was already way too late. His bullets got nowhere near Boom or Germ. He only decorated the hallway walls and the ceiling with holes. He kept pulling until he hit the floor though. That's when Germ let go of his triggers.

Boom and Germ caught each other's eyes, and without words, Boom showed his gratitude with a nod. Germ nodded back as if saying, *'It ain't nothun', my nigga!'*

All of a sudden they heard more rumbling coming from the top of the stairs on the second floor. They both turned with their weapons pointed as a man fell from the top and came rolling down to the bottom of the steps. When he landed at the foot of the steps, he had three holes in his chest and a surprised look still on his face.

"Oh shit," said Germ with a chuckle. "His homey over there just lit his ass up! That's some crazy shit right there. I ain't never ever in my life even *heard* about no shit like that!" Germ started laughing loudly, forcing a grin from Boom's tightly clenched lips. Even *he* had to see the humor in the freak occurrence.

"You aight, nigga?" Boom asked in whisper—as if he still had to be quiet.

"Yeah, man, it took forever to get that fat fuck off of me. Shit, the next time you get an idea, *you* standin' behind the muthafuckin' door! *Whew!*"

Besides the blood leaking from the bite marks on his arm, Germ looked fine from what Boom could tell. His clothes were covered with smeared blood, but it wasn't his own. It was the fat man's. Good thing he had thrown on his all-black Dickie suit, or he'd look like a used fuckin' tampon.

Boom's focus couldn't sway for too long. He quickly wiped the smile from his face and got back to the business at hand. He quickly reloaded his revolver and when he looked back up at Germ, his face was ice cold. Germ quickly got back on point, too. They proceeded up the stairs with caution. Once they reached the top, they heard crying coming from the bedroom in the back. Boom's face immediately lit up. It felt like a wave of joy came rushing through his body. He was visibly excited. He rushed to the back, following the sound until he reached the door of the room it was coming from. Boom stopped there and swallowed the lump in his throat and took a deep breath. As soon as he started twisting the knob, the crying stopped. He paused for just a second as his instincts told him that he shouldn't open the door. He disregarded his gut feeling and opened it anyway. The room was completely consumed with darkness. Thick velvet curtains shielded the sun from entering the few windows. He squinted to see as he searched the wall for the light switch. Then he heard a small whimper coming from the far left corner of the room. That's when his hand found the light switch, but before he could flip it on he heard a click like a hammer cocking... then all he heard was *BOOM!!!*

CHAPTER 13

Shonda was getting really frustrated now. She deeply needed to get in touch with Boom, but he wasn't answering his phone. "Damn it!" she blurted aloud. "What the fuck is the use of havin' a damn cell phone if you don't ever answer the shit???"

Between calls, she sent him brief text messages. If he would only read one of them, he'd know just how important it was that she spoke to him as soon as possible before anything bad happened. She could feel it deep down in her gut that something was going horribly wrong. She couldn't give up. Maybe he'd pick up her call, or maybe he'd read one of her messages. One of the two would be fabulous. All she needed was a second to speak to him and then she could breathe easy.

Her mind scrambled as she desperately thought of how she was gonna get to Boom. She was shaking uncontrollably now. She sat at the dining room table rocking back and forth. Her light brown eyes welled up...her pretty face turned red...her full lips twitched. "ANSWER THE PHONE!!!" she cried. "Goddamn it, ANSWER THE FUCKING PHONE!!!"

***

The impossible had just happened. He wasn't dreaming, nor did he imagine any of this shit. Wow! This was unheard of. He never thought it could happen, but it just did and there was nothing he could do about it. Ain't nobody untouchable in this world...NOBODY! Everybody is penetrable, and when it's your time, you'll get it too,...just like that!

What made it worse was that he didn't even see it coming. It was an obvious bait- and-switch move. It was damn near embarrassing that he'd be taken like that. He was supposed to be sharper. If there weren't a little girl's life hanging in the balance of all of this madness, maybe he'd have seen it coming. So seldom does he just disregard his gut feeling. Now he was paying for it.

Boom could feel a burning feeling in his left side now. He was already all numb, so he didn't even feel the dampness in his clothes. He couldn't even hear anything. The last sound he heard was a loud *BOOM*, and then everything just went silent. *'The last sound he heard was BOOM!'* That shit was crazy...ironic even that he could've been taken out in the exact same fashion as his victims; that he would live out their tragic fate. That's the only thing that went through his head once that bullet sunk in. It was almost relieving to him at first. At least all of the bullshit would be over with. Life was nothing but a big ball of stress rolling down a steep hill at him up to this point. He could use a break from it all. He felt like he had yet to experience a peaceful day. Then he thought of the repercussions if his life were to end right then and there. He was responsible for so much now. He had so much to live for. He couldn't die yet...he wasn't ready.

Boom blinked his eye for the first time since everything went blank. He was on the floor laid out on one side. He was more dazed than anything. He looked around to see if he could get a glimpse at who shot him, but he still could see nothing but black. At that point his instincts had come back to him, and he started feeling around for his pistol. When his search came to an end, he didn't have a nice big .44 in his clutches. There was someone standing over him. He knew because his hand grabbed onto a pair of fuzzy slippers. His eyes opened up wide. His buggy eyes still relentlessly searched the room blindly. He took a few short breaths and started toward the inside of his jacket for his secret weapon. All he needed was to get his hands wrapped around that fifty-round Calico and it would be a *good-fuckin'-night!* His breaths grew shorter as his nerves started to get the best of him. Unfortunately for Boom, the person standing over him had already adjusted their eyes to the darkness and saw Boom reaching. That's when Boom heard another *click* just like before he blacked out.

"Shit!" Boom said to himself.

The other person grinned devilishly, still not letting out a sound. "Stupid mutha-fucka. Who's dumb enough to come in here and think they ain't gon' die?"

All it would've taken was a small squeeze of the trigger and Boom would have been done for. His life rested on the tip of that small 9-milly's hammer. If it was allowed to snap, it only needed to move with lightning speed toward a slug not even a half-inch away. Too bad it was never granted that opportunity.

The lights came on as Germ eased into the room with his two toasts pointed. "Drop it, bitch!" he said. "You heard me???" he yelled when she didn't move quick enough. "Drop it or I'm lightin' ya up!"

When Boom looked up, he saw Patrice staring him back in the face biting on her bottom lip. She was looking at him like she wanted to kick herself in the ass for not emptying that clip into Boom's back sooner. That was the biggest mistake she'd ever made.

"Oh, you's a deaf bitch, huh?" Germ said as he approached Patrice, still acting as if she couldn't hear him. With one swing of the Uzi, a thump put Patrice to sleep. Her body collapsed to the ground lifelessly. Germ approached to quickly relieve her of her piece. With one foot on her arm to make sure she didn't move, he took her pistol and put it in his back pocket. He then turned his attention to his comrade.

"Yo, Boom…you hit, my nigga??? You i-ight, dog, say somethin'! Talk to me, baby; let me know you good!"

Boom didn't respond right away. He just shut his eyes and sunk into his thoughts for a second. He was quietly thanking God that Germ came in when he did. That was twice already that he stepped in and saved his ass today. Shit, imagine if he wouldn't have brought him. Just the thought sent a chill up Boom's spine that brought him back to reality. His eyes opened back up to see Patrice's face right in front of him. Once again, the urgency of the situation came rushing back to the forefront of his priorities.

Boom tried to get back to his feet, but stumbled. He wasn't prepared for the pain that would be caused from such a routine task. The gunshot went in to his deltoid muscle and just missed the bone on the way out of the back. It wasn't too serious but made it virtually impossible to use his left arm.

"Damn, son," Germ said. "That bitch caught you?" Before he even asked if his boy would be okay, he began delivering vicious kicks to Patrice's mid-section, as she lay unconscious. "Fuckin' whore!" he yelled. "Think you can just bang on my boy like that? Huh???" Germ kicked and stomped until he almost lost his balance. After he caught himself from falling, he took a break from savagely beating this defenseless woman. Then he glanced over at Boom, still resting on his good arm on the ground. He waited for Boom's approval, but he lay there staring up at him with a blank look.

"Done?" he simply said.

Germ shrugged at Boom's obvious sarcasm. "Yeah, I guess."

"Alright then, nigga, help me the fuck up!"

Germ quickly came to his partner's aid, helping him to his feet. When he was up, he took off his jacket and lifted his sweater to examine his wound.

"Fuck!" he said as he tried to lift his arm. "This shit hurt like hell, but fuck it, I'll be good. We got work to do." The only thing that pleased Boom was that the slug went in and out. Otherwise, he'd be fucked tryin' to explain that in the emergency room. Other than that, he was lucky it didn't hit a few inches to the right, or he would've really been doing bad.

Before anything, Boom tore up the sheet on the bed to wrap his arm. That should stop the bleeding, if not slow it down temporarily. Next, they needed to tie up Patrice and search the house, top to bottom.

"Yo, we gotta check every inch of this muthafucka, Germ," ordered Boom. "If Sabra's here, we need to find her and get the fuck outta here before somebody else comes through. We need to look out for this big muthafuckin' dread nigga that stops by periodically. This muthafucka is as big as this house; you can't miss him. If he wit' another nigga, small but brolic, that's our dude. He's that nigga we gotta get at. I'm gonna go start downstairs. In the meantime, this bitch needs to be gagged and wrapped the fuck up, feel me? Just put the bitch outta commission for now; get her outta the way. When that's done, start checkin' all of the rooms up here. I'll be right back up!"

"I got you; I'll shut this bitch up good!"

"Germ, none of that other shit, dog…for real! After all of this shit is done is another story. Trust me, you'll get yours, too, and soon!"

Germ understood Boom's orders and was ready and willing to carry them out fully. He started by yanking the socks off of Patrice's feet to gag her with. Then he threw a pillowcase over her head and wrapped her up in a comforter. He left her tied up on the bedroom floor, and then he proceeded to check the rest of the apartment for any signs that Sabra had been there.

The house was set up like two separate apartments. Both floors had a bathroom, a kitchen with a dining room, a family room, and two bedrooms. From what he could tell, the upstairs apartment was a lot different than the downstairs. A whole lot more work was put in to take care of it. It had nice, shiny hardwood floors throughout the halls, and plush carpeting covered the bedroom floors. The bathroom was all marble from the floor to the ceiling. The windows were all brand-new and crystal clear. The furniture was modest, but rich. You could tell someone had taken time to decorate. It wasn't for showing off or to be flashy, but just to be comfortable with how they'd become accustomed to living. It was obvious that this is where Patrice stayed. The downstairs apartment must've been for whomever they had on guard. It was completely different. The floors were old and rotted, and the paint on the wall was dull and chipped. The furniture was dusty and squeaky. It was like night and day.

Germ started in the upstairs kitchen. When he was done, he went downstairs to see if Boom had better luck. When he got downstairs, he found Boom sitting at the dining room table. He was on the verge of tears, and fighting hard to hold them back. Germ stood there at the doorway, without a clue how to approach him.

"Nothin'?" he finally asked when he couldn't think of anything else to say.

Boom had no response. He simply sat there. He was sunken in the seat leaned all the way back with his hand covering his face. His lips were tight and his jaw was clenched. He didn't know it, but his hand was twitching, and he was repeatedly tapping his feet. He was about to have a nervous breakdown. What really hurt was even as stressed as he was, he knew that Shonda had to have been ten times more fucked up. She had to feel a hundred times more lost, and a thousand times more helpless.

"Time's runnin' low on us, dog," Boom said with his face still buried below his hand. "All of this is startin' to get thin as shit, feel me. I don't know if we just keep takin' the wrong paths or what. I don't know what the fuck it is, but we just keep hittin' these brick fuckin' walls!" His voice raised a couple of notches above the soft tone he'd begun speaking with. "What the fuck!"

"Fall back, Boom; you can't think like that. All we gotta do is go back upstairs and take a lead pipe to that fuckin' whore til' she start singin' the song we wanna hear. Fuck all of this sittin' around shit! She can get us to that boy we need to see. That's the only missing link, my nigga. Once we get to this boy Winch, *or what-*

ever the nigga name is, it's a wrap! He gon' give up Sabe…we body that joker, and then it's muthafuckin' on like popcorn, nigga! We gotta go back to them old school days when we was hungry, man! We need to take it back to the street hard! Let's get it grimey."

At the end of Germ's motivational speech, Boom still wasn't feeling nearly as inspired or charged as he thought he would. He had a headache and he felt weak. He was still losing blood and, if he didn't get that wound checked soon, he wouldn't last long. On top of the woozy feeling, he just had a negative outlook on the whole damn situation. He had run into so many roadblocks since they started this quest that his pessimistic attitude was inevitable. He knew what he would have to do at this point. Before he flipped out and started burning these two cities down, he'd have to give Shonda a call. First, to find out if she'd heard something—if anything—from Sabra's captors. Second, to let her know that he hadn't exactly had the best of luck trying to find her. From there, they would figure out the best course of action.

He flipped out his cell phone and turned it on. When the backlight came on, and he realized how many missed calls, voicemail messages, and text messages he had, he knew that Shonda must've been ripping her hair out by now. It made him feel that much more fucked up. She would be devastated from the lack of good news he'd be reporting. But it was time for Boom to step up and stop acting childish. She deserved to know everything that was going on, and keeping her in the dark would have to cease from this point forward. What Boom didn't know was that Shonda, on the other hand, had some news that would bring a whole lot more light to the situation.

Boom bypassed checking the tons of messages Shonda had left him and started dialing her number directly. Shit, what was he gonna read in some damn text message that was gonna change things? *Fuck it!*

The phone didn't even ring one whole time before she picked up.

"Boom???" she said with an unusual mixture of excitement and nervousness in her voice. She had been stressing so hard the past few hours that she couldn't even speak a whole sentence without stuttering. "I…you need to know…did you get my messages…I gotta tell you…"

"OH SHIT!" blurted Germ. From the kitchen in the back of the house, he could see straight through the living room window in the front. From where he was standing, he caught a glimpse of a truck pulling up. He quickly moved to get a better look. That's when out of the truck appeared the man that Germ only knew as *"the enemy."*

Apollo was standing by the passenger side door looking from left to right. He had one hand on the door handle, and the other halfway reached into his overcoat. His cannon was only inches from his grasp. If his eye caught something out of the ordinary, the heat would be in his palm ready to blast off. It had happened before, and it might happen again. If it did, Apollo would be on point.

"What?" Boom said as Germ's behavior got his attention. "What the fuck is up, nigga?"

"That dread nigga just pulled up."

"What???"

Boom rose out of his chair to see if Germ was right. He was. The phone lowered from his ear without him even realizing it. Shonda had finally told him what she so desperately needed to, and was still waiting for a response to the bomb that she had just dropped. Sadly though, his mind was already in another place. He didn't even hear what she'd just said...what she had been so eagerly waiting hours to tell him...the reason she was damn near ready to bang her head on the wall because she couldn't reach him. All of that stress and worrying was for good reason, too. She was right about things getting worse and worse. Everything she anticipated was materializing right at that exact moment, and now there was nothing she could do to stop it.

"Boom, you there?" Shonda asked just before he hit the end button and stuffed the phone in his pocket as he scrambled for his tool. That's when the M-960 finally made its debut. Boom literally ran to the living room while Germ followed closely behind him. When they got there, Boom took position on the side of the window where he couldn't be seen and peeked through the side of the curtains. Germ knelt down low to the ground also out of sight. From there, he could also see everything going on.

As soon as Apollo gave a tug at that door handle, Boom started to see everything happening in slow motion. The first thing he saw was a red gator-skin shoe hit the curb from below the truck door. He had on a pair of royal blue pants that swayed in the breeze, revealing his matching royal blue dress socks. Winch's head came up as he eased his way out with the utmost grace and style. On his head he covered his thinning nappy Afro with a red Kangol cap turned slightly to one side. His eyes were covered by dark black shades.

He was visibly much older now than how Boom remembered, but his distinguishing features remained prominent in his face and throughout his muscular physique. His cleanly shaven face still accentuated the war scar that crossed his mug. His ice-grill was still chilling and rigid. The only differences were the wrinkles that had formed as he aged. It didn't take from his gangsta at all though. The thing is they only made him look meaner.

As he made his way to the front door, his silk Versace button-up shirt blew as the wind passed through it. It was flooded with radiant reds, bright blues, and hints of gold patterns. Underneath he had an icy white wife-beater fitting the form of his swollen chest and ripped abs.

With every blink, Boom saw his enemy switch from young Winch to the older version of this mean bastard that was now before him. With every step he took closer toward the house, Boom flashed back to that day all those years ago. He remembered his confident swagger and his enticing demeanor. He invited confrontation and you could see the invitation from a mile away. That request would be fulfilled more than he could imagine today, and he didn't even know it yet. He was boldly walking right into a slaughterhouse.

"Yo, this is what I need you to do…" directed Boom. "Go through the kitchen and out the back way. Come around the side of the house to the front. Just walk out like you own the muthafucka! As soon as they turn toward you, I'm openin' up the door and grab their attention back with this bad boy right here," he said, lifting the Calico to emphasize his point. "That's when you pull out and just back me up. We need to get them into the house as quick as possible before witnesses start creepin' out of everywhere…and I don't want not one fuckin' shot to be fired! You hear me??"

"I got you," affirmed Germ before making his way out the back.

As soon as Boom heard the back door close, Winch was stepping up on the porch, followed closely by Apollo. He wouldn't even know what hit him.

Boom quickly took his position behind the front door to wait for Germ's diversion. At that point Apollo rang the doorbell for the first time…*ding-dong.* Through the peephole all Boom could see was his massive frame standing directly in front of the door with Winch behind him. He rang the doorbell again...*ding-dong*. That's when Boom got the cue. From the right Apollo caught a glimpse of Germ coming around the side of the house in his peripheral vision. He immediately got on guard. Before Winch knew what was going on, Apollo was moving him out of the way. He took his position in front of him as a shield, at the same time making sure he wouldn't be obstructing his firing sights.

Germ did just as Boom had instructed him. He casually walked out from the side of the house with his hands in his pockets like he was taking a stroll in the park. He took his strides slowly. He even whistled a tune while he walked. He couldn't care less that there was this huge muthafucka only a few feet from him about to pull a long 12-gauge shotgun out from under his trench coat.

The shottie came out like it had wings on it. Apollo kept a lax grip on the cannon. He didn't let his nerves get the best of him. He was definitely experienced with the tool. There were plenty of times before this one where he used it with pinpoint precision, and if he had anything to do with it, there'd be plenty more. *Chic-chic!* He was ready, willing and able to tear a nigga's whole bottom half clean off. His focus was only disturbed when he heard the click from the lock on the door. He turned his eyes below his dark shades without budging his stance. He still stood firm, waiting for his mark to walk far enough around the front porch to get a good look at him before he squeezed his trigger. What he didn't know was that time wasn't a luxury he could afford at this point.

Boom turned the lock on the door and twisted the knob. He cracked the door enough to stick his arm through. The barrel of his weapon stopped squarely on the little kangaroo on the back of Winch's Kangol cap. Now his eyes were searching for the unknown. He never knew what hit him.

"Drop it, big man!" Boom yelled.

Of course Boom had Apollo's undivided attention by now. He had to have known deep down in his heart that they didn't have a chance, but he foolishly disregarded those feelings. He turned toward the door with the shottie pointed. It was a stupid move on his part. Sometimes when you're caught, you're caught, and there isn't anything you can do about it. The only problem was Apollo wasn't used to losing. He would have to get used to the idea that someone had gotten the drop on him sooner than later. He wasn't gonna go easily though.

Germ saw the focal point shift toward Boom and immediately drew down to back him up. In a hop, skip and a jump, Germ was up on the porch standing directly behind Apollo with his Glock pressed firmly in his back.

"Go ahead, lil' nigga," Germ whispered semi-jokingly into Apollo's ear. "Go ahead, please…I'm beggin' you! Pretty-please with a cherry on top, do some dumb shit. I'll empty out the rest of this muthafuckin' clip in ya back."

Apollo stood firm. His jaw locked. His grip got tighter and tighter on the handle. He wasn't ready to give up just yet. Luckily for him, he heard the voice of reason piercing through all those thick layers of stubbornness.

"Stand down, 'Pollo," ordered Winch. "Not yet, baby…not yet. Let's do as these fellas say and cooperate. You hear me, nigga???"

Apollo simply sucked his teeth in response to Winch's orders. Still, he fought back the urge to squeeze that trigger. He fought with all his might. But finally, he came to his senses. His grip on the banger loosened until it just dropped from his clutches.

As soon as Boom heard the shotgun hit the ground, his lips started twitching. He was fighting back a huge grin by then. But he had to remain focused. This wasn't the end by a long shot. There were still some twists and turns to steer through.

CHAPTER 14

"What now?" Shonda hopelessly said to herself. She could keep dialing Boom's cell number, but what good would it do? She could wait around for him to call her back, but what were the chances that was gonna happen? The only thing left for her to do was go all the way to New York to get him herself. At first the idea sounded preposterous. Imagine that shit! She'd have to be nuts!

Well, she thought. "Naaah, I wouldn't even know where to start looking," she said to herself as she came to her senses. She couldn't help but let out a chuckle at her own desperation. Even though she was laughing, it was no laughing matter. Her laughs quickly turned to cries. She cried long and loud as her options disappeared with her hope. At the moment she felt her lowest, the phone rang. Her eyes opened up wide and bright at the sound. She filled with joy. She hoped with all of her heart that it would be Boom.

"Hello," she nervously said. "Boom, is that you?"

"Naw, love," said the person on the other line. "It's me, Uncle Black."

***

"Hands up, fellas, and walk in slow," Boom directed as he backed away from the door, while making sure not to trip over the two dead bodies laid out on the floor behind him.

Winch followed Boom's directions and walked in slowly, followed closely by Apollo. Germ retrieved Apollo's trusty shotgun and closed the door behind him as he entered. When they were all in the living room they stood silent for a while. The silence was only broken when Winch sucked his teeth.

"The fuck you boys think you doin' here?" he asked in his raspy calm and collected voice. "Ya'll got the wrong fuckin' house this time, kids!"

Boom immediately responded. "Look around you, nigga!" he yelled. "Look to you like we got the wrong muthafuckin' house??? Nah, nigga, you the one that got it wrong. You know why we here."

"Hmm." Apollo smirked. "'Cause you wanna die."

Winch simply lifted his index finger to his lips. "Shhh."

Germ looked from Apollo to Winch, and then back to Apollo. He almost burst with laughter. "Can you make him roll over and play dead, too? Ha ha ha." He laughed aloud at his own joke.

Apollo didn't reply verbally, but his stare spoke loud and clear. He was looking right through Germ at this point. His mind was running through all the ways he could make him feel unimaginable pain before he killed him. He wanted to respond, but he bit his tongue and kept his mouth shut as he was told.

"Frisk 'em, Germ," Boom ordered.

Germ quickly started by patting down Apollo. When he didn't find anything, he started on Winch.

"Well, I imagine you boys came for more than to feed my pups," Winch said, noticing the bloody rags Germ's arm was wrapped in.

"Oh yeah? You's a jokester, huh?" Germ said with his pistol pointed. "You won't be laughin' long, old-timer."

"Ease up, shorty," Winch responded without even as much as a blink.

He only moved his eyes and lifted his brow to search Germ's face for signs of insincerity. To his surprise he saw none. Germ must've been one of those *'I ain't afraid of nothin'* type of dudes or he was just plain dumb. Of course there is a very fine line between balls and stupidity, but either way he'd be dangerous the same. Winch didn't give a fuck though. He was dangerous, too! He thought he'd make that known as he continued.

"Bitch, you just 'bout ready to make my dick hard you keep playin' me so fuckin' close. I'd tear you a new asshole just for me to rape, you sweet little faggot!"

"What you say to me, nigga???"

"Be easy, dog," Boom said, as he finally saw that all of this back and forth shit had gone too far. "Be the fuck easy. Don't forget why we here."

Germ backed out of Winch's face but mouthed the words *'fuck you, bitch'* as he did.

"Alright, now that we done playin' games..." Winch stated. "...you and him both know why ya'll here. That makes two of us. Is ya'll lil' bastards tryin' to be generous wit' that information at all?"

"Here this shit go again," said Boom as he recognized the familiar tone the conversation was taking. "I done heard enough of that talk in the last twenty-four hours. I ain't fittin' to go down that road with you. too!"

Boom flipped. He was consumed with rage now and could no longer keep his composure. He approached Winch as he lifted his toast in the air. He came down and landed a ferocious blow to the left side of his jaw.

Apollo had to catch himself from reacting. His orders were simple: shut the fuck up and don't make a move 'til told to do so. He was forced to watch as he bit his lip with anxiousness.

Germ was lovin' every minute of it. He was silently cheering on Boom to continue. In his head he was yelling, *'Yeah, now hit 'em wit a right!'*

Winch ate that first blow like it was cake and just tightened his jaw to brace for another. Just as he expected...*BONG!!!* Boom landed another damaging crack with the butt of his weapon. Winch's head was swinging back and forth from the force of Boom's sub, but he still turned back toward him after each strike. With every blow he met with Boom's eyes to welcome another. Even when Boom opened up a gash in the bridge of Winch's nose, he remained stone-faced. He just braced himself again and again as the blood poured down his face. He was like a volcano about to erupt at this point, but he was finally beginning to get a little dazed. His mouth was filling with blood. His legs started to wobble, but he remained on his feet as long as he could. Boom immediately saw that Winch was about to collapse, but he wanted to get one last good crack in before he went down for the count. He cocked his arm all the way back over his shoulder and swung back around with the speed and power of a vintage Tyson hook. When Boom's steel met with Winch's face, his head spun, sending blood and pieces of a shattered tooth flying. He fell backwards toward the wall, but he couldn't keep himself up on his feet anymore. When his back hit the wall, his head jerked. He looked like he was just about ready to fall asleep now. He hit the floor like a ton of bricks and didn't move. He was probably already in dreamland, amazed by the pretty colors the stars turned as they circled his head. Either that or the cute little bird whistling in his ear. Whatever the case, he was out cold and he'd be out for a good minute.

Boom was already perspiring profusely from the brief pistol-whipping session. You could see the veins bulging out of his forehead as he chased his breath. For a minute he simply stood there with his cannon in hand staring at Winch, as he lay napping in a small puddle of his own blood. He wanted to point and squeeze. It'd only take a second. If only it was that simple.

"Fuckin' pussy," he blurted in frustration still breathing heavily. He knew that Winch's time would be coming shortly, but not until they executed their primary objective. Boom finally shook off his desperation for murder and glanced up at Apollo. He had to quickly shake off the dizziness that such an abrupt workout caused. Now he was focused on his next victim.

Apollo's thirst for murder was obvious in how he stared back Boom. For the most part, he wasn't too expressive with his face, but the slightest variation was evident. Without even taking a second look, you could tell when he was in one of his three prominent moods: blasé, ornery, or pissed-the-fuck-off! The mood was extremely obvious at this point, but still he remembered that he was under strict and specific instructions: shut the fuck up and don't do shit! He was a soldier. He only hoped that he get the chance to act out the ferocious slaughter he was conducting inside of his head.

"You wanna say somethin', muthafucka?" Boom asked in a provocative manner. "What's up, dread? You wanna beat ya chest and pop off? Well go ahead, pussy! Jump off!"

Apollo didn't budge, but he also didn't alter the expression on his face not one bit. He was still fighting back the urges, and it was getting real tough.

Boom approached as he lifted his toast to Apollo's temple.

"I'm keepin' ya boss here alive for the time being, but I can dish you at any time. Keep that shit in mind and act right, nigga!

"Matter of fact, turn around," he directed Apollo by nudging him with the barrel of his gun. "Put your hands behind ya back and walk slow toward the kitchen."

It took a quick minute, but Apollo finally did as he was told.

"Wake that nigga up while I deal with this muthafucka here," Boom told Germ.

"Haha." Germ smirked. He couldn't even hide the joy he felt by the task he was given. "Got you, homey."

As Boom led Apollo to the back, he saw something he didn't expect out of the corner of his eye. It was so weird that it made him do a double-take. He saw Germ walk over to where Winch was laid out and pull down his zipper.

Ah shit, Boom thought. *Fuck am I thinkin'?* He didn't need to see none of that. As Boom got further in the back, he could hear Germ laughing louder as he relieved his bladder all over Winch's face. He just shook his head.

Just before they reached the kitchen, there were two doors to the right that led to the bedrooms. Boom had Apollo halt when they reached the door closest to the kitchen.

"Open the door and get the fuck in!" Boom ordered.

Apollo complied.

Upon entering the room he saw a little corner desk with a lamp and an old rotary phone. Sitting in front of it was a wooden chair. Boom ordered Apollo to take a seat in the chair. Then he ripped the phone cord out of the wall to tie him up. He didn't utter a word the whole time. That was how he dealt with situations like this one. The average person would piss himself trying to figure out what was in store for him. Apollo, on the other hand, was the farthest thing from the average person. He remained stone-faced, never saying a word. He wouldn't let anybody see him sweat...hell no!

Boom wrapped that cord around Apollo's wrists tight and knotted the other side around the back of the chair. When that was done, he walked back around to the front of the chair and knelt down to be face to face with Apollo. They exchanged an uncaring stare with neither one breaking or blinking; then Boom went on to his questioning.

"Where the girl at?" he asked.

Apollo had no response.

"You see ya boss? I ain't even start tearin' into his ass yet. I can guarantee that shit. I'm gonna find out what I wanna find out regardless of what. I'm just about ready to start taking some power tools to you muthafuckas 'till one of you talk. You hear me??? POWER TOOLS, NIGGA!!! Just think about that shit for a minute. You need to do what's right for the both of you. Now you have the advantage, 'cause you awake right now. That's it! Soon as my boy wake ya boss man, your lead is lost. Ya'll muthafuckas'll be neck and neck. You sure you don't wanna talk? Won't be long before Mr. Winchester in there'll be on ya back! Then what? What you gon' do when he all caught up?"

Apollo had no response.

Boom simply shrugged at his unwillingness. "That's cool. *Your limbs.*"

With that he left to join Germ back in the living room. He caught him still trying to wiggle more droplets of piss on Winch.

"Damn, nigga, cut that shit out already!" Boom yelled in frustration. "What the fuck!"

Germ's disappointment was apparent. If it were up to him, once he couldn't urinate anymore, he would go drink a few gallons of water until he had to go again. He would probably continue like this until he got bored with it. Then he'd think of a more creative way to have fun with the situation. Too bad for him Boom came when he did. It was back to business.

Germ quickly gave one more wiggle before he zipped his pants back up. Winch had already started waking. His eyes started to twitch as he shook his head. He was still dizzy and he just wanted the room to stop spinning. He squinted his right eye open first and kept the left one closed. That helped him see straight. That is until he lifted his head up off of the floor. He had a headache pounding behind his eyes like a sledgehammer, and it only made it worse when he started lifting himself up. He got as far as sitting straight up with his back up against the wall. When he lifted his hand to rub his eyes, he finally realized that he was drenched in piss. At first he thought it was sweat, but then he caught a whiff of the liquid that covered his hand. Now he was frantically wiping his head and face with both hands. He finally opened up both eyes to the sight of Germ and Boom standing over him. He was boiling inside and it was clearly illustrated with the way his face was screwed. When he saw a huge grin forming at Germ's mouth, it only fueled his fire. The straw that broke the camel's back was when Germ let out a chuckle. That's when he lost it. He turned his head to spit out the blood that had gathered in his mouth and then jumped to his feet. He snatched Germ and forced him up against the wall on the other side of the living room. He held him there staring into his face. Germ hadn't yet realized that Winch had a mean grip on his balls.

When Germ's back hit the wall, he felt Winch squeeze. His eyes opened up wide. He wanted to yell but he couldn't. His mouth opened up wide, but no sound came out.

"Yeah, bitch," Winch said as a jolt of energy went through his body. "You feel that, muthafucka?" His grip got tighter even as he twisted his sack. "What about now???"

Germ was on his tiptoes now trying his best to loosen Winch's vise-grip clutches and on his jewels. It didn't help at all. Winch didn't let up not one bit, not until he felt Boom's cold barrel on his temple.

"Let the boy nuts go, nigga, before I send ya thoughts all over them walls!"

Winch's face remained twisted. He didn't let go right away.

Germ had only gotten a taste of what was in his ability, and he should have been thankful for that. Right now he was just happy Winch's grip was loosening. Of course Winch couldn't just let him go without adding a little icing to the cake. He pulled him close enough to whisper in his ear.

"To be continued," Winch whispered in his menacing raspy tone. "You hear me? Sooner than later, I'm gon' make you my woman." With that he let go of Germ and lifted his hands in the air to surrender. Still he kept a chiseled mug. Not a hint of fear could be shown in his facial.

"Move it, nigga!" Boom ordered. "Back the fuck up! Get the fuck back and sit ya ass back down on the floor!"

Winch did what he was told at a slow pace. He never once took his eyes off Germ the whole time. He backed up slowly until he felt his back against the wall, and then he plopped down.

Boom looked from Winch to Germ, and then back to Winch. "Ya'll muthafuckas'll have all the time in the world to dance when our business is done here. I ain't gon' say this shit but one more time. I'm here for one reason and one reason only! I want my godchild back at home with her mother!"

Winch looked up at Boom for the first time. He bit down on his lip and didn't say a word.

"Alright, nigga, I know what you need," said Boom to Winch. "Germ, get that broad!"

The pain between Germ's legs was about gone now. Again, he was completely filled with joy at the directive he was just handed. He was nodding his head up and down while rubbing his hands together. "Yeah, no doubt!" he replied. He winked at Winch as he left.

Winch looked back to Boom. He was wondering what was going through his head at that exact moment. He was trying to figure out how far he'd go before he got what he wanted. He had to know how much room he had to maneuver before Boom completely lost it. What Winch didn't know was that Boom was willing to walk through fire if it meant bringing Sabra home safe. He'd soon find out.

CHAPTER 15

"What's the matter, baby girl?" asked Black.

"I'm trying to reach Boom, but I can't get through to him," Shonda hopelessly responded. "I must've left him a thousand messages on his damn cell phone already."

"Is that right? I thought he'd be over there with you at a time like this."

"Nope, him and Germ went back up to New York late last night."

"NEW YORK???"

***

"You know, ain't no way ya'll boys is gonna leave here alive," Winch boldly stated with all the confidence in the world.

"Is that right? See me shakin'?" Boom replied.

"Yeah, well it wouldn't be fair unless I warned you ahead of time. Consider yourself warned."

"You serious, too, ain't you? Look around you, Winchester. You ain't the one holdin' all the cards in this muthafucka. Now, I could just jump on you again with the butt of this here cannon, but I won't. It's chess now, *'king.'* I got ya queen; I'm droppin' all ya pawns one by one; plus I got whatever you consider this mute puppy-dog muthafucka over here. You ain't got no wins, so I suggest you just give it up. Maybe this shit don't gotta get no more bloody than it already has."

Winch simply sucked his teeth at Boom's clever analogy. He wasn't about to show his hand just yet. He was somewhat familiar with the game, too, and he had a couple of moves left in him before he was checkmated.

Boom waited for a response, but Winch gave none. They both sat there, staring the other down. That's when the thumps started from upstairs. Germ sounded like he was having a ball unraveling Patrice. Until now Winch was a stone, a block of impenetrable ice. He slipped up a bit when Patrice got added to the equation. He still stayed hard, but he was also concerned at the same time. He was fighting his feelings though. The worst thing you can do is let a nigga know when he's got you in check and that you didn't even see it comin'.

"Shut the fuck up, bitch!" they heard Germ yell just before another thump and a crash.

Patrice yelled, "Let me go! Let me go!"

"Come here," Germ said.

That's when the noise lowered to mumbles. Patrice was still yelling at the top of her lungs, but Germ had her face pressed up against a pillow while he put his knee in her back to keep her pinned down to the bed.

"So?" Boom said to Winch, as if offering him one last chance to cooperate.

Still, Winch tried his best to show as little signs of weakness as he could.

Boom didn't hesitate one bit. Once he realized that Winch was gonna be a hard ass, he called to Germ. "Ay yo, Germ!!!" he said, yelling over his shoulder.

"Yeah!"

"You know that thing we talked about earlier?"

"Yeah!" he replied excitedly. He knew exactly where Boom was going. He couldn't help but lick his lips with anticipation.

"That thing I said you could get later??"

"Uh-huh!!!"

"Well, now is later. Do ya thing, playa!" Boom said giving the OK for Germ to do with Patrice whatever came naturally.

That's when Boom looked back at Winch. He put his hand up to his mouth like he was whispering, even though he was all the way on the other side of the room. When he had Winch's undivided attention, he said, "He likes to take pussy." Then he started laughing out loud.

Germ started by running his hand slowly up Patrice's inner thigh. Beneath a silk robe, she had on a matching silk bra and panties. Her skin was surprisingly soft for her age. She wasn't an old hag or anything, but she was still getting up there. She kept nice care of herself though. Easily, she looked ten to fifteen years younger than her driver's license indicated. Germ was loving every minute of it.

When he reached her ass, he rubbed in circular motions. She had the perfect little tight butt to fit her shape. She was slim enough for her petite little curves to fit her just right.

Germ immediately slid two fingers—his index and middle finger—under her panties and ran them slowly down the crease of her buns. When he reached the area just above her pussy, he paused to tease himself. As the saliva welled up in his mouth, he savagely tugged at her underwear until he completely ripped them from her waist. With the same two fingers, he searched between her legs again.

Hock, thoof! He spit on his hand for a little bit of moisture and then forced them into her hole. He dug his fingers into her defenseless little pussy all the way down to his knuckles. "Mmmm," he moaned with his eyes closed.

Her cries grew louder, but she still lay unable to move as Germ kept her face planted firmly in the pillow with his other hand. She could hardly move at all, let alone fight off Germ once he set his mind to what he wanted. It was like stopping a pack of starving wolves from eating you alive.

Germ was getting more and more aroused as he continued his savage finger-fuck. It only added to the enjoyment that she fought every step of the way. He loved the idea of taking a woman unwillingly even more than the actual act. He felt like it gave him power. He got to be in complete control of things.

Before long he wanted to be inside of her. He wanted to feel her tenseness wrapped around his fully grown dick. He imagined that with every stroke her instincts would tighten her up more and more. Every terrified shiver would send splendid sensations through his body. Just thinking about it gave him the chills. She would desperately want nothing more than for him to be out of her. But tightening up those walls around him would only make the experience that much more electrifying.

Finally, he couldn't stand to wait any longer. He grabbed a handful of her hair and pulled her head from its secure position buried deep in the pillow. That's when the screams began to echo throughout the entire house. Over and over again Patrice yelled at the top of her lungs for Germ to get his perverted hands off her body. It was like she was having a seizure. She couldn't bear it, not even for a second. She would rather die than be raped.

"STOP IT! STOP! Don't you fuckin' touch me, you filthy pig!!!" she yelled. "You could kill me first!!!"

Unsurprisingly, the noise wasn't bothersome to Germ in the least. It only made the experience that much more enjoyable. In fact, he was the only one in the whole damn house who wasn't disturbed at all by Patrice's cries.

Apollo, for one, tried his best to completely phase out Patrice's hopeless whimpers. His fists balled up and his lips got tighter. Still, he sat there tied to that chair while this horrendous act continued in the room above him.

Winch's hard exterior was beginning to crack as Patrice's cries got louder and louder. Every time she let out a yell, it bounced around in his head and rested deep in his heart. He was hurting.

Even Boom, a heartless, cold-blooded killer, couldn't help but cringe at the sounds that Patrice had been making. He hid it a whole lot better than Winch, but he wouldn't have been able to let it continue for much longer before he stepped in himself. The only thing stopping him was the thought that this torture method might be the only way he was ever gonna get Sabra back. The end would have to justify the means. Still with his focus on that directive, he didn't know how long he'd be able to hold out. He lit up a cigarette to calm his nerves. He inhaled deep and blew a cloud into the air. That's just what he needed to relax. In fact, he looked so relaxed that it made Winch crack.

"Alright, you smug little punk bastards!" he finally yelled. "Put an end to this bullshit. I'll give you what you came for."

Boom was thanking God Winch reacted when he did. Another second and he would've been putting a halt to the shit himself.

"Oh, okay," Boom replied, still remaining as cool as a fan. "All of a sudden you got some shit you wanna tell me? Just a minute ago you were tellin' me to go fuck myself, but now that ya bitch about to get it stuck in her ass, you all forthcoming and shit? You fuckin' pussy!"

"Fuck you then, nigga," Winch viciously responded. He was desperate now and ready to try anything to assume a position of control in this situation. "Your little bitch goddaughter can die down there for all I care!"

"What you say, muthafucka???"

Winch simply sucked his teeth in response.

To that, Boom's reply was short, but sweet and straight to the point...*BOOM, BOOM!!!* He let two shots go off from the .44. The first one grazed Winch's right arm and went through the wall behind him. The second one flew right past the left side of his head, taking with it a small portion of his ear. It wasn't too serious, but the blood made it look a whole lot worse than it actually was.

"Aaaahhh!" he cried. He was so stunned after the first shot that he didn't even get a chance to make an attempt at getting out of the way of the second. He was caught completely off guard. Now what was left of his left ear was dripping blood all over his nice Versace shirt. Boom couldn't help but poke fun.

"My bad, dog," he said. "Were you saying something? I ain't mean to make a mess of your Sunday's best. And blood is a bitch to get out of silk, too, damn! I don't know from experience 'cause silk really ain't my thing, but I've heard, you know?"

Winch couldn't respond. He was too focused on the numbness he was feeling on the whole left side of his face. He was holding his head rocking back and forth on the chair, trying to stop the blood from pouring.

"You ready to talk now, nigga???" Boom yelled.

Still, Winch didn't respond quick enough. Boom immediately jumped to his feet and launched himself in Winch's direction with the burner pointed and cocked.

"What's the matter, Winchester? Can't you hear me talkin' to you??? I asked you a muthafuckin' question!" Boom was an inch away from Winch's face now, yelling in the ear that was still in one piece.

"Alright, you got it, nigga!" yelled Winch in desperation. "You got it! I got the girl downstairs. She in the basement, man. I'll take you to her."

"Bullshit, nigga!" replied Boom in disbelief. "Which way you think we came in, muthafucka??? Ain't shit down there but two dead poodles. You better not be lying to me!!!"

"I ain't lyin', muthafucka! I'm tellin' you I got her downstairs. There's a cage under the floor, like a trapdoor. I got her in there, man. There's no way you could've known it was there. Why you think I had them pups down there???"

Winch's story was starting to sound like it made sense now. Boom thought before he responded. He was getting close. He could feel it deep inside of his bones. He would be sure of Sabra's safety really soon now. That was for damn sure.

Boom slowly backed off of Winch to give some room to breathe. He held out his hand to help him to his feet, and Winch looked up at him with distrust in his eyes. Reluctantly, he finally accepted Boom's invitation and grabbed his hand. When he was on his feet, Boom stepped to the side.

"After you, sir," he said in a sarcastic but firm tone.

Winch was still looking at Boom through doubtful eyes, squinted low enough so that Boom couldn't get a clear picture of his thoughts through them.

Finally, Winch started toward the basement door and stopped at the stairwell. He looked over his shoulder at Boom as to signal it was his turn to hold up his end of the deal. Germ was about to get disappointed yet again.

"Yo, Germ!!!" he yelled.

Germ didn't respond. He was on top of Patrice with one hand wrapped around her neck and the other undoing his belt. He got the belt open and his zipper down before he finally heard Boom repeatedly yelling his name.

"What's up, dog?" he answered. "I'm just gonna be a minute; I'll be right down!!!"

"Nah, fuck that!" replied Boom.

Even Patrice had stopped yelling at that point to hear what was being said.

"Let the bitch be for now," Boom continued. "We about to get what we came for. If this nigga is bullshittin', full speed ahead on that fuckin' whore! Hear me?"

Germ sucked his teeth and sighed. He couldn't believe he was that close. With his dick hard and poking straight up, only a few inches away from Patrice's defenseless little pussy, he could do nothing but wait and anticipate. He knew what brought them there, but now his focus had shifted. In the back of his mind, he hoped that Winch would pull something to make Boom give the go-ahead. That would be all he needed, and he'd be just peachy with life.

"Let's go, nigga," Boom ordered.

Winch started walking, but stopped to deliver a message of comfort to his woman. "It's gon' be alright, baby girl!" he yelled.

"CARL???" Patrice yelled. "Carl, baby, is that you? Please tell me it's you!"

Patrice was almost fine until she heard her hubby's voice. Now she was feeling irate. She felt a bit of power come over her now. She didn't feel as unguarded. Her knight was there.

She immediately started to fight off Germ with ten times the power as her earlier efforts. She was actually backing him down now, too. Maybe it was the fact that his dick was sticking out, and his mind could only form visions of raping her until she bled. That's when he went for his weapon on the nightstand to assume his control back.

All Boom and Winch could hear from downstairs was...*BOOM!!!* The sound of a single shot went echoing throughout the entire house, and then it was silent.

Boom worried. He knew that Winch wouldn't be nearly as cooperative without the assurance of Patrice's well-being. He was one hundred percent right! Winch's first reaction was to throw Boom from his trail. He turned with his elbow swinging and landed a blow to Boom's chest that sent him flying toward the front door. With a bit of a head start, Winch went for the basement door. He threw the door open and leapt down the stairs in two steps.

By the time Boom was getting to his feet, he could hear rumbling coming from the room where he had Apollo stashed.

"Shit!!!" he said to himself aloud.

There were three more crashes before Apollo had completely shattered the chair he was tied to into pieces. With his hands still tied tightly behind his back he rammed into the door with his shoulder...*DOOM!!!* When the door didn't budge, he backed up for another try...*DOOM!!!* One more shot to the door with all of his weight took it off the hinges. The door came off just as Boom was about to turn into the basement. Apollo saw his enemy and charged at him. Even though his hands were bound, he didn't care. He was gonna do whatever he could to put Boom out of commission.

When he was finally close enough, he dropped his shoulder on Boom the same way he did the door. The shot sent Boom back to the floor, and threw the burner from his clutches. When he hit the floor, Apollo saw his window and went flying out of it with no parachute. He got to where Boom was on the floor before he got a chance to get back up and started sailing kicks at him. The first kick caught Boom in the face and threw his head back as he fought to get back to his feet. The second landed on his chest as he lay flat on his back. Apollo repeated this attack with relentlessness. He didn't even see Boom reaching.

Boom's hand came out of his pocket with unimaginable swiftness. He flipped out the blade with even more grace and quickness. The first swing split the back of Apollo's leg open, but he didn't even feel that one. He didn't know he was stabbed until the second one came. In a chopping motion, Boom brought the blade down on Apollo's pivot foot. It slid right through his boot and cut deep into his foot.

"Aaaahhhh!" he yelled.

Even quicker than the blade was inserted, Boom yanked it out to deliver another stab. The next incision went into Apollo's shin. He hit his bone with so much force that it chipped off the tip of the blade as Boom grabbed it back out.

That's when Apollo lost his balance and went crumbling to the ground. The pain took him right off his feet and now he lay on the floor, defenseless against Boom's continuing attacks.

Now that Boom had the upper hand once again, he didn't prolong things. He had to catch up to Winch. As much as he wanted to kill Apollo slowly, he didn't hesitate. He got his cannon back and started letting the shots go...*BOOM... BOOM... BOOM...BOOM!!!* The first two shots went into Apollo's back, and the last two went straight through the maze of dreads on his head, entering his brain from the back. Blood and bits of his insides flew onto the wall as the bullets blew out of his forehead. Boom knew that he wouldn't be any more trouble.

As he fled to the basement, he briefly glanced up the stairs. He wanted to check on Germ to find out what made him jump the gun like that, but first things first. He got halfway down the basement stairs just as Winch was unveiling his secret weapon.

Winch went straight for the couch that was covered with a dropcloth. He threw off the covers and all that could be seen was a cloud of dust sitting in the air. Winch felt around until he found what he was looking for.

"Yeah, you muthafuckas," he said to himself as if they were standing right there with him. "Take some of this."

Winch lifted the AK-47 assault rifle and cocked the hammer back to chamber a slug. Boom hit the bottom step, and Winch started letting shots fly through the dust in Boom's direction. Boom, although surprised, quickly jumped behind a work bench for cover and began returning fire with the Calico. They shot at each other blindly for the next few seconds as bullets littered the walls. That's when they heard something that surprised the shit out of them both.

"Carl??" yelled Patrice from the top of the steps. "I'm comin' down, baby! I'm comin'!!!"

"Noooo!!!" yelled Winch. He was trying to stop Patrice from engaging, but it was already too late. She was halfway down the steps and she had Germ's Glock in her hand pointed like she was ready to let a nigga have it! She didn't even hear Winch's warning over the shots that were being fired.

Boom's first reaction was something like, *How the fuck???* But he quickly used the situation to his advantage. As soon as she hit the bottom, he pounced. He got the drop on her before her eyes even adjusted to the darkness. He was standing right behind her as she held the cannon pointed in front of her. He effortlessly knocked the gun from her hand and grabbed onto her with the submachine gun at the side of her head. At that point, the shots came to halt.

"Yeah, nigga, now I got ya bitch!" Boom yelled into the darkness. "You wanna keep goin' or what? 'Cause I got plenty more clips, muthafucka, we can do this shit all night!"

In the midst of Boom's shit-talking, he got another surprise. First he heard steps coming from upstairs.

What the fuck now? he thought.

That's when the door opened.

Winch was still on the floor with his back against the couch, waiting for one more window of opportunity to open up for him. He was desperate at this point. Now that Patrice completely fucked up his major move, he was left at a disadvantage. He was damn near ready to force a window open for himself. The only problem was that at this point every possible path for him to take to save his own ass would almost certainly kill Patrice in the process. He almost wanted to start blowing away. Fuck it! Even if the slugs passed through her, he was just about willing to risk it. That's how badly he wanted Boom dead! His options were fading quickly, especially with this new development. If he would've known how bad Apollo got it, maybe he wouldn't have been banking on him being the one at the top of the basement steps. So sad…so sad.

"Oh shit, Germ?" blurted Boom in amazement. "You good, my nigga? I thought you was a goner for sure."

Germ took one step forward and stumbled down the first few steps at the top of the staircase. He got his balance back, but he didn't look good. His back was hunched over, and the only thing holding him up was the handrail. He made his way down the rest of the stairs as carefully as possible.

"Yo, what's wrong, Germ?" Boom said as he took his eye off of the couch Winch had taken cover behind. "You hit?"

"Boom, you gotta hear this…"

That was all Winch needed to hear. As far as he was concerned, his window was wide open right at that moment, and no way was he gonna get another chance to open things up. He jumped to his feet with the AK aimed at his enemies.

"Watch out!" yelled Germ as he got to the bottom of the steps. As Boom's animal instincts took over, he immediately lifted the sub to defend himself against Winch's fire. That's when the shots started again. Winch's slugs came flying first. Boom's followed closely behind though. Fully automatic shots rang out for what seemed like forever. At the end of it all, everyone was laid out on the ground surrounded by a sea of smoking bullet shells.

Boom thought he was dying already. Everything had gone silent and he could already feel himself getting numb. He felt like he was slowly fading away. He let the air out of his lungs and didn't even try to inhale again. That's when he could feel the blood soaking his chest. He figured he must've caught one in the midst of all the wild firing. A lot of slugs were traded in those short seconds, and it wouldn't have been a miracle for him to have caught one. He'd already decided that he was gonna die right then and there. Too bad for him it wasn't his decision to make.

"Boom, you gotta hear this," he heard Germ repeat. "You gotta hear this, Boom. Listen to me, nigga! You gotta hear this."

Finally Boom got the urge to breathe again and started coughing. He inhaled deeper than he'd ever inhaled before. The air filling his lungs back up let him know...he was alive. He couldn't believe it. But before he opened his eyes, he had to ask himself, *Am I the one bleedin'?*

He opened his eyes to see what he had envisioned for himself only seconds ago—death. Patrice was right on top of him. Her eyes were wide open and pointed directly at his eyes. He could see from the lifelessness in them that she had gone to see her maker. It wasn't the first time he had seen that look. In fact, eyes like hers had haunted his dreams for years. Those same eyes would probably be waking him in a cold sweat sometime in the near future, but he was used to it by now. Boom and death were like first cousins. They knew each other very well.

As Boom gazed into Patrice's emptiness, he heard Germ's voice again repeating the same sentence over and over again.

"Boom, you gotta hear this. You gotta hear this, Boom. You gotta hear it."

Finally Boom looked over and saw his comrade laid out with his body littered with bullet holes. He looked like he was bleeding from everywhere. He quickly threw Patrice to the side to attend to his brother.

Germ was lying on his stomach unable to move an inch in either direction. He had too many holes in back for Boom to even count. Boom knelt down beside him and turned him over. On the other side were more bullet wounds and a whole lot more blood. He held him in his arms.

"You gonna be alright," he said. He knew otherwise though. "You gonna be good, my nigga. I promise you, you'll be fine."

When Germ tried to talk, he coughed up and blood came leaking from the sides of his mouth. He tried again to talk, but it only brought up more blood.

"Don't talk, son," Boom advised. "Stop tryin' to talk. Just sit tight; we gon' get you all patched up and you'll be good. Don't even worry about it."

Once more Germ spit out the blood that gathered in his mouth and tried to talk. "Boom, you…you gotta hear…this," he repeated.

"Hear what?" Boom finally asked.

Germ bowed his chin as if to try and point at something. He was holding something in his hands.

"What's that?" asked Boom before gently loosening Germ's grip on what he had for him. It was his cell phone.

Germ tried to take a breath before he continued, "I wanted...to call…Shonda. I wanted…to let her know…to let her know we found her…that we found Sabra."

Boom's eyes welled up with tears. He was fighting with all of himself to hold them back. He didn't want to just break like that, not in front of Germ. Especially not in the condition he was in. He just took a deep breath. He sniffled and fought to remain strong.

"Guess what, Boom?" Germ asked.

"What's that?"

"She…sh-sh-she f-found…"

"Yeah," Boom said, trying to coach him along.

"Sh-sh…she found her first."

"Wha?" Boom asked in disbelief. At first he thought his boy must've been tripping. Then that's when he heard the most beautiful thing coming from the cell phone. It was Sabra's voice on a message that Shonda had left on Germ's voicemail.

Boom reached for the phone, and just as he got it from Germ's clutches, he coughed. At the end of that cough, he simply stopped moving altogether. His eyes froze with emptiness just as Patrice's did. He was gone now, too. Boom couldn't bring himself to look. He didn't want Germ's soul haunting him with the others. They were somehow acceptable to him, like a chosen sufferance for the wrongs that he'd done during his short stay on this planet.

"To replay this message, press 1," the machine said as Boom lifted it to his ears.

He hesitated at first, but then quickly pressed the button as his anxiousness got the best of him. When the message restarted from the beginning, Boom could no longer hold back the tears. As soon as he heard little Sabra's voice, the crying started. He was bawling by the time Shonda got on. She went on to explain that she didn't know who, why, or when her kidnapper *decided* to bring her back home, but that's what they *did*. She didn't know and she didn't care. All she cared about was having her little girl back unharmed. Nothing more, nothing less.

It seems as though after Patrice shot him, the first thing Germ thought about was calling Shonda and telling her that they had found Sabra. He promised he would call and he was making good on that promise, even if it meant that it was the last thing he did. Just as he did after he dipped out of the back of Shampoo when they got the drop on Beast. She was also the one he called before he and Boom got on the road to come to N.Y. Germ was definitely a man of his word. The only thing that stopped him from calling this time were the many text and voicemail messages he realized he had once he cut his phone back on. He could gather the gist of the story from reading it, but he had to check one of the voicemails to be sure. That's when he heard Sabra coming out of the phone. Everything changed at that point. He couldn't just lay there as blood leaked out of his chest. He was shot as he and Patrice struggled for his gun. He knew he was gonna die, but he had to get to Boom first. He needed to know that they had traveled so far for no reason.

Maybe Beast was the culprit. Maybe he lied to Boom to get him to let him go, and then returned the girl on good faith. Sounds pretty fuckin' thin, huh? Whatever the case, Sabra was home. Now Boom had dug himself in so deep that it was impossible for him to turn back. Too many people had died. Besides, there were still some blank areas to fill in. All of the answers were right in front of him, and Boom only needed to keep his eyes open to see them.

CHAPTER 16

"Fuckin' pussy...you couldn't even finish me, could you? I swear you fuckin' kids nowadays don't know how to do shit right! You little fuckers ain't got it in you to complete nothin' you fuckin' start! You know what? I wish I did have that little bitch! I would've twisted her little sweat ass out. She'd have been on the stroll by thirteen!"

Winch's taunting mumbles brought Boom back to the reality that was his life. He was still cradling his homey's corpse without a clue as to why he was even there. He couldn't figure it out for shit.

"What the fuck is goin' on?" he asked himself. It was the only sentence he could bring his mouth to form. No doubt he had a mission ahead of him to try and answer that question, but first things first. He bowed his head to say a prayer for another one of his fallen comrades.

"The Father, the Son, and the Holy Spirit...Amen."

Just as he finished praying to most high that his boy be granted the privilege of resting in peace, he searched for his weapon to send another one of God's children back to their father.

"What's that you talkin', joker?" asked Boom as he approached with the sub in hand.

"You heard me, punk!" replied Winch, spilling blood from his mouth.

The closer Boom got to him, the more fucked up he looked. It was a wonder he was still talking shit at all with all the holes he had in him. The nigga definitely should've been dead by now. He was on the floor sitting with his back up against the wall. His hands were at his side, and his head was slumped over to one side.

"You just want me to finish you off, huh? You can't even imagine goin' on livin' ya worthless life after today, that it? Who's the punk again???"

Boom was standing right over Winch. He saw him differently than he had a few minutes ago. Now, he was just a mark and that was it. He'd lost all of his importance at this point. Shit, if he wasn't already littered with shots, maybe Boom could've taken some joy in torturing him just for G.P. That much would have closure at least. He had bigger fish to fry though. There was still a mystery out there that needed solving. Boom didn't even want to waste any more time.

"Hmm," Boom thought out loud. "I should just let you die slow, muthafucka!" He turned around to leave, but Winch wasn't having any parts of that. He had his own questions he needed answered.

"What the fuck is this? You about to just leave?" Even though it hurt like hell, Winch couldn't help but laugh aloud. "Not even a *'my bad'*...not even as much as an apologetic gesture? You muthafuckas came in here guns blazin', huh? Probably got a brain not even as big as my dick between the both of you!"

"Apologetic?" Boom said as he paused mid-stride. "You want *me* to apologize to *you?* You can't be fuckin' serious!!!"

"Yeah I am, ya stubborn bastard!" he yelled. "I'm dead serious! You think you can just leave???"

"You should be happy that I am, nigga!!!" Boom yelled. He turned back. When he got close enough, he knelt down so that he and Winch were eye to eye. "You don't even realize what just happened, do you? You don't even know who I am."

Winch had no response. He lay there breathing every breath like it could've been his last.

"Answer me, muthafucka!" Boom ordered.

"Fuck you, youngster!" Winch snarled. "You ain't no-fuckin'-body! Why the fuck should I know *you? I'm* the big boss here, not you. *I'm* the man, not you!"

"Shit, I don't even know why I bothered," Boom said, thinking out loud. "Why should you remember me? That was a long time ago. How many years passed now since that day? I was just a kid." Boom started to play devil's advocate as the flip side of the argument started to make sense now, too. "But you had to know that I would be coming for you though. You should've been prepared for this to happen. You knew they had a son. You should've been expecting me."

Winch was thinking hard about what Boom had just said. Things were beginning to calculate in his head. Other things had happened that didn't make sense. Now everything was beginning to come together.

"You Vester and Grace's boy, ain't you?" Winch said, finally putting everything in perspective.

Boom's silence was enough for Winch to assume that he'd hit the nail on the head.

"But all of this ain't because of what happened that day at ya pop's wake, is it? There was somethin' else goin' on. You said somethin' about a girl."

"Yeah, that's what brought me this time. A little girl was missin' and everything was pointin' at you."

"Why?"

"What???" Boom yelled. "What the fuck you mean, *why?*"

"What would I have gained by snatchin' up some little girl?"

"Nigga, 'cause you knew I was on ya ass, that's what. Makes perfect sense. I asked a couple of people about you and the word got back. You grab up my goddaughter for insurance."

"Lil' nigga, if you had a brain, you'd be dangerous. All of this for what? 'Cause you *thought* I had somethin' to do with a missin' kid? Nah, there's gotta be more to it than that. What the fuck was you doin' lookin' for me in the damn first place then?"

"Revenge," Boom simply replied. "Why else?"

"Well," Winch said before pointing toward Patrice's lifeless body. "I guess you got what you came for then, huh? I guess the debt she thought she paid to society wasn't enough."

"Not in the least homeboy. She should've been put to death!"

"Hmm." Winch chuckled. "Jury of her peers didn't think so. They thought eight years was more than enough."

"EIGHT YEARS??? FOR A BODY???"

"Hmm." Winch chuckled again. "My lips are sealed. Somebody's playin' you good, lil' nigga!"

"FUCK YOU!!!" Boom yelled. "You just tryin' to throw me off ya scent. But I smell you; you dried-up piece of shit! That fuckin' whore is dead now, and that's it! She got what she deserved!"

"So, how does it feel? Better?"

Boom looked over at Patrice, and then back at Winch, then down at his burner.

"Almost," he said before looking back up at Winch.

All of a sudden, it hit Winch like a ton of bricks. He had finally realized just how fucked up this whole situation was. He could see everything for what it was now. Most importantly, he knew what brought Boom back to the Bronx after all of this time.

"This is about your father."

Boom gave Winch a look like he didn't know what to say. He could think of plenty of ways to respond but nothing came out of his mouth right away. He finally said, "Nigga, you just as stupid as you look!"

"Well, I guess you ain't lyin'. I must've been stupid to think you knew the whole story. I should've known you would've been kept in the dark. You're right, kid. I am a fuckin' idiot! That does explain a whole lot, though, including what that fucking snake was doing back in the old hood. Yup, what else would he be doin' here after all of this time? Then, out of nowhere, you just pop up looking for revenge. I should've seen it comin'."

"What you tryin' to say?"

"Aaahahaha..." Winch laughed aloud. He couldn't believe that Boom could be that naive. When he finally stopped laughing enough to reply, he said, "You got ya eyes wide open...but they behind a thick, dark blindfold, kept tied tight by someone standing right behind you. You lookin' to find the muthafucka responsible for that there killing, you in the wrong place and you ain't even warm, youngster. You see, Jr., that there...was what we used to call a *black-tie affair*."

Even while experiencing the deepest pain he'd ever felt in his entire life, Winch found it inside of himself to smile. A face that was usually as cold as a block of ice was warmed with smug sarcasm. As he leaked out the last little bit of life he had left, a knowing look froze in his facial expression. He exhaled his last breath as his eyes stared vacantly into the sky. He was gone.

Boom hopelessly stared as Winch went. His face described his thoughts exactly. *What the fuck???*

CHAPTER 17

When Boom got back to the car he just sat there. He was getting a little sleepy and he desperately wanted to rest his eyes, even if for only a few minutes. He felt his head leaning to the right; his eyelids got heavier and heavier. When his head hit the window, he quickly woke back up. He couldn't be overpowered by the urge to fall asleep. The consequences could be deadly. He was realizing now what was making him feel this way. The reality of it scared him enough to keep his eyes wide open.

His clothes were soaked in blood by now. The awkward thing was that most of it wasn't even his. He couldn't believe that he had killed so many in such a short period of time. On top of that he was the only one to walk away, and with only minor damage.

He couldn't think about all that he'd just gone through for too much longer. He couldn't forget that he still had a whole mountain of shit to climb ahead of him, too. He knew exactly where to start. It would be just what he needed. Of course he needed to make moves as quick as possible. He couldn't chance someone spotting him looking the way did.

After a fifteen-minute drive, Boom was pulling back up to the motel he stayed in a couple of nights ago. Good thing he kept that stash in the room or else he'd be stuck without a move to make. Originally, this was something he was saving for Germ, but he didn't need it where he was, and now Boom was gonna need it more than anything. He pulled into the driveway right past the front office where he could see the owner of the establishment through the window. He gave him a nod as to ask, *'Everything copasetic?'*

The owner gave him thumbs up in response. Boom knew that everything they had discussed was taken care of. Before Boom left, he gave strict instructions that no one try and get into the room to clean it. Just leaving the "Do Not Disturb" sign hanging from the door wouldn't have done the job. That wouldn't have had the same comforting feeling at all. Boom even left a couple of thousand dollars to ensure that his words would have that lasting impression. It would've been a month before anyone went into that room without Boom's authorization, and that's exactly what he wanted.

He parked in the lot and after grabbing his knapsack out of the trunk, he made his way to the room as quickly as possible. The last thing he needed was for someone to bump into him and get blood smeared all over their clothes.

When he got to the door, he threw it open and quickly closed it behind him. *Click-clack*...he locked both locks on the door and took a deep breath.

"Shit!" he said to himself in frustration. "Gotta make this quick."

He went through his bag, got out a fresh change of clothes, and laid it out on the bed. Then he emptied everything in his pockets on the dresser. From there he made his way to the bathroom to make sure things were just how he left them.

"Perfect!" he said when he was satisfied with what he found.

He needed to jump in that tub to handle some business, but first he removed each article of bloody clothing and carefully stuffed them into his backpack. he ran himself a nice hot shower and then jumped in. He made sure to scrub everything three times just to make absolutely certain he was completely rid of any evidence. He watched enough Discovery Channel to know that no one is exempt from all of the shit science could do nowadays. Shit, if you're too careless, it ain't a question of *if* you get caught, it's *when*.

Twenty-five minutes later, he was finally done. He got out of the shower and grabbed a couple of towels to dry off with. He stood just outside the bathroom in front of the mirror as he dried off. He examined his wound. It didn't look any prettier than it did earlier. It still hurt like hell but he was gonna have to hack it. He ripped one of the towels into narrow strips to wrap it. When that was done, he really got down to business.

He started by getting himself a fresh cigarette. Then, still wearing nothing but a towel wrapped around his waist, Boom went back into the bathroom and took a seat on the edge of the tub. He sat there nonchalantly blowing smoke into the air. He was just looking way too cool, and it was beginning to get difficult for his prisoner to keep her composure. Before he even spoke a word, Phylecia was already on the verge of hyperventilation as all she could do was imagine what was in store for her. It had been over forty-eight hours now since Boom had left her tied to the toilet bowl, and she looked like she could've been bawling the entire time. Now she was sniveling and twitching, trying to stop herself from making too much noise. She actually thought that if she stayed quiet enough that maybe Boom would just leave again, for good this time.

As naked as the day she was born, she was bound with her head down and her ass up, positioned perfectly for what Boom originally had planned for her. Germ would've been extremely grateful, and he would've deserved every moment of it after all he sacrificed. Boom had the whole thing planned out. He couldn't think of a better way to deal with this whole Phylecia situation. Now, everything was different. But Boom was always good at adjusting to unexpected conditions.

Boom could tell that Phylecia was about to break just as he was finishing his cigarette. He calmly lifted one finger to his lips. "Shhh."

Phylecia had no response besides more tears. It was a wonder that her body could even still produce them.

"I'm only gonna ask you this question once," Boom said as he lit another cigarette with what was left of the first one. He took a pull and inhaled slowly. Then he quickly removed the gag from her mouth. "Who sent you?"

Phylecia didn't waste any time beating around the bush. "It was my uncle; he sent me," she spat. "He told me where to find you and what I needed to know about you. His name is Russell…Russell Hynes. He said there was a lot of money in it for us if I kept a tab on you, maybe slow you down a bit."

"That it?" asked Boom. "Just slow me down? You weren't supposed to off me or set me up to get wacked?"

"No, it wasn't nothin' like that. Honestly, I was supposed to turn you out… you know, get ya nose open. I just thought somebody thought you needed to get you some pussy, that's all! Some guys have a problem with paying for it, so other people pay…kinda like a gift, you know?"

"A gift, huh?" From what Boom could tell she was being somewhat honest.

There were still some holes in her story that needed to be filled before he decided what he should do with her.

"So this dude Russell, that's the 7-1-8 number on your cell?"

"Yeah."

"You say he's ya uncle?"

"Right."

"And he's pimping you?"

"No, it's not like that. We take care of each other. He doesn't beat on me or anything like that. And he doesn't just take *all* of my money neither. He needs me just as much as I need him. We're like a team."

"A team?"

"Yeah, it's been this way for as long as I can remember. It wasn't even his idea at first. He only has my best interest in mind; he always has. He cares about me. Look, when my parents both OD'd on dope, he was the only person that looked out for me. No one else, just him!"

Boom was getting a better understanding of Phylecia's thought process now. This nigga Russell definitely had her brainwashed. He wasn't buying all of that, *'It wasn't even his idea at first'* shit! That piece of shit manipulated his own niece into being a whore for him. He was gonna get what was coming to him, and Boom would be enjoying every second of it.

"Well, I need to talk to this nigga. Where's he at?"

"I can take you to him, but you have to promise me that you won't hurt him. He's an old, weak man. And he has habits. Trust me; he's no threat to you."

Boom didn't respond right away. He sat there and looked at her. *Stupid bitch,* he thought.

"So...do you promise?"

"Yeah, I promise." But that was just the words that his mouth produced out loud. In his mind he was saying, *Fuck that shit! I'm about to find out what this nigga is about, and then he's gettin' dished...him and his fool-ass whore he got for a niece, too!*

Surprisingly, Phylecia's face produced a little smile. She was confident that knowing the story would make Boom more comfortable. Hopefully, everything would be a whole lot clearer once he spoke with Russell. They could clear up whatever else Boom needed to know.

"I need a favor before we go," Boom said just as he got the knot out of the phone cord that he had tied around Phylecia's wrists.

As soon as she was free, she went right back into her mode. "Just gimme a minute to get cleaned up and I'll do whatever you want," she said with a big smile. She stood up and she was face to face with Boom. She reached for his crotch as she approached, leaning in like she was about to kiss him.

"Bitch," he said, halting her advance by grabbing her by the chin. "You're fuckin' disgusting already!" He pushed her away from him. "That ain't what I meant!"

Phylecia frowned at Boom's response. She had the wrong idea, but she was straightened out now. She had to get used to the fact that maybe sex wasn't always gonna be the only thing a man wanted from her. There were other things more important than sex, especially at a time like this. Boom couldn't think of pussy. This time, he needed her for that other thing that she was probably good for... cleaning up! He immediately ordered her to get some rags and some soap to start scrubbing any and everything he may have touched, bled on, or dropped someone else's blood on. Meanwhile, he finished getting dressed. After that, he went outside to make a phone call that he'd been anticipating for the past few hours.

★★★

"Oh my God, Boom, is that you? Please tell me it's you!"

"Yeah, it's me. My bad about earlier. We was in the trenches, you know? I couldn't really talk. How are you doing?"

"I'm wonderful, Boom," Shonda responded. "She's home. They brought her home without a scratch on her. I don't know what you did, but you did it!"

"This one wasn't me," Boom replied in all honesty. "I don't know what the fuck is goin' on. But I won't be back home 'til I get a better understanding. I can't wait to see the little girl. So, you say they ain't harm her none, right?"

"No, not even as much as a paper cut."

"Good. Where's she at now?"

"She's right here beside me asleep. I ain't ever gonna let her outta my sight again, Boom."

"Well, I don' know about that," Boom said with a giggle. "We definitely gon' have to get her outta that crumb-ass school though! Soon as I get back down to the hood, we can start on that. Until then, you just keep her close."

"You're still in New York?"

"Yeah...how did you know where I was?"

"Germ called me and told me before you guys left. First he called and told me about what happened at Shampoo with Beast. A couple of hours went by and he called back to tell me that you guys had fingered the wrong guy. I was so upset at first, but then I got my hope back when he said that you guys were on to someone else. I had all the faith in the world that you would fix this for us."

Just hearing Germ's name caught Boom off guard. He hadn't dealt with that loss just yet, and he definitely wasn't ready for that shit. He quickly changed the subject back to his mission at hand. "Yeah, but I couldn't carry this one out all the way. I was all off point and the shit was right in front of my face. I'm on it now though."

"Please, Boom, just come home. I've been stressing the last few hours since Sabra's been home, and I have a really bad feeling about this whole situation. Honestly, something deep inside of me told me that I'd never see or speak to you again. I can't go on feeling like this. This is supposed to be a happy time. I'm over here pulling my hair out already! I spoke to Uncle Black and he's worried out of his mind about you, too! I told him where you went and he started going ballistic on me."

"I didn't mean to stress you guys out, but this is something that I had to do. Sure, I should've called you to let you know what I was up to instead of being a pussy about it. I honestly didn't think you could stand more bad news. I underestimated you; you're a fuckin' trooper and I'm proud of you. But I still feel like this is something that I gotta do. Trust me, I came this far knowing that I would be no good to you or Sabra dead. I *will* come home, but not until I wrap this shit up. It ain't just gon' go away; not as long as I'm here...not as long as I'm alive and breathing. It's either me or them, Shonda."

Shonda had already started tearing up before Boom even finished speaking. She knew that it wasn't in her power to make him leave all of that behind. She knew that he couldn't just leave the wound open like that. In essence, he was right. What happens the next time? Just as easily as they got Sabra this time they could get her again, or someone else close to him. In one way he was the security they needed to be safe, but at the same time he was the negative figure that brought on all of the unwanted attention. If he wasn't around, they probably wouldn't even need security. He was a gift and a curse, no doubt about it. But it was up to him to make sure that he was more of a gift than a curse.

"You know..." Boom said, changing the subject to another touchy topic. "...What happened between us that night? I don't know how to explain that. I don't know what it means. But I don't think it's too good for us right now."

"I know," Shonda simply replied. She was already ten steps ahead of him. "I thought about that, too...and you're right."

"I don't want nothin' to mess us up though, feel me? Let's just take one day at a time, cool?"

"Yeah, of course. I was thinking the same thing."

"So, you knew about Ivan and Travis, right?" Boom asked, giving Shonda all the credit she deserved for being the ride-or-die bitch that she was. "You knew what that was all about, didn't you?"

"Yeah, I knew. I knew the whole time. But that was my man, you know? Nothing was gonna end that, especially not some stupid little bitch!"

"You're one bad muthafucka, you know that?"

"Hmmm," she simply replied with a smile. "Yea, I know!"

★★★

Their conversation was interrupted when Phylecia came out of the room into the hall to report that she had completed the task Boom handed her.

"All done, baby," she said with a confident smile.

"Good," Boom firmly replied. "And don't fuckin' call me 'baby'!"

Phylecia sat her chin in her chest and walked back into the room. Boom waited until the door closed behind to begin talking. "Listen, Shonda, I'll call you back when I have something."

"Alright, tell Germ I said, 'holla at ya boy'!" Shonda said in a lighter tone.

Boom had no response. He couldn't tell her what happened right then and there. He didn't even want to deal with it, let alone comfort someone else.

"Yeah, alright," he said, trying not to crack. "If you see Uncle Black before me, tell him that I love him and that I had to do what I had to do. Talk to you later. One."

***

When Boom went back into the room, he was shocked and amazed at the job that Phylecia had done. Everything was spotless. She carried out her directive to perfection, and with limited resources.

"See," Boom said. "You aren't only good for *one* thing!"

"Thanks," Phylecia replied, mistaking Boom's sarcasm for a compliment.

"Alright, we gotta get up outta here. Wash up and get dressed."

"Umm," Phylecia said nervously stuttering into a question. "Before we go... shouldn't you get that looked at?"

"What? This?" Boom said, pointing at his shoulder wound where blood had already begun leaking through his quick patch job. "This ain't nothin'; I'll be alright. Don't worry."

"It doesn't look good; you sure you don't wanna get it treated?"

"What the fuck am I supposed to do? You want me to walk into an emergency room and try and explain why I have a bullet hole in my chest?"

"Well...no...I suppose..."

"What???"

"Well, I was gonna say I could probably stitch you up myself if I had a needle and some thread. It couldn't be *that* much different from sewing fabrics."

"Are you serious?"

"Yeah," Phylecia honestly replied. "Remember I told you I was into fashion designing and all of that. I wasn't lying about that!"

After a moment of consideration Boom finally said, "Fuck it, what's there to lose?" He called down to the front desk for a needle and thread. When it came, Phylecia got busy. She was careful and neat. When she was done, Boom looked in the mirror at the job she'd done. *Not bad,* he thought. Phylecia proved to be so much more help than Boom had ever thought. If she wasn't such a ditz, he could probably use her services. Oh well.

"How does it look, Sylvester?" she asked proud of her performance.

Boom looked over his shoulder at her and then back at himself in the mirror. "It looks good. I can't front; you know what you doin' wit a needle and thread."

Phylecia couldn't help showing how she happy she was that Boom had such endearing things to say about her. She was blushing, but that would change once Boom continued.

"But don't ever fuckin' call me Sylvester," he ordered. "My name is Boom."

★★★

From there they were off, on the road again. Boom had an unimaginable thirst to find out who this Russell Hynes guy was, and what their connection could possibly be.

He would know as soon as their eyes met what ways he could make him talk. He had enough experience with interrogation and torture methods, but he was actually getting a bit rusty. His most recent victims were giving up the information all too easily. They weren't giving him a chance to brush up on his skills, but it was all good as long as he was getting what he needed from them. He secretly hoped that Russell would be just a bit hesitant. As much as he wanted to know what the hell was goin' on, he also wanted to have some fun. This could serve as a celebration of sorts. That would lift his spirits. Besides the fact that Sabra was home safe, Winch and Patrice were where they were supposed to be. He felt like he was rounding third base about to hit home with this goose-chase he'd been on for the past few days. He'd find more corners once he found out about Mr. Hynes. Boom was in for the shock of his life.

CHAPTER 18

At Phylecia's direction, Boom drove through the back blocks of the Bronx to their destination. Each turn brought him that much closer to closure. Every stop sign or red light he caught only prolonged his anxiousness. It was obvious that he was fluttered with nervous energy about to burst from his body.

They weren't too far from where they needed to be now. As they got closer, the funniest thing started happening to Boom. A feeling of familiarity started getting stronger and stronger. He was definitely in a place where he'd been before. The only thing was that it was too long ago for him to remember.

When they turned onto Westchester Avenue, Boom wasn't even paying any attention to Phylecia's directions anymore. He knew where he was going. He made a left onto Jackson Avenue alongside of St. Mary's Park. Halfway into the long block, he turned on his right-turn signal. That's when Phylecia realized that Boom knew where he was going. Her surprise kept her silent as Boom navigated his own way through his childhood stomping grounds. When he got to the next corner, he made a right turn onto St. Mary's Street. He slowed down at the corner of Powers and St. Mary's and crept the rest of the way into the block. Just before he reached the next corner, he pulled over by a fire hydrant and put the car in park. Boom and Phylecia sat there for a few minutes not saying a word. They both remained quiet, trying to figure out what the hell had just happened.

"How'd you know where I live at?" Phylecia asked.

"I *don't* know where you live. I used to live here."

Phylecia was in disbelief. She couldn't quite get it yet. "Wait, what you sayin'? You used to live where?"

"Here. Right here!!"

Boom pointed to the third floor of the building where they were parked across the street. "That was my bedroom window."

Phylecia looked up at the window that Boom was referring to, and then she looked back at Boom. She did this once more before her head went blank. She still wasn't grasping the concept. "I don't understand. This ain't makin' no sense. Ummm...but that's where I...hmmm...and you used to live...naw, but that can't be right..."

Phylecia's rambling got as low as a whisper in Boom's ears, and then he just completely phased her out. What did this mean? What significance did this have? How was his past still connected to all of these things happening to him now?

"It was so long ago," he said to himself aloud. "What the fuck is goin' on???"

Without thought, Boom pulled his Glock to make sure his clip was full with a slug chambered. That's when Phylecia started to panic, and for good reason, too.

"But wait, you told me you wasn't gonna hurt him," she said. "You promised. He's just an old man. He can't do you any harm."

"Bitch, if you don't shut the fuck up, I'ma stick my foot knee-deep in ya ass!" Boom had enough of the games. He was ready to get down to business and his first directive was to reestablish authority. "Now if you play this shit right, maybe I won't have to throw you off of the roof of this muthafuckin' building! You hear me???"

Phylecia didn't respond right away so Boom gave her some incentive to go along with him. He placed the burner at her temple and repeated his question slowly, "Are we gonna have any problems? I will splatter you all over the inside of this car if you play with me!"

"No, we won't have any problems," Phylecia finally replied. "I promise...and you can trust *my* word!"

"You know what, fuck ya word!" Boom quickly responded to her sarcasm. "I don't give a fuck about words. You shouldn't be givin' a fuck about words either. Think about these bullets I got loaded in this here clip. Think about them cutting through you like a hot knife through butter. Think about that!"

He snatched the key out of the ignition and pulled the handle to open the door. He cracked the door and paused to ensure that she was doing the same. Phylecia was just sitting there pouting like a child. Boom was soft enough for long enough.

"Come on and get outta this car before I drag ya ass out!" he spat.

Phylecia had no choice but to obey. The same thought repeated over and over again in her mind as she exited the car. *What have I done?*

The walk across the street was devastating for Phylecia. She really thought that she was safe with Boom now that she'd come clean about the whole story. She was so naive. She didn't take into consideration all that he'd gone through since he left her in that bathroom tied to the toilet. How could she have known...so sad, so sad.

As soon as Boom walked into the front lobby, he was taken back to his childhood once again. It was almost making him lightheaded. There were so many memories here that he had long forgotten.

Everything was exactly how he remembered it. The paint was chipped. The brass mailboxes were dinged and in dire need of a good coat of polish. The fluorescent light on the wall above the mailboxes was dim and blinking. The air carried a scent of aged urine, and colorful graffiti tags decorated every wall. In the intercom door glass, he even pinpointed a tag he threw up himself. Scratched into the corner was the name: "Lil' Silly."

"Shit," he said to himself out loud. "This shit is unreal."

Phylecia took notice to Boom's apparent reminiscing and fought not to comment. Even with all that had happened she still found the want to delve into his deepest and most personal thoughts. Maybe she thought that if she and Boom connected in some way those feelings might hinder any harm he was planning for her and her uncle. On the other hand, maybe she was just stupid, either that or she thought that Boom was.

"Any good memories coming back to you from this place?" she asked.

Boom simply gave her a look like she was out of pocket. His lips got tighter and his eyes squinted. He was about to spit fire on her and make her sit that chin back in her chest, but he didn't. He contained the fire he had growing inside for the time-being.

"Let's go," he simply said.

Phlyecia led the way up three flights of stairs while Boom followed closely behind her with his burner in hand. When they got to the door, Boom stood to the side just in case someone checked the peephole. Then she knocked on the door for the first time. A few seconds passed without a response, so she knocked again. When there still was no response, Boom took it upon himself to pound on the door a few times to make sure.

"Fuck it, just open the door," he said.

"What you mean, *'just open the door'*?" Phylecia replied. "I ain't even got the key!"

Boom's eyes scanned Phylecia's. She didn't look him directly in the face. She would lift her head up to see if he was looking at her and then look away. Her arms slowly came down to her side and then around behind her. She looked like she didn't know what to do with herself. Her body language was contradicting the words that had actually come out of her mouth, and she was completely oblivious to it. She was hiding something.

"Listen, you can't possibly think that just 'cause this nigga ain't answerin' the door that I'd just call it a wrap and go the fuck home...did you??? I hope not, 'cause that ain't even close to what'll happen if you lyin' to me. If he ain't home and I gotta wait for him, then so be it. Whether it's inside the apartment or out here is fine by me. The only difference is if he roll up on me out here he's more likely to try somethin'. You know what that means, right? I'm gonna have to splatter that nigga ass all over this here muthafuckin' hall!"

Phylecia wanted to respond but she was hesitant. She didn't know what it would mean if Boom were to find out now that she was trying to deceive him. Then she asked herself, *What's worse than him just killing us both as soon as Uncle Russell gets here?* She couldn't think of the answer right then and there. If she had a train of thought like Boom did, she'd have thought of a hundred things that could be worse than dying a quick and painless death. Inside the confines of an enclosed space to maneuver, Boom could go at them for days without anyone knowing. Phylecia's somewhat untainted mind couldn't ponder such realities though. She hadn't experienced enough to predict those kinds of circumstances.

"Okay, okay," she said when her judgment finally took over. "Alright, Uncle Russell usually keeps a key under the welcome mat."

"You can't be fuckin' serious!" Boom replied in disbelief. "People actually do that shit??? That's gotta be the dumbest shit I ever heard!"

"Yeah, well I guess that's what he was hoping. Usually, people wouldn't think to look there because it's such a stupid thing to do. Besides, he wasn't dumb about it. He dug out one of the floor tiles to hide it under...see!"

Boom looked down at the floor below the welcome mat and nothing was there. It looked perfectly normal.

"You got a knife?" Phylecia asked.

In response, Boom simply flipped out the trusty blade that he'd recently put in so much work with. It was still covered in dried blood. Phylecia quickly regretted her request.

"Umm…here you can probably do it better than I can," she said. "It's that one right there."

Boom sucked his teeth at Phylecia's obvious uneasiness. "It's only blood," he said. "Fuck it, which one is it again?"

"That one." Phylecia pointed and moved out of his way. She didn't want the knife to even come near her.

Boom quickly knelt down in front of the door and began poking around the floor tiles to find the one that was loose. When he found it, he forced the knife under it and popped it out. Underneath was a key dug into the grout.

"Tricky little bastards," he said to himself. "Here." He handed the key to Phylecia. "Get it open and make it quick!"

A couple twists of the key later the door was open. As soon as the hinge squeaked as Phylecia eased it open, Boom drew his heat. Phylecia automatically got second thoughts and hesitated. She stopped at the door and didn't move. Then she started to slowly back out of the doorway. Her stomach was rumbling now and her heart rate sped up to a million beats a second. She started to breathe heavily and the feeling of Boom's barrel touching her back didn't help much. In the very least it halted the yelling she was about to start.

"Listen," Boom whispered in her ear. "If you play this shit right, it won't get messy. Now, just walk in slow and don't make a sound. You hear me?"

"Yes." She took a deep breath and started back into the apartment. Boom followed close enough behind her so that the feeling of his burner never escaped her thoughts.

On the other side of the door, immediately to the right as you walked in, was the entrance for the kitchen. Next to that was the entrance for the bathroom. Straight ahead was a hall that led to the living room and the two bedrooms. The windows in the living room and one of the bedrooms faced the front of the building. This would have been a great vantage point for Boom to keep a close eye to the street. That way he could see Mr. Hynes coming from a block away and prepare to welcome his arrival. By the time he saw him coming down the block, he could post up in the kitchen right next to the door to attack immediately upon his entrance. He could stash Phylecia in the bedroom furthest away from the door so that she couldn't send any warnings. Russell would be caught completely off guard. That shit would've been perfect. Unfortunately, Boom wasn't gonna get a chance to use any of these circumstances to his advantage.

"Walk slow and step lightly," Boom whispered to Phylecia. "If you fuck around, you gonna end up on the ten o'clock news. I guarantee it!"

His message was clear. Phylecia knew not to mess with him. There was already enough indication that Boom just wasn't the type of nigga you could play in no shape or form. He was too sharp. Even though Phylecia wasn't used to not having any control over a man, she was quickly getting used to it.

Boom followed Phylecia's every step. He stayed behind her ducked low. If anybody was waiting for him on the other end of that hall, they'd have to shoot through Phylecia first. He checked the kitchen as they passed, and there wasn't anything out of the ordinary. They walked a bit further and ended up at the door leading to the bathroom. Boom placed Phylecia in front of it and threw the door open…nobody there! The only thing that seemed a little weird was that the sink was running. The water was hot enough to slightly steam up the bathroom. Once Boom looked a little closer, he saw something that really made him thinkg something was wrong. There was what looked like blood smeared in some areas of the sink. Boom looked a bit closer and there was also blood on one of the hand towels that hung from the wall adjacent to the sink. That put Boom on point. Something wasn't right. He could feel it. They proceeded down the hall toward the living room with caution. Every step Boom took was on his heels to make the least amount of noise possible. Halfway down the hall Boom could almost get a good glimpse into the living room. He would have to approach from another angle to get a better look, but there was an old beaded curtain hanging from the doorway stopping him from seeing much of anything.

All of a sudden, while walking down that long hall, something caught Boom's attention from his peripheral vision. He immediately stopped to take another look. He was looking at a picture on the wall. He couldn't take his eyes off it. He froze. He couldn't even move his feet any further. He just stood there with his jaw dropped.

"What the fuck is goin' on?" he quietly asked himself.

In the picture that Boom couldn't take his eyes off of was Grace and Vester, his mother and father. They were so young and vibrant back then. They were so visibly pleased with life. It was obviously old, and it must've been taken when Boom was a kid. He was certain that it was them. Even though they were both sporting Afros and bell-bottom pants, those faces were unmistakable. Boom had no doubt in his mind.

Along with them was another familiar face in the picture. Boom couldn't quite remember where he knew the face, but he was sure he knew him. From how they were all hugged up in the picture, the guy must've been someone really close to the family. Boom studied him relentlessly. He was dead-set on figuring out who this strange character was. He immediately started looking at the other pictures that hung from the wall. He saw more pictures of this unknown person. He also saw some more of his parents and even saw a picture of himself hanging from the wall.

As Boom searched for more familiar images, he noticed something weird. There were empty spaces on the wall where the pictures once were. He could tell because of the discoloration of the wall. On the places where the pictures were removed, the wall was lighter. That's how long they must've been there. Years of soot and settling dust marked the spot on the wall where those frames should've been hanging. Apparently someone didn't want them to be there anymore.

Now the curiosity that had been stewing deep down inside of Boom's gut was multiplied by a hundred.

"Hurry up," he ordered Phylecia.

She didn't hesitate. She knew that anything could set Boom off at this point and didn't want to give him a reason to flip out.

When she finally got to the beaded curtain, she leaned in toward it slowly. She was trying to see if anyone was on the other side of the doorway. From where they were standing they could only see half of the living room. On the other side could've been twenty thugs with machine guns.

Fortunately, Phylecia couldn't see anything. Everything was just how it was supposed to be. So she pulled the curtain to one side and entered the living room. Boom came in pointing his gat in every direction he looked...nothing!

The living room had a throwback look. It was about directly on top of that line that separates rich antique furniture from old shit. It was definitely something right out of the eighties. The sofa and loveseat had wooden arms and legs. The cushions were decorated with fancy patterns but they didn't look like they were comfortable at all. In some areas you could even still see the old plastic that they were covered in still protecting whatever it could hold on to. There were matching nightstands and lamps, and this huge china set on the wall beside the bedroom doors. The furniture was positioned around the floor-model television that sat in front of the wall where the windows looked out to the street.

Boom directed with his hands for Phylecia to sit while he walked over to the window to check on his view of the street. As soon as he peeked out, the flashbacks started. He remembered looking out that window when he was a kid. He stared down at the block and remembered playing there. He remembered the winter days filled with snowball fights, and remembered the summer mornings when it was hot enough to pop the fire hydrant on to cool off in the nice cold water.

As his mind went back to all of those years, he started to feel like a completely different person. The killer that he'd grown to become couldn't have come from such a pleasant childhood. Hard times make hard people. He shouldn't have had to live the life he'd been leading. If only his father were there for him. His uncle was good for teaching him how to be tuff and defending himself, but he wasn't good for all of the other stuff. When it came to showing love and affection, that's where Black lacked ability. He taught Boom everything he needed to know about the streets and stopping at nothing to get your hustle on, but what he didn't know was that he had created a chiseled monster that found it difficult to express his feelings.

"I was happier here," Boom said. "I don't know *what* the fuck happened to me!"

"How much do you remember from back then?" Phylecia asked.

"Nothing until now," Boom replied honestly. "I ain't remember none of this shit before I came back here. It's like I just buried those memories of being a regular kid inside me...maybe to hide it like it was a weakness...maybe to protect it like untarnished treasure. For whatever reason, I made myself forget about all of this shit."

"So, it was just you, your mom and your dad?"

"Yeah."

"So then this must've been your room, right?" Phylecia said before jumping up to show Boom his old room. "OH MY GOD!!!" she cried. "OH GOD, NOOOO, NOOOO!!!"

Boom quickly reacted. He flew over to where Phylecia was standing. She paused in the doorway of her bedroom, hopelessly staring at the most horrific image she had ever seen in her life. When Boom got to the door, he pushed her to the side and came in with his gun drawn. When his eyes were finally exposed to the vision, he realized that his burner wouldn't be doing him any good. All Boom could see was blood splattered all over the place. It was on the walls; it was all over the carpet. It was on the windows. Most of all it was on the bed where Russell Hynes was laid out with his neck slit from ear to ear.

"Oh shit!!!" Boom said. "What the fuck???"

He was lying there with a shocked look like he was woken from a sound sleep to the feeling of someone slicing him to shreds. With his head pointed straight up, eyes bulging and mouth wide open, he looked like he had to have died a horrible death. He had multiple stab wounds throughout his chest and stomach. He may have put up a fight but must've been overpowered. He was simply too weak. His bones held almost no weight. He had dark bags under his eyes and burned fingertips. His habits were evident.

"Wait, hold on," Boom said, now studying his face a bit longer. "Could it be?"

Boom was realizing that he was the mysterious face in the pictures. He didn't recognize who it was because he had so much more weight on him. He had to have dropped a good two hundred pounds since those pictures were taken. Now he could tell where he knew him from. Russell Hynes was one of his father's oldest friends. He was the one who had gotten up to speak at his wake. He was the one who sang "It's So Hard" for him. Most memorably, he was the only one who shielded Boom from the devastating events that occurred that day. While everyone else disregarded the ceremony, Russell was the one who knew this wasn't the time or the place for what was about to happen. He figured the best thing to do was to protect innocent little Sylvester from harm. Boom remembered now with great detail how caring he was to him. He remembered how endearing and sincere he was. This wasn't a man who would pimp a family member just to make a buck. Boom had a difficult time putting these two completely different entities together. But when you thought about how powerful crack was in the eighties, you had to imagine that anything was possible. Muthafuckas would've done whatever to secure that next hit, and manipulating your niece to sell her body for money fell into the category of doable shit. It was just as simple as that. Maybe by the time he realized how low he'd sunk it was too late. Maybe he was so blinded by the smoke that he couldn't even see that it was wrong. Whatever the case, Russell had fell hard since the memories of him that Boom could recall.

"I know him," said Boom. "I remember this nigga from my dad's wake. He's your uncle? He's the one that sent you after me???"

The sound of Boom's voice brought Phylecia out of her somewhat catatonic state. She was curled up on the floor in the corner hysterically crying, until she stopped. She heard Boom's voice and looked up at him with big glossy brown eyes. Her facial expression changed from hopelessness to rage. Her leg was twitching with nervous energy. She was like a volcano about to erupt.

Boom didn't even know that Phylecia was in the corner boiling, ready to explode. All he did was stare in amazement. He didn't even blink; that's how hard he was gazing at Russell, or what was left of him. When he finally blinked, it was like a bunch of flashing red lights in his face. His mind was moving now. His brain was processing a million thoughts a second. He started to search the room for clues. He needed to move fast if he was gonna find anything because he didn't really know how long ago this shit had actually happened. What if the muthafucka that killed him just left? What if they were in here rumbling around and someone already called the police to report it? He knew he had to get the fuck outta here, but he couldn't leave empty-handed. From the look of the room, it wasn't a robbery situation. It didn't look like there was anything worth stealing; it also appeared that no one had tried to search for anything. Besides a few things that appeared like they were thrown around during the fight, the room didn't seem too ransacked. That's when Boom came to the realization that Russell must've known his murderer. There was little tampering, and the door wasn't broken in to. It was actually locked. That made all the difference in the world. His killer must've had a key, or knew where he kept the spare.

Boom looked a bit deeper and saw there was a cell phone on the floor beside the nightstand. He figured there could be some valuable information in there. He made sure not to step in the areas of the floor that were soaked with blood. When he got the phone, he immediately looked for the most recent calls. He absolutely couldn't believe what he saw when the first number popped up.

"OH MY FUCKIN' GOD!!!"

CHAPTER 19

Boom was about to leave, and then he got another surprise. He turned around to find that Phylecia was gone.

"What the fuck?" he blurted aloud. "Fuck this shit! I'm getting' outta here!"

Boom didn't have time to bullshit anymore. He could only think one thought over and over again. *This shit ends tonight!*

He was halfway to the door when he finally found Phylecia. She caught him by surprise. She came out of the kitchen walking directly toward him. Her body language was stiff and quick. She had her head down but her eyes were pointed directly up at Boom. She looked like she had something hidden behind her back. She looked really focused; almost to the point that it was scary. Boom hadn't seen this expression on her face before. By the time he realized he was the target, it was too late.

Phylecia rushed his stance and revealed the butcher knife she was holding. As soon as she got in arm's distance of Boom, she started swinging wildly. The first slice caught his left shoulder and tore through his sweater and carved a nice-size gash in his skin. That's when Boom jumped back. He was on guard now but Phylecia didn't waste any time before she approached for another attack.

"It's all your fault!!!" she yelled as she swung the knife again. "You did this!!!"

Boom was in a difficult situation. He didn't want to hurt her, but she wasn't letting up enough for him to calm her down. He could understand her frustration, but she had to know that he wasn't the one who had done this to her uncle.

"Whoa!" Boom said as he weaved another slice just in the nick of time. He was still backing up to get out of her swinging range but she kept on charging. "Be easy, Phylecia. I ain't the one that did this. You know I ain't do this shit so just chill out! We need to get the fuck outta here!!!"

"Noooooo!" Phylecia was only fueled by Boom's reluctance to admit his responsibility in the situation. Even if he wasn't the one who dug that knife into Russell, he was the one responsible. These two situations could not be coincidental. They were connected somehow, and the only connection Phylecia could see was the man standing before her. She swung again, and again, and again.

Boom was weaving through her attacks but not by much. He wasn't that fast. It wasn't until she caught him with another slice on his forearm as he threw it up to defend his neck. That's when Boom retaliated. He waited for an opening and threw a quick left jab and followed up with a right hook. The punches threw her head back but that's it. They didn't slow her down one bit. She was still coming straight for Boom at full speed.

Finally, they collided. Boom grabbed onto her arm as she attempted a downward chop. He held on and didn't let go, but she kept coming forward. By now they had reached the living room. As Boom backed up blindly, he was tripped by the arm of the sofa. He fell backwards and took Phylecia with him. They hit the couch and then rolled over onto the floor. Phylecia was on top of Boom with the blade lifted into the air about ready to bring it down into his chest. Boom acted quickly. He lifted her with both arms and legs and managed to throw her from on top of him. She flew to the left toward the huge china set that was up against the wall. Upon impact, shattered glass flew through the air in every direction. She hit the floor with a thump as tiny pieces of glass rained down on her. She was in a daze now. She almost didn't even know where she was. But she still kept the knife tightly in her clutches. It took her a second, but she managed to shake it off. By the time she was coming back to her senses, Boom had already gotten back to his feet and had his burner pulled and pointed.

"Phylecia, you need to calm the fuck down!" he yelled in an attempt to get through to her. "You ain't helpin' shit! He's gone now and he ain't comin' back. Forcin' me to kill you won't help, I'm tellin' you. You hear me, Phylecia??? I don't wanna do something I'm gonna regret."

"Aaaahhhh!!!!" Phylecia yelled at the top of her lungs before jumping to her feet and launching herself in Boom's direction.

"NO!" Boom cried. He was giving her one last chance. He would be forced to shoot. "STOP...DON'T!!!"

All Phylecia got a chance to do was lift the blade into the air to get ready to swing, and then...*BOOM!!!*

The bullet went into her body dead center of her chest and halted her advance. She looked up at him like she had just awoken from a nightmare. She had finally come back to her senses, but now it was too late. She checked her chest and put her hand over the hole. When she saw her hand, it was covered in her own blood. She looked back up at Boom. The knife finally loosened from her grip and dropped to the ground. She dropped next. She fell to one side in the middle of the living room.

Boom looked into her dead eyes and recognized the look all too well. He took a deep breath. *"Damn!!!"* he roared. *"SHIT!!!"* He didn't wanna kill her but she left him no choice. There was nothing else he could do. He tried his best to avoid this. What happened to her uncle may have been because of him but it wasn't his fault. Had he realized who he was, chances are Boom would've let him live once he found out what he needed to know. He wouldn't have been able to kill him. He would've left and that would've been that...case closed, end of story. The muthafucka responsible for all of this shit would suffer enough for everybody. That was for damn sure.

For a while Boom simply stood. He was stared at the wall like he didn't know what to do. He was stuck, unable to budge from that position. His eyes welled up with tears and he could feel himself about to break. That's when he heard the sirens sounding in the distance.

"Oh shit!"

Probably someone did call for the rumbling that was going on when Russell got murdered. Boom knew that it was impossible for them to respond so quickly to the shot he had just fired.

In any case, he didn't have time to think about it. He dipped out the front door, taking a picture off the wall with him as he dashed. Boom could already hear the walkie-talkies in the lobby downstairs so he had to think quickly on his toes. Instead of running down the three flights of stairs to run right into the police, he went up. The building was only four flights high. He ran all the way up to the roof. Luckily the door that led out onto the roof didn't have an alarm. He kicked it open and ran to the front to see how much of a shit-storm he was in for. He could see a marked car parked in front of the building and three more coming from both directions.

"Goddamn!!!" he spat. "What the fuck now?"

He looked to the left. He looked to the right. Then he saw his exit strategy and took off running toward the left edge of the roof where there was another building right next to it. When he got to the edge there was a fence separating this roof from the roof of the building next to it. He climbed the fence without a problem and threw himself over to the other side. From there he went straight for the door that led to the stairs. He flew down whole flights of stairs in single leaps. By the time he got to the second floor he slowed down. He walked down the remainder of the steps with ease, confident that he made a large enough margin between him and the police. They would be right next door when he exited the building so he couldn't look like he was running a damn marathon. That would've defeated the purpose.

As Boom expected, there were still officers outside of the building next door when he reached the sidewalk. He made sure to walk past them like he could care less that they were there. On his way to his car, he overheard a couple of them speaking and that gave him a better idea of the sudden urgency.

"Yeah, we got the domestic dispute call first," said Officer Moore to the other officers on the scene.

"All I heard was *'shots fired'* come over the airwaves from the same location!" another officer added. "Shit, I put the pedal to the metal!"

"Same here," another officer responded. "I thought you guys were engaged."

"Fuck," blurted Officer Hargrove. "Then we could've had some real fun!"

"Yeah!" they all agreed and shared a healthy laugh.

"So how long before Homicide gets here?"

"Shit, your guess is good as mine!" They all started laughing as loud as they could again. They didn't even notice Boom walking right past them. New York's finest strike again!

After escaping the clutches of the law, Boom felt like he was untouchable. That added to the piece of the puzzle that he'd discovered in Russell's place gave a strong sense of accomplishment. He knew exactly where he needed to go.

Just before hopping back in his car Boom took a peek at his wristwatch. It was just a little past three o'clock.

"Should be there by sundown," he told himself. "Just gotta hurry."

FINAL CHAPTER

It was around seven when Black got home from the pub. The sun was almost gone. Soon the moon would light the night's sky, a full moon at that. It should be a beautiful night. On nights like this Black liked to go out into his big back yard and sit under the stars. He could kick back in a lawn chair for hours staring into the sky. All he needed was maybe a nice cigar and a glass of cognac. He'd be good.

Only tonight, he wasn't thinking of the stars. He had other things on his mind. When he got like this he was hard to even talk to because he was so oblivious to the world around him. He couldn't concentrate long enough to carry a conversation, let alone admire the way the bright stars accentuated the night. The only thing that Black needed at times like these was booze...lots of it! He'd bury all of his problems in the bottom of a bottle of scotch and drink the pain away.

Black had just gotten home from a long stressful trip. He stopped at the pub around the corner from his house on the way home. He told himself that he was only going to have a drink, maybe two. Yet here he was, eight double scotches later, piss drunk and stumbling all over the place.

He put his key in the lock to find that the door was already open. Without even giving it a second thought, he pushed the door open and went in. He locked the door behind him and then started to get undressed. He started by taking his hat off and carelessly tossing it into the air. He didn't care where it landed but it managed to find a space on the dining room table. That's when he smelled something that caught his attention. There was a hint of smoke in the air like something was burning. Black squinted his eyes to try and see in the dark room, but the room still shaking kinda threw him off. That's when he saw a small light coming from the area of the couch. It was all he was able to see at that point. That's when the light moved. It went up about a foot or two and got brighter, and then it went back down. Black thought he was going crazy for a second. Finally he got to the lamp and flipped the lights on.

"Sylvester?" he mumbled. "That you?"

"Yeah, it's me, Unc'," Boom replied as he blew smoke into the air. "Surprised to see me?"

"Naw. I mean, well yeah…but you know you ain't supposed to be up in here smokin' them stankin'-ass cigarettes though! It ain't been that long, lil' nigga. The rules ain't changed!"

Boom simply replied with a giggle. "Hmm," he said before taking another long drag from his Newport and blowing the smoke in the air.

"You don't hear me talkin' to you, youngster???" Black yelled as he approached Boom to speak to him face to face. "I look like I should be taken for jokes???" Black could hardly hold the tone before his head started hurting and he started coughing uncontrollably. He was obviously regretting even raising his voice to begin with.

"Take it easy, Unc'. Maybe the *rules* ain't change…but shit definitely ain't like it used to be. At least not in my eyes."

Boom reached into his back pocket. When he pulled out what he had he simply tossed it onto the coffee table. It was the picture he got off of Russell's wall. In the picture was Boom's mom and dad alongside Russell hugging and looking as happy as they wanted to be.

"Or maybe shit ain't change," Boom added. "Maybe you've always been a deceitful, manipulative, back-stabber!"

Black looked down at the picture. He couldn't take his eyes off of it for what seemed like hours. He didn't even blink.

"Where did you get that?" he asked, his voice cracking like he was about to burst into tears. He took the photo in his hands and cradled it like it was a child that needed to be handled with care. He rubbed the glass free of dust and smiled.

"You know where I got it from. You were there before I was. You took the pictures you wanted. You left this one behind. Why is that? Would it hurt too much to look them in their faces and realize how happy they were…before you fucked it all up!!!"

"What are you talking about?" Black asked like he hadn't a clue what Boom meant by the harsh accusations he was throwing around.

"Don't play me, Unc'. You had me fooled long enough. That shit is over!"

"I don't know what the hell you're talking about!!!" he yelled as his eyes welled.

Boom took a good look into Black's eyes. He was almost convincing, but Boom knew better. He wasn't about to be taken again. He refused.

"I already know what happened," Boom stated. "I just wanted to hear it come right from your mouth."

Black didn't respond. He simply stared down at the photo with loving eyes. All Boom could do was sit there watching Black for signs of dishonesty. He saw none. Either Black's lying skills were just that on point, or he was telling the truth. Nah, no way could he be telling the truth. He definitely had something to do with all that was going on. It was the only thing that made sense. Boom couldn't have hit another brick wall. He wouldn't know what to do with himself if he did.

The first sound that came out of Black after minutes of silence was a sniffle. He hesitated at first, but he had a question that he wanted to ask Boom. Everything inside of him told him that he shouldn't have had to ask the question at all. He didn't want to but he had to nonetheless.

"Are you trying to ask me if I had something to do with their murder?" he finally asked. A single tear dropped from his eye that brought on a waterfall of tears. "Is that what this is all about?"

Boom swallowed a huge lump in his throat. He'd never seen Black let go of so much emotion. He was so used to him being so calm, collected, and in control of shit. He almost didn't want to answer. What if he wasn't ready for how Black would respond to his answer? He had come so far. He already lost too much. If this was how it had to go down, then so-fuckin'-be it! "Yeah," he said with assurance. "That's *exactly* what I'm sayin'!"

Black looked up at Boom and their eyes locked. He was still holding back more tears but he lifted his chin with confidence. He cleared his throat before he responded to make certain his voice didn't crack again. Then he plainly said, "Get the fuck outta my house...NOW!!! You done lost it, kid. All of this mess with that little girl has your head spinnin' or somethin'. You need some time to chill out and get your fuckin' head straight! That don't happen, God help me, I'll straighten you right the fuck out myself!"

Boom's lip curled to one side. Never once had he ever let someone speak to him like that. Black had never even used those kind of words directed toward him before. He was boiling. His mind was going into autopilot and he didn't even realize it. His hand was inches from his burner. It wouldn't be a thing to get to it and blow a couple of shots off before Black even knew what hit him. It was that simple.

Then Boom thought reasonably about whom it was he was considering murdering, and why. Could he be so reckless? "What the fuck am I thinking?" he asked himself. He stood up. His and Black's eyes never disengaged. Then he put his head down. He stuck his hands in his pockets and started toward the door. He took his steps short and slow while he fumbled through his pockets in haste.

Just as Boom was about to reach the door, Black's cell phone started to ring. He ignored it at first, but the sheer relentlessness of the caller finally made him reach for the inside pocket of his blazer. He wiped the tears from his eyes and looked at the name in the phone. He absolutely couldn't believe what he was seeing.

"What's wrong?" Boom asked with his back still turned to Black. "Ain't you gonna answer that?"

Black looked up as Boom was turning around. Black could see the fire in Boom's eyes as he stared at him, but what he didn't see right away was that he had his gun in one hand and Russell's cell phone in the other.

"Who's that, an old friend?" Boom asked as he lifted the cell phone up in front of him to make sure that Black could see it.

Black's facial expression illustrated his fret. It was evident in the nonstop movement of his eyes that he was calculating every possible exit strategy to the predicament that he found himself in. He didn't know what else to do at this point. He did what came naturally.

When Boom saw Black reaching for the inside of his coat where he kept his pistol, he reacted quicker. He didn't even lift the toast to take aim. He blasted from his hip...*BOOM!* He let a shot go from his Glock that halted Black's advance. The bullet made its entrance through Black's right forearm to stop him from getting to his heat. It exited through the other side of his arm and entered his chest just below his right shoulder. The impact of the slug sent him flying backwards. He was unable to move.

"You put that muthafucka Russell and his little whore niece on me, didn't you???" Boom yelled as he walked toward Black with his weapon drawn and pointed. "They were just supposed to keep tabs on me, right!!! It wasn't until you realized that I was still getting closer and closer to finding out the truth about what happened to my parents that you went ahead and snatched up Sabra to bring me back home. You even used Russell down at the school as the diversion you needed to scoop her up without any witnesses!!! You knew no way could you have a local fiend do that shit without me ever finding out! You thought I had learned my lesson, huh??? DIDN'T YOU??? No fuckin' way would I go back up there and leave them exposed like that again!!! You didn't take into consideration that I just might've assumed that Winch had something to do with her disappearance, 'cause of how close I was on his ass. You ain't think I would connect that shit up and take that muthafucka's head off!!! AM I RIGHT SO FAR???"

Black gave no response. He was unable to. He was in too much pain.

Boom continued in a lower, more menacing one, "So as soon as you find out where I was, you flip out...think about it...then drop a line to your old pal, Russell. Perhaps he tells you that he ain't seen or heard from his niece in over a day. You figured she must've fucked up...she blew her cover. You knew it was only a matter of time before I could get to the one person that could connect you to all of this. So what do you do? You get there before me and off that nigga. You even leave his crib with the pictures on the wall that had you in them. You thought of everything, didn't you?"

Black still bit his tongue. He stared down the barrel of Boom's Glock...anticipating the flaming bullet to fly at him with fierce relentlessness.

"You didn't cover your trail well enough though, *Unc'!*" Boom continued. "I ain't the brightest nigga in the world, but I ain't the dumbest neither. I let you play me long enough! Only thing I don't understand is why...why'd you murder my father???"

It was silent for what seemed like forever after Boom finally asked the question that had been bothering him since that flashback at Ivan's wake. This was the hunger that drove him harder and harder these past days. It was all he could think about. He went to bed with the question on his mind and woke up with it being the first thought in his head...*Why was my father murdered?*

Boom's eyes were bloodshot red by now and glossy. A second after he asked the question tears started finding their way from his eyes down his face. He sniffled and wiped the tears with his free hand while he kept his cannon pointed directly at Black's skull. He was damn near ready to pull the trigger prematurely, and then Black finally let out a response.

"I loved her," he said. "I loved her with all my heart. I was just silly with love for that woman, Boom." Black was smiling thinking about Grace, and he didn't even know it. He couldn't even stop himself from grinning ear to ear as he cried. "Let me tell you somethin' about your mother, boy," he continued. "She could walk into a room and it would be all eyes on her. She lit the place up. She just had a way about her. It was like her aura was felt from across the room. She had a strong presence. I loved everything about her...even you, Sylvester. You were her creation, and for that I wanted you to be *my* son. I wanted *us* to be a family.

"And she loved me, too," Black continued.

He had Boom's undivided attention now. He was watching with fierce absorption. The moment Black made the suggestion that his mother was somewhat at fault for what happened his blood began to boil. It was only a matter of time now before he just flipped out completely if Black didn't watch what he said.

"She never told me flat-out but I could tell. I wasn't the only one either. Your father could tell, too. It was probably his fault in a way...he always idolized me. In his eyes I was a superhero. He painted the picture of a man that Grace could see herself getting swept off of her feet by. That drew us together. It drew closer and closer until the unimaginable happened. It was while your father was away doing that brief stretch up in the pen. She was all down about the shit and I was there to console her...you know, for support...to keep her strong. One thing led to another and..."

"Stop that shit right there, you piece of shit!" Boom yelled. "You mean to tell me that while my father was away doing a bid for a crime you committed, you moved in on my mother?"

"I couldn't control it, Sylvester," he replied in his own defense. "Besides, that was a long time ago...before you were born. It just happened and that was it! It only happened that one time, and we never spoke about it ever again. That was all it took anyway. The damage was already done. Anyway, a few weeks later Vester was back home. Then, all of a sudden, Grace was knocked up with you. I knew then that we would never be together. They got married and I supported them every step of the way."

"Even if what you're saying is true, what does that have to do with my father's death?"

"I was getting to that," Black replied with hesitation. His voice dropped a few octaves as he tried with all of his heart to get the rest of the story out. It was getting more and more difficult though. "The day he died was the day the truth came out."

"How did he find out?"

"I told him."

"Why am I not surprised? I should just kill you now, you pig!" Boom placed his burner between Black's eyes. His hand was shaking and his finger was twitching on the trigger. Something was stopping him from pulling it though. The want was still there for Black to finish the story. Boom gave him just enough time to deliver the kicker.

"I only told him because of what your mother told me, Sylvester," Black explained. "The truth had been eating out her insides for long enough. She wanted me to know the truth...the truth about you, Sylvester...the truth about us."

"What the fuck are you tryin' to say???"

"You know what I'm trying to say. You just don't wanna admit it. Maybe it's because you've dedicated so much time to trying to find out who killed your father...when your father isn't even dead! Don't you understand??? Vester's not your dad! Your mother was already pregnant when he got out of jail! She just never admitted it until then!"

"WHAT???" Boom cried. "YOU A DAMN LIE!!!"

"Believe what you want, lil' nigga!" Black darted back at Boom. "It is what it is. If you can't be proud to call me your father, then I don't want you as my boy! But no matter how we end up after today, that's still my blood you got runnin' through them veins."

Boom was so in a daze that he slowly released Black from his clutches and lowered the weapon. He sat down on the couch beside him. His face was blank. He was staring off at the wall in disbelief. He was shocked at first, then depression took over his emotions. That's when denial set in. He was completely rejecting the whole notion that Black had been his father the whole time, and he never once even tried to tell him.

"Why didn't you ever tell me?" he asked without even realizing that he had spoken a word.

"I didn't wanna taint the memories you had of your mom. The last thing I wanted to do was ruin your memories of such a wonderful woman. I could go without having you call me dad. I was only concerned with the bigger picture. You didn't need to know that Vester wasn't your pop."

"But...why'd you kill him?"

"It wasn't my fault, Sylvester," Black replied as he sat straight up in the couch. "He blacked out on me. He started yelling like he was crazy and acting all erratic and whatnot. He ran up on me, and we fought for a little, until he got hold of a kitchen knife. I ain't know *what* to do. He was so relentless with that carver, boy. I ain't never seen that look in his face. He kept swinging it at me and I couldn't do shit to stop him. I caught a few slices before we started rolling around on the damn floor, fighting for the blade. And just like that, he got stuck. That's when he stopped fighting. There was blood everywhere, all over the place. I didn't know what to do. I panicked. So I made it look like it was somebody settling a score. What I told you about Vester and Patrice was true...except for the part that they might've still been seeing each other. I knew otherwise. In any case it only helped the look of it all. I knew Winchester was good with a carver, so I did what I had to do."

"Oh, so that wasn't one of your 'black-tie affair' signature killings?" Boom could hardly get the sentence out before his eyes welled.

"Hmm." Black couldn't help but let out a chuckle. He was surprised at how much intel Boom had actually collected. In some weird way, it made him proud because Boom was a product of his influence. It just so happened that all the work he'd put into making Boom a street-smart, stone-cold killer had come back to bite him in the ass. He'd created a monster. "I see you've been talkin' to Carl, or Winch, or whatever the fuck his name is. That was a long time ago though, son. My murder-for-hire days have long gone."

"You know you're a piece of shit, right?" Boom said while tears rained from his eyes. "You better know that shit, muthafucka! You know what you put me through? Do you know how much better my life could've been??? I thought I was your godchild."

"I thought I was helping you...and your mom, Sylvester! I didn't mean to..."

"BULLSHIT!!!" Boom said, slicing into Black's sentence. "That's bullshit! You weren't helping us. You were helping yourself. Helping yourself to my mother, that's what you were doing."

"BUT I LOVED HER!!!" Black cried. "What was I supposed to do?"

"You only love yourself!"

"That ain't true and you know it!"

"But she was your best friend's wife."

"Sylvester, I'll just tell you like this since this may be the last bit of advice I ever give you…ain't no fuckin' friends when it comes to women like her!"

"You a fuckin' crab," Boom stated with disgust. "You make me sick!"

"Oh, is that right?" Black replied, now going to the offensive. "So you probably think you better than me, don't you? You gon' just sit there and judge me? How dare you. You have no right…especially with the way you and old girl gettin' all chummy so soon after ya boy's untimely passing."

"WHAT???" Boom yelled at the top of his lungs. He couldn't believe what Black had just said. "You think I'm like you??? That's where you wrong, nigga! I ain't like you, not in the least bit. My main concern is my family, not myself! You just a selfish, pathetic, lonely piece of shit! I'll never be like you!"

"Oh yeah?" Black responded with a smirk creeping out of his facial expression. "You're more me than you know it, *playboy*. You used to be a scared little punk. I made you the man you are today. Everything you know is because of me. Every day of your life that goes by you owe to me!!! There ain't no one else, Boom. I'm all you got! Without me, you'd just be a crumbled-up piece of trash in a landfill…just like your so-called dad!"

"You the one gon' end up in a landfill, you keep runnin' off at the gipper!" Boom got up from the couch and stood before Black. He looked down at the man he'd grown to love more than anything else in the world. He was sickened by the thought that he was his father.

"Kill me if you want, boy. I ain't got nothin' else to live for. But you might need me alive."

"Why the fuck would I need you alive? When are you gonna get it through ya fuckin' head that I don't need you for shit??? I never have, and I never will!"

"That's right, you so smart, huh? Did you go off and kill Winchester before you got a chance to get all the details. I taught you better than that, didn't I? He ain't tell you why Patrice wasn't locked up; why she ain't spend the rest of her natural life behind bars?"

Boom didn't respond right away. He had given that some thought, especially because of how shifty Winch sounded when they spoke. His curiosity was getting the best of him now.

"What the fuck you talkin' about?"

"Just think about it. You don't get life in prison for attempted murder."

"What are you tryin' to say?"

"I know where she is, Sylvester. Me and me only. I can take you to her."

"You lyin' little piece of shit!!!" Boom cried as he placed his burner back between Black's eyes. "STOP FUCKIN' WIT MY HEAD!!!"

"She never died that day! She's still alive! It's the truth, I'm not…"

BOOM!!! The sound of the last shot being let go from his clip echoed nonstop. It sounded like a cannon ball was blown through the wall. Even after the shot went off the sound kept playing over and over in the room.

"Oh shit!" Boom murmured jumping backwards as blood splattered all over him. He couldn't even open his eyes; his whole face was covered with Black's blood and bits of his flesh. He started having shortness of breath. When he finally got his breath back, that's when all of the sound returned. He was looking left to right hysterically and hyperventilating. "What did I do?"

He couldn't believe he pulled the trigger. It was almost involuntary. He didn't even have control over himself. It was like he didn't want Black to finish saying what he had to say. He just blacked out.

Now what? If what Black was saying was true, then his path couldn't end here. He couldn't continue with his life the way he was. If there was a possibility that his mother was somewhere out there, he'd have to reevaluate his priorities yet again. Besides taking care of his inherited family and looking toward the future, he'd have to follow the paths that he was shown to fully resolve his issues with his past. If that meant that he'd have to turn the whole goddamn city upside-fuckin'-down, that's just what he'd do.

★★★

As Boom sat there with his back up against the wall, he gazed out of the window. He could see the moon peeking from the clouds from right there and that calmed him. It made him think about Shonda and Sabra. His promise was kept and everything was fine. That was where he found his tranquility, as crazy as it seemed. With all that had happened to Boom in the last week, he could sit there…and breathe easy. He wasn't on the warpath anymore, or at least for that minute, he didn't feel like it. Tomorrow was another day. Who knows, maybe this was just the beginning…or maybe it *was* just…

THE END

AUTHOR BIO

Michael Baptiste, born April 23, 1980 in the Bronx, New York, discovered his love for writing while he attended Evander Childs High School. At the age of sixteen, Michael's heart was not in his schoolwork and he would seldom attend class. He probably spent more time in the school's halls than in the classrooms. With the exception of art, he later found that writing was the only subject in which his attention could be held for more than a few seconds at a time.

Growing up in the BX during the Hip-Hop age drew Michael into rap music, and this is probably where his hunger to become a wordsmith was born. Add to that the fact that he was reading authors that were greatly praised and critically acclaimed. His detail-oriented style of writing is influenced heavily by Dean Koontz. Donald Goines' work let him know that he could write tales that he himself could relate to, in turn making his impact on the urban fiction genre that much more powerful. These novelists gave him a window into the world of writing...true writing. The urge to create vivid images with incredible detail grew stronger and stronger inside of him.

Michael finally had the chance to let all of his skills be shown when his writing teacher issued an assignment to scribe a graphic composition about your location of choice, and the things that go on in that particular place. Michael could've chosen anyplace in the world, but he chose what he had grown to know best...the streets! In this tale, which Michael wrote in only a few minutes when pressured with a deadline that had come before he knew it, he told the story about a young man that wanted out of the drug game. It would become the first version of his first published novel, *Cracked Dreams*, when it was simply called "A Drug Dealer's Dream." He got an "A" on the paper, and the rest was history!

Now that Michael is a published author, he can tap into a life he left behind to create the life he always wanted for himself in the future. The fact that he is rewarded for merely doing what comes natural is enough for him to keep writing realistic and relatable crime stories for the rest of his days. He hasn't even begun to reach his full potential, and this is demonstrated in the growth and maturity from his first publication to his second. Hopefully, he can stay on the right path and there's no telling how far he can take his writing career. This is only the beginning!

A producer and freehand artist, *Godchild* is Michael's sophomore release following his bestselling first novel, *Cracked Dreams*. Please visit Michael Baptiste at www.OnlyMike.com to learn more, or email him at mbaptiste@onlymike.com with your thoughts and questions...and yes, he does answer all of his emails!

EXCERPT FROM

CRACKED DREAMS

BY MICHAEL BAPTISTE

STREBOR BOOKS

My heart stopped. I couldn't even breathe. It didn't hit me until I looked up at Ginger, and she had tears in her eyes. She thought I knew. I couldn't contain myself any longer. Once Ginger looked up at me, I saw the pain that she felt for me and for Pop and for Trigger. As tears began forming in my eyes, I quickly buried the emotions deep inside me as Trigger continued telling me the story.

"He came to pick me up early yesterday morning. The night before had been real good for our spot on 219th. Shit was moving like water. We thought it would be best to keep it fully stocked. So that morning we cut up half a brick to re-up the spot with. On our way out, we weren't even halfway out of the door before the police rushed us. When I saw them approaching, I went to shut the door, but they beat me to the drop. Pop had already run back upstairs for the Mac-10. Like eight of those pigs went upstairs after Pop, and as soon as the first one hit the top step, the shots started. They had me pinned down at the bottom of the stairs when I screamed to him to that we were caught. All I could hear was the rattle of the shots being let off from the Mac, one after the other, while Pop screamed like a maniac."

"What happened next?" I spat into the phone in suspense.

"He took out like six of those mu'fuckas before they got him. He gave it to five of them upstairs, and then he got away from them to come back toward the stairs where they had me pinned down. He hit one of the dudes holdin' me down in the head twice before another cop caught up to him from behind. Yo, I saw his brains hit the fuckin' wall, my nigga. He went out like a straight-up gangsta though, dog. After I saw that shit, it took five more of them to hold me down. Then when they finally got me to the precinct, those punk mu'-fuckas beat the shit out of me for what seemed like forever, I guess for they partners, and shit."

"Yo, I'm gonna get you out of there, son. I got you, don't even worry about it. I got you," I said with redness in my eyes. I wasn't playing one bit neither. Whatever it took, I was going to get my man out of there.

I reassured Trigger that I would hold him down like steel. He, in turn, reassured me that police wouldn't be waiting for me when I got back to the Bronx. I should have known that he wasn't a rat, especially as long as we'd known each other, but sometimes you have to put your brain before your heart. Besides, I didn't even know who snitched to begin with. How the fuck did they know about our little organization anyway?

Seeing the stress in my face as I sat there with my head in my lap, Ginger came over to me in an attempt to comfort me. She stood up in front of me and began rubbing my shoulders. When I looked up at her, she wiped the tears from her eyes, kissed my forehead, and got on her knees in front of me resting my head on her shoulders. Just the feeling of her soft, warm body up against mine as we hugged immediately made me feel much better. She then began kissing my neck passionately, and then unbuttoned my shirt kissing my chest with more intensity. In seconds, my shirt was off, and she slowly started to undo my pants while she gently kissed down to my stomach. Before my pants were even all the way off, I had already grown to the extent of my erection as the anticipation grew. Once I was completely naked, she looked at me and smiled as she stroked my fully enlarged penis with both hands. Without her even breaking eye contact, I watched myself disappear into her mouth. It felt like I was in heaven as she motioned up and down, but unfortunately I couldn't stay in this heavenly place for much longer before I would explode. I soon felt myself ready to ejaculate, so I lifted her head back up and began kissing her deeply. I took her in my arms and carried her upstairs to her bedroom where we would continue what she started.

As I laid her down on the bed, I removed all of her clothes slowly. When she was completely nude, I began caressing her breasts and kissing them softly. Soon, she was pushing my head further down her torso until I was between her legs. I began tenderly kissing her inner thigh, and slowly moving inward. When I reached her clitoris, I teased it with the tip of my tongue making her jerk and moan until she begged me to stop so she would not cum prematurely. Laying me flat on my back, she mounted my throbbing penis, and inserted me inside of her moaning more and more as I sunk deeper and deeper.

"Cum for me, daddy," she said with the sexiest, most sensual voice I could imagine. That's all it took. Within seconds I was ready to explode. The intensity grew with every movement. I felt a rippling wave flow through my body as I began to erupt. With her hands clenched into my chest, her grip grew tighter and tighter as she came right along with me. When we were both through, she laid her head on my chest, and fell asleep to the sound of my heartbeat.

All over again, my mind started to race as I lay in Ginger's bed smoking a cigarette, while she slept beside me. All of the stress from when I first hung up the phone with Trigger came rushing back. I would need to get a lot of money together for this shit. Bail money wasn't the least of my worries; we were going to need a good lawyer for Trigger, and for any one of us who caught a case. It was time for grind mode.

I called Tone first. I had to see if he was really serious about all that shit he was talking in Daytona. If I was sure of his dedication, I would call Louie and Rob next. I had to set up a meeting with them to propose that they transport in and out of the States through me for a reasonable price, while I bought directly from Mr. Ortiz. That shit would be perfect.

9 781593 090449

Printed in the United States
by Baker & Taylor Publisher Services